MARIE CADIEUX

AND THE

FEVER COAST

DAVID GENNARD

ARE YOU READY FOR ADVENTURE?

Thank you for purchasing this book. I'd love for you to become a part of my reading crew and keep up to date with all of my latest stories, news and special offers. Feel free to head over to: www.davidgennardauthor.com

CHAPTER 1

1889

It's everything Marie expects a narrow, sandy street in Cairo to be. Stall holders vie for her francs. A merchant sprinkles spice from his chubby stained fingers. The pungent smell of cumin lingers in the air, and orange, yellow and red spice cones rise from sacks.

At the next stall, watermelons and dates ripen in the sunshine. Playing up to the passing trade, the young seller juggles pomegranates.

A skeletal hand thrusts a lamp towards Marie, and the perforated brass shimmers in the sunlight. Dappled light reflects onto the whitewashed walls. She waves the offer away.

A few strides on, a man with crenellated teeth grins. He rushes to keep ahead of her and uncurls a scroll of hieroglyph-covered papyrus. She shakes her head, and he pretends to cry. Then she has to stop beside a fabric merchant's stall to let a couple of camels waddle through. Two men in pith helmets sway in the saddles between the humps. The camels stink of sweat and straw.

She continues. Women lean in doorways, and their mascaraed eyes peer from their niqabs. A group of men circle a hookah and pass the pipe between them.

Marie slows. René Binet paints at his easel. On the canvas is the white minaret at the end of the street with its golden, gleaming crescent perched atop.

She curses under her breath and pulls her wide-brimmed hat lower covering her eyes. She had hoped not to see anybody she knew here, but there was always a good chance she would. As a cover story, she carries an easel like a rifle against her shoulder and a rucksack full of art supplies. She would rather sit and paint the scene herself than do what she is there to do. She turns to the shop windows, hoping he won't recognise her. They are full of more luxurious and expensive antiques than the cheap tat on the stalls.

'Madame Blanchet!' René shouts.

She rolls her eyes. She should lie about being there to paint, but she's running late, so she pretends not to hear. She only relaxes when a donkey pulling a cart trundles past blocking René's view of her.

After two years of marriage she still thinks it sounds strange to be called Madame Blanchet. 'Cadieux,' she whispers to herself. Don't forget who you are, she thinks.

Further along, the scent of coffee fills the street. Marie wants to sit at a table among the other people and bask in the sunshine. If only, she thinks, and she keeps walking.

A snake charmer sits cross-legged on the street, playing the Arabian riff on a flute. A black cobra sways in a basket entranced by the tune, and people steer their route away from the snake. Opposite them is her destination. The tall narrow building has turquoise tiles surrounding the scalloped archway entrance. She pushes through the dangling beads, unhooks the sign that reads private, and climbs the steep steps.

In the single room, her contact Matthieu lurks in the mashrabiya. Sunrays stream through the hexagonal latticework into the dusty room. The floorboards creak, and he glances over his shoulder.

'You've made it,' Matthieu says. He peers back out through the latticework. He is down to his shirt and braces, sleeves rolled up, and sweat stains creeping from his armpits.

6

Matthieu is podgy around the middle. His greying curly hair circles his bald, sunburnt crown.

'This is ridiculous,' she says. 'You're ridiculous. What are you even looking at?'

'You'll see in a minute.'

'I'd rather not. René Binet saw me out there, and god knows who else.'

'Well, it's your job to have a cover story.'

'Don't worry. I have one.' She drops her bag and easel onto the floor.

He bites into a shawarma. And then he motions with it to what Marie's brought with her. Onion falls onto the floor. 'You should've come as a belly dancer instead. Bare midriff, veil covering your face, nobody would've recognised you. And less to carry,' he says, with a mouthful of flatbread and chicken.

'Keep your mind on...whatever it is you're eating. What's happening?'

'A drop.'

'The only thing I see dropping is your food. Down your shirt. Why do you need me here for this?'

He strokes crumbs off his belly. 'Because the boss thinks you should be doing more.'

Marie grinds her teeth. 'I wasn't aware I'd been activated.' She sits on a carved wooden chair in the corner of the room. An oriental rug covers most of the floor, cushions lie scattered against the walls, and a couple of unlit copper lamps sit on a chest.

'Well, you know Max. He's as impatient as they come.'

Marie looks up to the ceiling. A rope, tied to a hook, leads outside between the gap in the shutters.

She leans forwards. 'Where does that go? Has it got something to do with this drop?'

Matthieu looks up at the taut rope. He smiles, and then he swings open the shutters. Daylight floods the room. Marie squints. 'Come and watch this,' he says.

She goes over to the mashrabiya. Opposite, across the square below, two hieroglyph-decorated obelisks guard the temple. On the temple's roof, a man waits beneath the rope.

'It's a zip wire.' Marie's says. 'He's not actually going to ride that thing across here?'

Matthieu waves. The man flings something over the top of the rope. Then, he runs off the edge of the temple's roof and slides towards them. Behind him, two gunmen appear on the roof. They shoot. A stray bullet hits one of the wooden shutters beside Marie. Another round hits the wall. She jumps back from the mashrabiya. A bullet hits the man. He falls from the zip wire. He's dead before his body smashes into the market stalls below. Marie covers her mouth. She turns to Matthieu, but he's gone pale and grave. He holds his chest. Blood seeps through his fingers. Marie grabs him and holds him upright against the wall.

'What the hell is happening? Are you—'

He grits his teeth. 'I'm okay.'

She peels his shirt back. The bullet wound is beneath his shoulder. 'You're lucky it missed anything important. You need a doctor though. I know one. I can take you to him.'

'Never mind,' he says. 'Get to him down there. Get what he was carrying.'

'No way! Are you mad?'

'He's got a statue of Tefnut. Get it before they find it.'

Marie grabs her bag and easel off the floor. She heads for the stairs. 'What are you going to do?'

Matthieu staggers towards her. 'I'll be fine, now go.'

8

Marie runs down the stairs. In the street, she catches her breath. Her heart races. Everyone is oblivious to what's happening in the square at the rear of the house.

'Go!' Matthieu shouts as he lurches down the stairs.

Marie runs. Her easel whacks the corner of a fruit stall sending a pile of mangos and melons crashing onto the floor. The stall-holder shouts at her in Arabic. She turns into an alley between the buildings. It leads to the cobbled square at the back of the house. A shocked crowd stares at the dead man. His limbs strike out at awkward angles among the shattered pottery. The potter gestures at the sky and his stall and then holds his hands to his head. At the far end of the square, the two gunmen arrive, and they observe the carnage. Their eyes meet Marie's. She's sure they're going to come for her. She tenses to run, but they push through the crowd towards the man they killed.

'Merde,' Marie says. She cannot get to Matthieu's contact or the statue now. They search him. The potter tries to stop them. They push him away.

'He must've dropped it,' one of them says. The men start sifting through the broken pottery.

That is when the boy, a shifty gamin, with a yellowing shiner on his cheek, edges his way out of the crowd.

Heading towards Marie, he glances over his shoulder and clutches something to his chest. The two men haven't seen him. Marie leans against the alley wall. The route is open and as inviting to the child as a cake left unattended. She jabs her easel across his exit as he is about to escape the square. He turns on his heels. She grabs his weathered collar. It rips. She swings the easel around and strikes his ankle. He stumbles to his knees, and Marie is on him quicker than a lion.

'Give it to me, you filthy little gutter-snipe, and I'll let you go,' she says.

The boy spits in her face. She grimaces and clings on. But as he wriggles his bony body free of her grip, he drops the statue. They hesitate. The statue is of a slender woman's body with a lioness's head crowned by a sun disk. The figure is the length of a forearm. Scuffs and scratches mark the polished black wood. They both grab it. Neither of them lets go. The commotion attracts attention from the crowd, and the two men's gaze snaps like a hawk's on its prey.

'Don't move! Stay there,' one of them shouts. Marie freezes. Used to such situations, the boy yanks the statue of Tefnut from Marie, and he runs. Marie gets up and runs after him, and the men chase them both.

Running through the alley, she drops the easel behind her. As it bounces on the floor, one of the men mistimes their jump over it, and they both fall over each other.

On the main street, the cobra snaps at the child who runs too close. Marie shoves through the crowd. Heading past the minaret, they come to the end of Rue du Caire, an area at the Paris Exposition Universelle designed to look like a street in Cairo.

The boy heads for the Javanese village opposite, and he goes into the crowd outside the tall gates made of palm. Marie follows. She removes her hat, discards it on the floor, and unpins her light-brown hair, letting it drop to her shoulders. She glances back towards the two men. They both also head into the crowd away from Marie. The boy has disappeared, but she runs in the direction he'd gone.

It's like she's stepped into another country. She goes past a house with a thatched roof and walls made of woven bamboo. A couple of men stand outside wearing sarongs and batik jackets. She keeps walking. A pack of children catch her attention. They're wearing patterned sarongs and a variety of headdresses and necklaces. Except one. The gamin. He's taken off his top in an attempt to blend in. It has almost worked, but his dark hair is where the similarities with the Javanese children end.

'If you run, they'll spot us,' she says.

'Then let me go.'

'I can't. I need that statue.'

The child shakes his head.

'I'll pay you,' she says.

The child's eyes narrow as if considering the deal. Then they go wide. The gunmen push through the crowd towards them, and the child bolts. Marie turns away, and they go straight past her chasing the boy.

There's no way Marie can catch up with them. Regardless, she follows where they'd ran, towards the recently constructed Eiffel Tower. Arriving beneath it, they've vanished. Had the boy climbed the tower? The latticework of iron reaches up into the sky. The tower's height is dizzying. She shakes her head. It's a dead end. He wouldn't have gone up there. She jogs the short distance towards the River Seine. Her legs ache, so she leans against a wall to catch her breath. Then, she spots them on the bridge.

The gamin has climbed onto the railing, and he holds the statue out threatening to drop it into the river. One of the men steps towards him and shoves him off the bridge. The statue falls out of the boy's hand and plunges beneath the murky surface. The boy hits the water with a splash. He thrashes around as the current sweeps him away under the bridge and out of Marie's sight.

CHAPTER 2

That evening while pacing between the exotic plants inside the orangery, Marie pulls at and adjusts her evening dress and squints as the sunset glints off the glass. The breeze drifts through the open windows, brushes the leaves and caresses her skin. Goosebumps rise on her chest. She shudders. Then her bare shoulders slump.

She lifts the plunging neckline of the black, silk evening dress she's been told to wear by her husband.

That boy must've made it back to the riverbank, she thinks. All those urchins swim in the river and play to the crowds walking by. Someone would've dragged him out. All she can think of is the current sweeping him away.

The housemaid walks into the orangery and asks, 'Madame, is there anything I can—' On seeing Marie's dress, the maid looks down at the tiled floor.

'Is there anything you can what?' Marie asks.

'Is there anything I can get you, madame?'

Marie plants her hands on her hips. 'You might look at me when you talk instead of mumbling at the floor.'

The maid trembles. She is maybe sixteen or seventeen, with a porcelain disposition. She holds her hands behind her back. She looks up, but her innocent brown eyes can't make contact. She can't look at the dress, so she looks back at the floor.

'Oh, for goodness sake,' Marie says, exasperation more than anger in her voice. 'Look at me.' Marie glares at the maid. As the girl pales, Marie feels bad. She might've ended up being that girl doing a job like that. Play the part. Be the bitch you're expected to be. 'Where on earth did he find you?' Marie asks.

'Find me, madame?'

'My husband...'

'At the agency, madame.'

Marie rolls her eyes. 'Tell me,' she says, gesturing at her dress. 'What do you think?'

The maid keeps looking at the floor.

Marie clicks her fingers, and the maid looks back up.

'It's not my place to say, madame.'

'It's not your place to compliment me?'

'I—'

'Don't bother. I know what you think. I agree.'

The maid swallows. 'It's like nothing I've ever seen before.'

'Isn't it. Do you think I'll cause a scandal tonight at the art salon?'

The maid's eyes widen. 'It is very daring, madame.'

'Go. Fetch me a drink. You can manage that?'

'Yes, madame,' the maid says, and then she scuttles off out of the orangery.

Marie turns to walk through the glazed room, but the maid comes back. She keeps her head down and holds out an envelope. 'I'm sorry, madame. I meant to give this to you.'

'What's this? Your resignation?' Marie snatches the envelope. The maid goes to leave. 'Wait,' Marie says. She takes out a folded piece of paper. Written on it are the words: We need information tonight. M.S.

'Who delivered this?' Marie asks.

'A man, he didn't—'

'When?'

'Earlier madame—'

'And you didn't think to give it to me immediately?'

'Sorry, madame, I was going to give it to the master—'

'Any letter addressed to me comes straight to me, do you hear? You don't give it to my husband. You give it to me.'

'Of course, madame. Sorry, madame.' Tears well in her eyes.

'Good, now get me that drink. God knows I need it.'

Marie pushes aside the date palm and lemon plant leaves, walks through the orangery and comes to her easel in a clearing. Sighing, she rereads the letter. Then, she pushes it back into the envelope, folds it and wedges it into the frame at the back of the canvas on the easel.

The urchin is now the least of her worries. The letter was signed off with the initials M.S. It seems Maxwell Steiner's patience has ended. What was so special about that statue of Tefnut? What could it possibly have to do with her mission? She closes her eyes and takes a deep breath. The smell of the citrus fragrance from the potted trees calms her. When she opens her eyes again, she studies the half-finished painting of a crane lily sitting on the easel. The painting bothers her. She frowns and then she examines the lily behind it. She closes one eye. Then, as clear as a crisp morning over the Pyrenees, she spots the problem. The foreshortening on one of the flowers she's painted is off.

She pulls her baggy artist's smock over herself and covers the dress and her bare skin. She immediately feels better. She mixes yellow and crimson oil paints onto a palette, scoops up a blob of the viscous, orange mixture onto her brush and slides a sluggish line onto the canvas.

The maid eventually returns. Her footsteps slow when she finds Marie at the easel wearing the smock. 'Where would you like your drink, madame?'

Marie holds the paintbrush between her teeth like a ciga-

14

rette in a holder, and the maid places the glass into Marie's outstretched hand. It is water. Marie sighs.

'Are you not going out now, madame?'

'Yes, of course I am,' Marie says.

The maid frowns.

'Victor will take an age,' Marie explains. 'That's one thing you'll learn. He takes longer than me to get ready. And I won't stand in this dress a minute longer than I need to.'

Upstairs, Victor Blanchet closes the shutters on the blood-red sunset and turns up the gas lamps on the wall.

He takes an ironed shirt off a hanger in the wardrobe and slips his arms into the sleeves. Standing straight, he admires his reflection in the mirror. Then, he breathes in as he fastens the buttons.

From a selection of five, he chooses a navy silk tie with a gold geometric design. He picks out a pair of gold cufflinks from a box and fastens his sleeves. He puts on his waistcoat and attaches the chain of his eighteen-carat gold pocket watch. The time is seven fifty-two, but the clock on the mantlepiece confirms it's slow. He winds the watch forwards and drops it into his pocket.

After the events today, at the mock temple, which is the pavilion of the Suez Canal Company, he thinks it wise to carry protection. He puts on his morning jacket and his top hat. Then, he takes out a palm-sized, pearl-handled pistol from his chest of drawers. He drapes his overcoat on his arm and slips the gun into a pocket. Finally, he selects a walking cane with a gold pommel and goes down the stairs.

'Really? You're painting.' Victor says when he finds Marie in the orangery.

She leans towards the canvas and applies a dab of paint.

15

'Our carriage waits.' He slaps a leaf away from his face with the walking cane's pommel.

'It can wait.'

'It can, but I can't. This could have waited.' Victor says.

Marie remains silent.

'It's like a bloody jungle in here. I'll have it cut back.'

'You don't appreciate wild things do you, Victor? Besides, I like it.'

He opens his pocket watch. 'We'll be late.' He clips the lid shut. Then he walks past Marie and goes behind the canvas. She stops painting. She wishes she'd buried the letter in the soil inside one of the large pots instead of hiding it in the canvas frame. She wipes her hands on a rag as he inspects the crane lily.

'Don't move it, darling. It needs to be exactly how I painted it.'

Victor faces her.

Marie peels off the smock revealing the dress. He studies her as if she's his bank statement. 'Good,' he says. 'There, now you see. When it's tamed, I do appreciate beauty. Now come.'

He goes away from the canvas, and she sighs. She stands between the plants and trees, watching him walk down the corridor. His cane swings and merrily taps the floor, and when he opens the front door, he is a silhouette against the sunset. She wonders whether he had anything to do with that statue of Tefnut. 'What are you hiding, you sly bastard,' she whispers to herself.

The maid is standing there. Marie jumps on seeing her.

'Good god!' Marie says. She doesn't know how long the maid has been there, but it's long enough to have heard what Marie has whispered. 'Don't you have a home to go to?'

16

Marie asks, glaring at the maid. Then Marie leaves to join the man she married to spy on.

CHAPTER 3

The driver swings open the carriage door outside the tall townhouse on Rue de l'Élysée. Victor climbs in ignoring his wife. The driver offers Marie his hand, and she smiles, takes it and climbs up. Inside the carriage, Marie faces away from Victor.

'Move on,' the driver says, and the horses pull the carriage over the cobbles and onto the well-lit, tree-lined avenues and boulevards. People stride and stroll and scurry to their evening entertainment.

After a while, Victor says, 'I suppose you had another wasted day?'

Marie shakes her head. 'I spent it at the Académie if that's what you mean?'

'Well, maybe my investment might finally pay off tonight.'

'Please try and enjoy art for how it moves you and makes you feel, Victor.'

'I'll be thrilled if it makes me a profit.'

'Art is not a commodity. What I mean is, I'm sure you'd make more money trading corn or gold.'

'I'm glad you're here to advise me.'

Her jaw tenses. She says nothing more. After a short ride, the driver pulls into the courtyard of the Baron's hôtel particulier, and a footman opens the carriage doors. Victor climbs out first. Marie hesitates in the carriage doorway. A string quartet struggles to be heard over the many voices inside.

'What are you waiting for?'

'Nothing, darling.' She steps down into the courtyard.

'Come, take off your coat.'

'Once I'm inside,' she says, pulling her coat around her. Oblivious to her discomfort, Victor admires the neo-classical courtyard.

'I couldn't imagine acquiring such wealth. Is it possible?' Marie asks, trying to ingratiate herself.

'I could've had something like this if it wasn't for the damned Paris commune.'

'Well, I'm sure you could still achieve this. If anyone can, you can.'

'Once I return.'

'You're going away again?'

'Yes.'

As he turns his back on her, Marie smiles. 'How long is it for this time, weeks? Months?'

A couple of gentlemen walk past and touch the brim of their hats. One of them, René Binet, stops and recognises her.

'Ah, Marie,' he says.

'René, it's good to see you.'

'And not for the first time today—'

'René, let me introduce you to my husband,' she says, trying to steer the subject away from where she was earlier that day.

'Ah, good evening,' he says.

Victor shakes the outstretched hand of René and his friend. 'If you know my wife, you must be an artist.'

'Yes, monsieur. In fact, I was painting a scene today in Cairo Street at the exhibition. Marie, I saw you there. You went right past. I tried calling you, but you didn't hear.'

'I'm sorry, no, I didn't hear you.'

'Not to worry, you seemed to be in an awful hurry. I'll see

19

you inside,' René says.

Marie smiles as he walks off with his friend.

'You were at Cairo Street this morning?' Victor asks. His eyes narrow on René's back. Then, he turns his attention to Marie.

'Briefly,' she says.

'Why?'

'To paint.'

'You said you'd only been to the Académie today.'

'Well, it was hardly worth mentioning because I didn't stay long.'

'Because you were in a hurry?'

'What's this, an inquisition? René, of course. It may sound stupid, but he beat me to it.'

'To what?'

'The scene I wished to paint. He was already there, set up, painting happily away.'

'You can't move for bloody artists there.'

'So you've been too?'

'Yes. Anyway, listen. Focus. Tonight, I need you to give me a reason why I should continue paying for your tuition at the Académie.' Victor faces Marie and towers over her.

Marie rolls her eyes. 'Darling, your business is dull.'

'Yet you enjoy the comfort it brings and the art you're free to do.'

'Remember, I am your wife. I don't work for you.'

'Then you have a bigger stake. You will do as I ask.' He cups her cheek. 'Jacque Comtois has been avoiding me at every opportunity. When I see him tonight, I want him alone. I don't want his damned wife at his side. Listen. When you're with Vérité, you will find a pretty young man and make sure he entertains her so Jacque can see.'

Marie sighs. 'Can't we just go in and enjoy the night?'

'I haven't finished. When I talk to Vérité, I want you to make him not take his eyes off you.'

Marie takes off her coat. Goosebumps rise on her bare shoulders and chest. 'Well then,' she says. 'I guess that won't be difficult.' She walks into the reception hall between the marble pillars and breezes up an imperial staircase to the grand reception room's open doors.

Fine paintings on easels, marble statues and expensive people fill the room at the exhibition's opening night. But it is Marie Blanchet who captivates Dr Gabriel Bertrand. He blows out a low whistle of approval when she enters the room. Everyone stares at her. Their reactions ripple across the room. The women gasp and frown. The men ogle and leer. Marie keeps her chin high, and she charms people with her smile.

'She's catching everyone's attention in that dress,' says Michel. 'Close your mouth, Gabe.'

Gabriel half turns to his friend but refuses to take his eyes off Marie. 'She looks incredible,' he says.

'Dangerous, I believe is a better word.'

'She's not, she's....'

'Trouble?'

'Trouble's good. Especially when it looks like that.'

The pair grin.

A rotund man wearing a monocle comes over and inspects Michel's painting. 'A scene from the Exposition Universelle, I suppose?'

'Actually, I painted it while in Algeria.'

He ignores Michel, turns to the grey-haired necklace-laden woman accompanying him, and criticises how light falls on the Algerian street scene. Then they walk away.

'Why the crusty old fool,' Gabriel says in defence of his friend. 'I bet he's never even been to—'

'Forget him.' Michel touches Gabriel's arm.

'Remember what they say about people and opinions?'

Gabriel laughs. 'I don't know how you do it.'

'Me? You're the doctor. You'll be inspecting their arseholes.'

'Then it's a good job I'll get paid more than an artist for doing so.'

When they stop grinning, Michel says, 'That Exposition is a pain. Everyone presumes any painting of a foreign scene is down there. Are you even listening?'

Gabriel is gazing across the crowd at Marie. With her light-brown hair pinned up, his eyes linger on her neck, then her bare shoulders, and then her cleavage. The black dress clings to her waist and sweeps down to the floor. He knows what it's like to undress her, but he wants to peel that dress off her body. His balls tingle at the thought. As Gabriel admires her from afar, a man stands before her blocking his view. Gabriel frowns. He presumes it's her husband, Victor. She'd told him Victor was old, and he'd assumed her husband wouldn't look dashing. Jealousies rise in him. His stomach twists.

'Maybe I should paint her instead of street scenes,' Michel says.

'What?' Gabriel asks.

'Well, at least you might buy one of my paintings then.'

'You mean I haven't already.'

'I'm going to miss you, my friend,' Michel says, shaking his head.

'No. You'll miss the trouble we get up to.'

'And the drinking.'

'And the gambling. Listen, I've been thinking,' Gabriel says. 'I'm going to ask her to come.'

Michel laughs. 'You're crazy.'

'I know Madame Durand told me not to, but I'll regret it if I don't.'

Michel shakes his head. 'You're serious?'

'Yes.'

'Here?'

'Why not?'

'In front of him?'

'What a way to leave Paris, hey?'

'Now I know you're joking, Gabe.'

'Why?'

'He'd kill you.' Michel's smile fades. 'Listen, I know you're joking about asking her in front of her husband—'

'I'm not,' Gabriel says.

'Yes, well, don't be disappointed, old friend. She won't leave him. You're not rich enough.'

'Don't. Marie's not like that.' But even Gabriel doesn't believe himself.

'Look, I don't want you to get—'

'She loves me. I know it.'

Michel shakes his head.

'Care to wager?' Gabriel asks, holding out his hand.

Michel shakes it. 'I hate taking your money.'

'You don't.'

'You know, I might actually become destitute without you,' Michel says.

A short man wearing a military uniform waddles over to Gabriel. 'Ah, monsieur, you are the artist?'

'No, Michel, my friend here is, please...' Gabriel steps aside and lets the two men talk.

'Algiers, if I'm not mistaken? You've captured the light perfectly. I served there myself. Do you see these medals here...'

Gabriel winks at Michel and walks away. Though Gabriel thinks the paintings displayed are incredible, none of them steals his attention more than Marie. Top hats block his view of her. He keeps moving, watching her between the marble statues and the canvases. She still hasn't seen him. But her eyes search the room for him, and that makes Gabriel smile.

Jacque Comtois doesn't see Victor coming.

'My dear man,' Victor says. 'And his charming wife.'

Vérité turns and already has her lip upturned in disgust. Victor leans in and kisses her on the cheek before she can pull away. After the couples greet each other, she raises an eyebrow at Marie. 'How daring you are. You'll cause an absolute scandal in a dress like that.'

Marie smiles. 'People will only be jealous for so long. Then they'll start trying to copy.'

'Well,' Victor says, examining the room. 'I hope you haven't bought all of the good pieces yet. Are there many?'

Jacque says, 'The paintings—'

'There are some fine paintings,' Vérité says, speaking over her husband.

'Truly?' Victor says. 'I'd welcome your opinion.'

'I imagine your wife knows more about art than me,' she says.

Marie smiles.

'Then, with both your opinions, I'm sure to acquire a fantastic painting tonight.'

The group falls silent. Victor touches the small of Marie's back, but she smiles, choosing not to act upon his hint. Their

24

attention turns to the impressionist painting next to them. Waves lap on a tropical beach with jungle and mountains rising behind it.

'We intend to go on a trip ourselves soon,' Victor says.

'We?' Marie asks, raising her eyebrows at her husband.

'Panama, I suppose.' Vérité says.

On hearing the word Panama, Marie studies her husband's reaction. Her skin tingles. Adrenaline surges through her body down to her toes as if lightning has struck her heart and forked through her veins. Yet, her demeanour remains calm and unflinching.

'What was all the commotion today down in Cairo Street? Did it have something to do with Panama?' Jacque asks.

Victor shakes his head. 'It was nothing.'

'Nothing?' Vérité raises her eyebrows. 'A man was shot. And fell from the pavilion roof.'

'Shot? I was down there this morning,' Marie says.

'That's when it happened.'

'I didn't see anything. That's awful.'

Victor sighs. 'It was a thief by all accounts. He stole an Egyptian artefact on display in the Canal Company's office. It had nothing to do with Panama. Anyway, Marie, why don't you put that training to good use and find me a painting to buy?'

A waiter steps beside them, holding a tray of clinking champagne flutes, and they all take a glass.

'I'm sure their conversation will be boring anyway,' Marie says to Vérité. After all, she knows Victor won't disclose any more information in her presence. However, she might be able to learn something from Vérité. 'Shall we?' Marie asks.

The two women walk off and pass several paintings of landscapes with water; shimmering seas, lakes and rivers. People in the room treat Marie with admiration and shock as if she is a work of art. She holds her head high and acknowledges only the people she knows. She is about to start questioning Vérité when somebody taps a fan on her shoulder.

'Good evening Marie.'

'Madame Gage,' Marie says, facing the older woman. 'What a pleasant surprise. It's good to see you. I didn't think you'd be here at a show like this. May I introduce Vérité Comtois.'

The two women greet each other.

'Madame Gage studies with me at Académie Julian,' Marie says.

'Ah, I see. Are you enjoying the exhibition?' Vérité asks.

Madame Gage's nostril flares, and her lip raises in disgust. 'There are a lot of vulgar displays on show,' she says, raising her eyebrows at Marie. 'I see little skill, just crude attempts at eliciting emotion and reaction.'

Marie smiles. 'Then not for the first time Madame, though I respect your views, I have to disagree. Art should break convention. It should disrupt. Creativity should shake society.'

'But not at the expense of taste.'

'Art has to be provocative. Else, what's the point?'

Madame Gage flicks open her fan cooling herself. 'It's very warm in here. Wouldn't you concur, Vérité?'

'Yes. I—'

'I'm sure you'd agree, Marie, but alas, I'm sure you feel quite cold in that dress. Excuse me while I go and get some fresh air,' Madame Gage says before leaving.

'The wonderful Madame Gage,' Marie says, scowling in the woman's direction.

'Yes,' Vérité says. 'She was friendly.'

Marie knows Vérité is trying to aggravate her. But why?

She knows it will be something to do with Victor, something regarding Panama and the woman's husband, Jacque. She bites the inside of her cheek to stop herself from scolding the woman, and they continue through the exhibition. Marie stops at a painting of a woman walking through tall grass holding an umbrella.

'This is beautiful,' Marie says.

'Then why don't you tell Victor to buy it?'

'Maybe.' Marie says. 'Though I think he's interested in buying something else.' Across the room, their husbands laugh. 'Jacque seems surprised about us going to Panama—'

'Don't talk to me about Panama!' Vérité says. 'He wants Jacque to invest all of my inheritance in that damn canal.'

'Invest in the Panama Canal, really?'

'Yes. I told Jacque he's a bloody fool if he gambles my money.'

'But Victor's stayed clear of the dig all this time.' Marie says. 'Why get involved now when it's failing?'

Vérité is about to answer when somebody approaches them from behind and says, 'It's not bad. But my friend's painting is better.'

The interruption annoys Marie. She is finally discovering information about her husband's dealings that will appease Maxwell Steiner. But her frown fades when she recognises the voice. They turn from the painting to a handsome man with dusty blonde hair, blue eyes and a strong jaw. His hand is tucked into his trouser pocket, and his coat tail sweeps behind it.

'And you are?' Vérité asks.

'My name is Gabriel. Dr Gabriel Bertrand.'

He kisses Vérité on each cheek in greeting. Then Gabriel turns to Marie, and they also kiss each other on the cheek, savouring each other's scent as they do.

'It's my friend you must meet,' Gabriel says. 'He's currently having his ear chewed off by an old general. You should see his work. It's fantastic.'

'Is it, really?' Marie asks.

'And what is your friend's name?' asks Vérité.

'Michel DuPont. You might know him?'

Vérité shakes her head.

'I'm aware of Monsieur DuPont and his work,' Marie says.

'You are? Splendid. Have you ever been to Africa?'

The two women shake their heads.

'Well, even the old general said how well he'd captured the light. But anyway, it's the subjects Michel paints. They're what's incredible. They're full of a...beguiling mystery and beauty,' he says, fixing his gaze on Marie.

Vérité bats her eyelashes. 'Why don't you lead the way then, doctor,' she says.

Gabriel leads them towards his friend's painting, and when they are deep in the crowd he reaches back and touches Marie's hand for the briefest moment.

Later that night, as Marie strolls back from the bathroom, a man in a dark suit, wearing a red rose in his lapel, turns to face her and says in English, 'You're a hard woman to get on your own.'

She recognises the American accent of the United States ambassador to France, Maxwell Steiner.

'We shouldn't be talking like this,' Marie says, continuing in French. 'And you shouldn't have sent me that note. The maid nearly gave it to Victor.'

He smiles. 'Needs must,' he says, switching to perfect French. 'After your failure today.'

'I did not fail at anything today.'

'Did you retrieve the statue?'

'No, but—'

'Then you failed.'

'Why are you going in like a bunch of cowboys? This is Paris. It's not the Wild West. Matthieu was nearly killed. I take it he got to you without bleeding to death?'

'Washington is pushing for information, and you've not been to visit us for months.'

'If I had something, I would have. Besides I wasn't aware I'd been activated.'

'Maybe you're not trying hard enough.' He puts his hand on her waist. She shoves it away and stands back.

'You're mad. If he saw you do that...'

'Victor? Or your boyfriend?'

She is surprised he knows about Gabriel, but she doesn't react.

'You're good,' he says. 'Oh, you're good, but if we know, then there's a chance Victor will find out too. Ditch the cute young doctor and do what you're paid to do.'

'I'm a sleeper agent. I don't get paid.'

'So that's what it is? You've gotten used to the life you're living, and you don't want it to end. Get information, and we'll talk. Okay?'

Marie looks over her shoulder. There's nobody around who she knows. 'I've found out something tonight. He's investing in Panama,' she says. 'Whatever they plan to do to save the Panama Canal must be significant because Victor wouldn't invest otherwise.'

'That statue is the key to all this.'

Marie shakes her head. 'The statue is gone. I saw it sink in the Seine.'

'What?'

'A street rat got the statue before those men or I could get it. They pursued him and pushed him into the river. Who are they, those men? Maybe it's you who needs to be careful, Max. They knew somebody was onto them,' she says, leaning closer and whispering into his ear. 'What if they knew it was you Americans. Maybe you should stop the espionage and do what you're paid to do. Be a diplomat.'

Maxwell smiles. 'Sweetheart, you wouldn't believe what I'm paid to do on behalf of the American government.'

Victor is telling jokes and recounting stories to the group that has formed around him. Marie takes a drink and goes to his side. She gives Jacque attention like Victor had instructed. As the night goes on, their host, the Baron, gives a speech. Such is the applause led by Victor that even the Baron joins their gathering. Throughout the night, Gabriel downs drink after drink. A band of artists gather around him and Michel, but they are subdued by the sheer exuberance Victor collects in his orbit.

'Tell me,' Victor says, leaning into Marie. 'Are those the men you spoke to earlier?'

Gabriel whispers something into Michel's ear.

'Yes, I think so,' Marie says.

Victor lurches forwards. Drink spills. People laugh. 'Gentlemen,' Victor shouts towards Gabriel and Michel. 'You! I believe you know my wife?'

CHAPTER 4

Gabriel casually keeps one hand in his pocket and a champagne flute in the other as a weapon. Victor stalks towards him.

'I had the pleasure to meet your wife, monsieur,' Michel says, stepping past Gabriel.

Victor brushes past Michel's outstretched hand and approaches Gabriel. But he also marches past him and goes to the painting.

Gabriel locates Marie across the room. She smiles and nods. Gabriel puts the glass on a table and rolls his tense shoulders.

'Yes, yes. Very good. Marrakech?' Victor says, studying Michel's painting.

'Algiers,' Michel says.

'My wife tells me we should buy it.'

'Then your wife,' Gabriel says. 'Has an excellent eye.'

'Yes, she bloody well should have,' Victor says, holding Gabriel's gaze. 'Is it still for sale?'

'Yes, monsieur,' Michel says. 'Though I've had interested parties.'

'How much?'

'Three hundred francs, Monsieur.'

Victor's eyes narrow. The painting cost a hundred francs more than Michel had planned to sell it for. 'Alright, you have yourself a deal. Will you deliver it?'

'Of course, Monsieur,' Michel says, and Victor shakes his hand. He also extends his hand to Gabriel, and their handshake is firm.

'Come,' Victor says. 'Join me for a drink.'

Michel holds up his hands. 'I wouldn't wish to intrude.'

'Nonsense. I want you to.'

'He wants us to join him, Michel,' Gabriel says. 'Don't be rude. He's just bought your painting.'

Marie's eyes widen. Michel's eyebrows raise. 'Okay,' he says. 'Lead the way.'

Gabriel and Michel join the raucous group. Victor laughs at the Baron's jokes and ensures the Baron's glass is always topped up with champagne. Marie can't quite believe that her lover and her husband are standing and drinking so close to each other. She's relieved she has a task to do, though it doesn't really distract her. She continues paying Jacque attention, much to his wife Véritè's annoyance. In return, Véritè flirts with Gabriel and Michel. And so the night goes on until Victor announces it is time for himself and Marie to leave.

'We're leaving far too early. It's not even midnight yet,' Marie says, walking over to the carriage.

'I have business to attend to in the morning with Jacque.' Happy with how the night has progressed, Victor holds Marie's hand as she climbs into the carriage.

'I'm not sure Jacque will be in the right state for anything in the morning,' Marie says.

'Good. The weaker Jacque is, the less he'll resist.'

The carriage jolts forwards rattling from the Baron's courtyard onto Boulevard Haussmann.

Victor holds her knee. His face turns grave. 'What did the American want?' he asks.

Marie doesn't flinch. 'Which American?'

'The one you spoke to.'

'There was more than one, and what do you think Americans want when they see a woman dressed like this?'

The answer satisfies him. They ride along the boulevard, and Marie waits a minute before changing the subject and asking, 'You're happy with how the night went then?'

'Indeed.' Victor smiles. 'Very pleased.'

'Well, you and the baron seemed to get on—'

The carriage's wheel hits a rut in the road. The axle cracks. The carriage jolts to a halt. Marie lurches forward into Victor. The driver jumps onto the road, scratches his head and curses as he surveys the damage. Then he appears at their door and knocks on it.

Victor lowers the window.

'I'm sorry, Sir, but the axle has snapped. This carriage isn't going anywhere tonight.'

Victor shakes his head but smiles. 'How convenient.'

The driver frowns at this strange assessment. 'For your safety, Sir, I suggest you wait here, and I'll run back and get another carriage.'

'I'm sure that's exactly what they want. No. We'll walk.'

'With respect, Sir, I wouldn't advise people of your stature—'

Victor stands and pushes open the door. The driver staggers backwards. 'I said we'll walk.'

'But Sir, I really—'

'Who hired you?' Victor asks as he steps out and stands before the driver.

'You did, Sir.'

Victor narrows his eyes. The driver edges back, holding up his hands. 'It's up to you, Sir. Do as you please.'

Marie steps out of the carriage, whispers sorry to the driver and gives him a coin for his troubles. She joins Victor as he walks away. The Parisian boulevards are so light and bright from the many gas lamps that the full moon can't lay its silver blanket over the city.

'What's happening, Victor? Why walk?'

'I don't trust the driver. It's a strange coincidence, don't you think?'

'I'm not sure I follow.'

'When have you known an axel to break like that? No, they're trying to find out what's happening.'

'Victor, I am completely lost. Who, what? What are you caught up in? Does it have something to do with what happened at the expo on Cairo Street?'

'There are forces that want us to fail at building it,' he says.

'Building what?'

'The canal, in Panama.'

'Why?'

'So they can take control of the dig.'

She's never seen Victor so paranoid, but she is sure he doesn't suspect her. He eyes the narrow alleys and doorways as they walk.

Then he turns them off the bright boulevard. The further they walk along Rue de Miromesnil towards the Seine, the darker and quieter the connecting side streets become.

'The people haunting these streets belong in the dark. You take me to the best places,' she says. 'Are you sure we're going the right way, Victor?'

'We are,' he says.

The buildings loom over them, blocking the sky. Marie can see candles behind the cracked windows, but no light spills through the grimy glass onto the cobbles. It's difficult to see where she walks. She fears standing in something fresh. The stench of excrement and urine stings her nostrils. She thinks this is where she could end up living in a place like this if she's not careful.

'Are you sure you're not being paranoid? Why would they sabotage the carriage, though? What do they want from you?'

'The company's plans are only known to a trusted few. They will do what they can to find out. You heard what they did at the expo.'

'You said an Egyptian artefact was stolen.'

'They're hiding the plans inside them—'

A man's silhouette moves in the shadows between the ill-fitting buildings. Marie wishes she hadn't spotted him. Their eyes meet, and it's all the excuse he needs to step out from the darkness. He blocks their path. Sallow skin clings to his gaunt face, and he clutches a tarnished blade.

Victor shakes his arm free from Marie's grip. 'Who sent you?'

The man waves the knife at them. Marie edges back, but Victor stands entrenched like the barricades that crossed Parisian streets years earlier.

'Shut it,' the man says. 'Jewellery. Money. Give them, or I'll gut your fancy whore right here in the street.'

'Who sent you?' Victor asks.

The man angles the knife at Victor's head.

'He's a thief, Victor, not a spy,' Marie says, grabbing his sleeve, but he shakes her off and steps towards the man.

'Who are you working for?'

CHAPTER 5

In the dark street, dripping water from a broken pipe punctuates Marie's shallow breathing.

'I'll cut you,' the man warns.

But as Victor stalks forwards, the thief's threatening stature shrinks. He edges back. He shakes his head. He holds his hands up in defeat.

Victor holds a gun low at his waist aimed at the man.

'I asked, who sent you?'

The knife falls from the man's trembling hand. 'I'm hungry, that's all. I haven't—'

Victor slams his cane against the man's head, and he crumples to the floor.

Marie sighs.

Victor pokes the thief with the cane. He is either unconscious or dead. Then, Victor wipes the blood off the gold pommel onto the man's coat.

'Scum,' Victor says. 'Utter scum.' He points his gun at the man's head.

'No! What are you doing? Don't.' Marie grabs Victor's arm, but she can't pull it away.

'We need to send them a message,' he says.

Marie blocks the muzzle with her hand.

Victor's finger is on the trigger. His eyes bulge with anger.

'Don't. Don't have it on your conscience.'

Victor shakes with rage. The muzzle presses into her palm. If he shot, she'd never paint again. She pulls her hand away.

'No. Victor!' She puts her hand back over the muzzle and stands between the two men. 'He's not one of them. He's just a thief,' Marie says.

Victor's attention snaps back to her. He drops the gun to his side. 'Alright,' he growls, sliding the weapon into his coat pocket. 'Come, let's go.'

The following day, Marie wipes her brow on her forearm. No air comes in through the open windows of the orangery. As she mixes paint on her palette, she thinks about the man Victor struck the night before. She was sure the man was a thief and not a spy. She shakes her head. Of course, he wasn't a spy. Victor was paranoid. And she was surprised by how paranoid he was. What would he do to her if he found out she was spying on him? No, the man was an opportunistic thief. She also wonders if the blow Victor dealt killed the thief. Then she daydreams about Victor going to prison for it. While adding cadmium scarlet to the crane lily, Marie imagines Victor lying in the guillotine. Continuing to paint, she gets oil paint on her fingers, and it's like blood.

The front door opens, breaking her daydreaming. She wipes her hand down her smock removing some of the paint as she listens. A walking cane taps against the parquet floor in the corridor; it's Victor.

As he walks into the orangery, she greets him over her shoulder. He holds a briefcase and his cane. He smiles.

'You seem happy. I take it Jacque complied?'

'Indeed he did.'

'Good. So, when can we open our own gallery?'

'By the time I'm finished, they'll name galleries after me.'

'Really?' She rolls her eyes as she leans into the painting and adds cross-hatching to the leaves. 'Well, that sounds a tad more interesting than your normal business. Care to share?'

'No, you'll know soon enough,' he says, tapping his nose with the cane's pommel. Then he places the cane and his briefcase onto a wicker chair and removes his suit jacket.

'And all this before eleven. I take it you're not done for the day?'

'No, just getting started. In fact, it's going to be a long day. I must entertain Marcel Jacobs tonight.'

'What? Oh please, I do hope it's not here.'

'We'll be going out. Marcel needs entertaining in a way you can't offer,' he says.

Marie continues to paint. Victor devours one of her sandwiches. 'Why aren't you eating these? They're going stale.'

'My appetite deserts me.'

He picks up another and waves it at her. 'It'll be the drink from last night.'

'No, I remember our walk sobering me quite quickly,' she says.

He stands in the doorway with the manicured garden behind him. 'Where is she?' he asks.

'Who?'

'The maid.'

'Where do you find such staff?'

'At the agency.'

'That's what she said. Well, it's a good job you employ better people for your businesses.'

Victor turns to Marie. 'She wasn't hired for her mind. She was hired to be told what to do. Maybe it's you that has the problem.'

'With what?'

'Giving and obeying orders. You're of a certain stature now. You must act accordingly.'

Marie says nothing. She continues to paint.

'Where is she anyway?' he asks.

'Out. I sent her on an errand.' The doorbell rings. 'Get that would you, Victor.'

Victor rolls his sleeves as he returns to the house. Marie listens to his footsteps, and she goes over to the chair when she's sure he's gone. She wipes her hands down her smock again and pulls a pin from her hair. She twists it inside the lock on the briefcase until it pops open. Voices come from the door. She opens the flap closing the case. Inside there are various written and typed documents, deeds and maps. On the map's edge is the title; The Isthmus of Panama. Her eyes narrow. Then she curses when she sees the smudged red fingerprint she's left on it.

Marie hesitates. Footsteps approach down the corridor towards the orangery. She pushes the document back into the briefcase, closes the flap and fastens the lock. Two steps, and she is back over to the easel.

Turning to their visitors, her mouth drops open. Gabriel winks at her. Victor follows behind him, and Michel comes in carrying a canvas wrapped in a tarpaulin.

'You remember my wife? You have her to thank for your sale.'

'Yes, indeed. Hello Mademoiselle, and thank you,' Michel says.

'My wife thinks she's a painter—'

'I'd say she's very accomplished,' Gabriel says.

'You're an authority?' Victor asks. 'I didn't think you were an artist. Aren't you a...'

'Doctor. I'm a doctor.'

'You've only just graduated,' says Michel. He goes over and admires Marie's painting. 'It is terrific. Your wife has talent. She has an artist's eye.'

39

'Thank you,' Marie says. 'And well, I'm shocked to see this here so quick. The exhibition only opened last night.'

'I bought the damn thing, so I should damn well have it when I want it.'

'Don't worry, I had another painting the Baron was gracious enough to accept in its place,' Michel says. 'Monsieur, shall I unwrap it for you?'

Victor waves the offer away. 'Not here.' He fetches his jacket and briefcase off the chair and collects his cane. 'Bring it up, follow me,' he says, going out of the orangery, followed by Michel.

Gabriel nods in the men's direction. 'You never told me he's a cripple?'

'He's not. It's an old injury from fighting against the Commune. What the hell are you doing coming here anyway?' she asks.

Gabriel slips his hand around her waist. 'You looked incredible last night.'

She pushes him away. 'Are you mad?'

'Possibly,' Gabriel says, and they kiss. She steps back. 'This is madness. You're mad.'

Gabriel laughs.

'If he knew,' she says.

'He'd what?'

She shakes her head at Gabriel. 'Oh darn it.' Paint is on his shirt and on her fingers.

'Don't worry about it.'

'You can't let him see it.' Marie goes to hold her forehead and then stops herself from getting paint on her head. Michel and Victor's footsteps come closer down the corridor.

'Don't you have a jacket with you?'

'No, but I've got an idea,' he says, pointing at her painting.

CHAPTER 6

Gabriel takes the painting off the easel. As Michel and Victor come back into the orangery, Michel raises his voice, warning his friend, 'I do hope you're not boring the Madame with tales of your medical sketches—'

'Oh dear, I should've listened,' Gabriel says. 'I've gone and gotten paint on my shirt.'

Victor puts his hands on his hips. 'What's going on,' he asks.

'I'm the proud owner of this fine piece of art,' Gabriel says, grinning and looking between the two men and the painting.

Victor raises an eyebrow.

Marie shakes her head. 'I did tell him he should collect it when it was dry, but what do I know?'

'It will take pride of place in my surgery,' Gabriel says.

'Oh, and just where is your surgery?' asks Victor.

'He hasn't got one,' Michel says.

'Yet. I mean, it will take pride of place. When I get one.'

'Well, if he values it so much, I hope he paid handsomely for it?' Victor asks.

Marie sighs. 'I said he could pay me when he moves into his surgery.'

Victor shakes his head. 'Well, you should charge him interest.'

'Ah, imagine?' Michel says. 'To be an artist that could give away work without worrying about money.'

'Indeed.' Victor nods. 'Too comfortable. Good artists need to struggle. It makes them better.'

'Precisely,' Michel says. 'Which is why we should leave,

and I'll let you get back to your business.' Michel taps the chest pocket where he'd put Victor's payment. 'And I must paint because this will only last so long.'

'Let me show you out,' Marie says.

As Gabriel walks, he bumps the canvas into a large terracotta pot holding an orange tree. The letter Marie had hidden in the frame of the canvas falls onto the floor. Victor, closer than Marie to it, picks it up.

'You seem to have dropped a letter,' Victor tells Gabriel.

Before Gabriel's brow could furrow, Marie says, 'It's not his.'

Victor opens the envelope.

'It's nothing,' she says.

Victor's eyes narrow at the letter. 'Who needs information?'

Marie shakes her head. 'I used it as a wedge to make the canvas tighter.'

Victor stares at her, wanting an answer to his question.

'Madeline at the Académie,' Marie lies. 'She wanted information on which competitions I wanted to send work to.'

Victor's stern expression brakes into a smile. 'Competitions? You?' He laughs. 'Goodbye, gentlemen. Thank you for the painting.'

As she leads Michel and Gabriel to the front door, she sighs. Victor's desire to ridicule her ambitions always outweighs any distrust he might have.

Michel says, 'You should enter a competition, Marie—'

'What was that all about?' Gabriel asks. She needs to get him out of the house before he loses his temper.

'Nothing,' she says.

'But the way he talks to you.'

'The last thing I need is my honour defending Gabe,' she says, placing her hand on Gabriel's back.

'Marie!' Victor says from down the corridor. She pulls her hand away from Gabriel and spins to face her husband stalking towards them.

Victor holds up a paintbrush. Her face blushes as he approaches. She frowns.

'I thought real artists sign their work.'

The lower right corner of the canvas has no signature. 'Monsieur Blanchet is correct, Marie.'

'Yes, Marie, I'm correct,' Victor says, giving her the brush.

She signs the painting on the doorstep and then says good-bye to the two men.

Later that afternoon, in Académie Julian's rooftop studio, fifteen women apply the last brushstrokes to their portraits of the model. Apart from the different angles, all paintings were the same except for Marie's. She has captured a scene of the class on her canvas. She'd painted the other women, in smocks or aprons with palettes and brushes, stood and sat at their easels. The model is wearing a Grecian dress and posing against a backdrop. Marie has even captured the glass roof and the sun streaming through clouds that now bring the thunder.

Marie stares out the windows, drumming her paintbrush against her hand in time with the rain slapping against the glass roof. Her teacher, Amélie Beaury-Saurel, leans into the canvas and admires the short brushstrokes. 'Ladies, gather please.' she says.

Marie puts her brush down and sits on a stool as the women gather around her easel.

'Marie has created a painting very different to what the rest of you have done. Why do you think that is?'

'I like it,' Anna, Marie's friend, says.

'No. I don't want to hear what you like,' Amélie says. 'That isn't going to make her painting or any of yours any better, so you can cut that out immediately.'

The class falls silent. Then the group's oldest member, Madame Gage, pushes her shoulders back. 'The composition is cluttered. I don't know what to focus on.'

'The composition is fine. Marie, Maybe you should explain why you focused your painting on the class rather than just the model?'

'I thought it was a more interesting story to tell,' Marie says.

'Good. Now we're getting somewhere. Story. All great art tells a story.'

'It's like a photograph,' Madame Gage says.

'And that's a bad thing?' Amélie asks. 'Marie was brave enough to try something different. I want you to all think about that tonight. What risks can you take that will change what you do. That's it for today. Thank you, ladies. I'll see you tomorrow.'

Marie cleans her brushes and packs away her oil paints. As she heads to the door with Anna, Madame Gage ingratiates herself with their teacher, Amélie.

Amélie motions from behind Madame Gage and says, 'Marie, could I speak with you before you leave?'

Marie nods.

'I'd wait for you,' Anna says, but she thumbs over at Madame Gage, 'however, I fear you'll be waiting all evening.'

Marie laughs. 'I'll see you tomorrow then.' Anna leaves the studio, and Marie puts her bag on a table and goes over to the window. She sits on the sill. Rain runs down the glass and the rooftops of Paris, the nearby library, and the convent and the rows of buildings to the Louvre on the banks of

44

the Seine.

'Goodbye, Marie,' Madame Gage says but doesn't wait for a reply as she closes the door behind her.

Amélie joins Marie. The Louvre's roof glistens.

'Ultramarine and Mars black,' she says.

Marie's brow creases. 'Crimson too. To capture the warmth. To get that hint of the sun on the tiles after the rain.'

'Technically,' Amélie says, 'you're the best in the class.'

'Thank you.'

'Do you paint much in your free time?'

'As much as I can.'

'You see things differently, Marie. Your view of the world is wonderful. Have you seen much of it?'

'A little. Before I married.'

'The Prix de Rome is a prestigious scholarship allowing artists to study in the Italian capital for three years at the expense of the French state. I want you to apply for it.'

'Me?'

Amélie smiles and nods.

'I'm honoured you'd think—'

'I don't think,' Amélie says. 'I know, and you'd stand a good chance.'

Marie's smile fades. 'I'm really honoured. But I'm afraid my husband would never entertain the idea of me studying in Rome for one year, let alone three.'

'Ah. You're certain?'

Marie nods.

'He allows you to come here. I guess he pays your fees?'

'I know you mean well—'

'You'd want such an opportunity, though?'

Marie goes over to her painting. 'Asking him's not an option. I told you. I know what his response will be.'

45

Amélie follows her to the painting. 'Would you want this more than anything you currently have? More than living the comfortable life you lead now?'

'I...'

Amélie shakes her head. 'It's fine, Marie. I just needed to know. You have no problem taking risks with your art, but if you have no desire to—'

'I have the desire, but what am I to do? All I want in life is to paint.'

'I just meant there are others who would jump at such a chance.'

'It's not that I don't want it, I just...I can't, not now.'

Amélie puts a hand on Marie's shoulder. 'You should at least think about it.'

'I will,' Marie says. 'Thank you.'

The rain falls heavily as Marie steps out of Académie Julian onto Rue de Vivienne. She says goodbye to the women sheltering on the steps of the building. Then, she puts up her umbrella and heads down the street.

As she goes past the colonnaded stock exchange building, Palais Brongniart, she spots her lover, Gabriel, who waits for her under a row of linden trees across the street. She smiles and pretends not to see him. Gabriel throws his cigarette onto the cobbles and walks after her. He keeps his distance while they are still in view of the Académie; when they aren't, he jogs to catch up with her. But before he reaches her, she goes into a watchmaker's shop in a galleria to collect her repaired watch.

The rain has stopped by the time Marie comes out. Though her boots are already wet, she avoids the puddles. Then she spots him leaning against an alley wall. He grins. She goes over to him, and he puts his hand around her waist, and they kiss.

'I couldn't wait. I had to see you again,' Gabriel says. 'I've wanted you since I saw you this morning.' They kiss again. Gabriel has completed his studies at Hôpital Universitaire Pitié-Salpêtrière. Since graduation, his lack of lectures and exams has increased his demands on her. Something she has willingly indulged. But this isn't a sudden trend. Over the year they'd been together, their relationship had evolved beyond the simple arrangement they'd started with.

Nobody on the street pays them attention, so she steps from the alley, and Gabriel follows.

'You shouldn't have come this morning,' she says. 'It was too dangerous.'

'You loved me showing up like that.'

'And what about now? What if I was meeting Victor in that watchmaker's shop?' Marie says.

'He wouldn't have met you,' Gabriel says, but he glances over his shoulder anyway. 'Come home with me?'

'I'll see you later when he goes out.'

'No, I need you now.'

Marie grins. She wants him too. 'Okay. But I can't stay for long.'

Moonlight covers Gabriel's bedsit. Marie sits on Gabriel's bed, buttoning her bodice, then pushes her feet into her boots and ties the laces. 'I can't believe we fell asleep like that,' she says.

Gabriel laughs. 'Come here.'

'No, I've got to get home.'

'Don't you like being with me?'

'You know I do. I feel like me when I'm with you.'

'Stop worrying about him. He'll have gone out by now.'

'I hope. Victor will want to know where I've been.'

'Then tell him you were at the Académie.' Gabriel kneels among the sheets. He pulls Marie into him, and she can't help but kiss him.

'You're going to get me into so much trouble one day. Imagine if we'd slept longer?'

'But we didn't. Listen, Marie, we need to talk.'

'We can talk while you walk me home.'

Gabriel slumps back onto the bed and lights a cigarette with a match. 'No. We need to talk here.'

'Are you not going to walk me home? Do you know what happened last night to Victor and—'

'Victor, Victor. Always bloody, Victor.'

'Don't act like a child, Gabe.'

'I'm leaving,' he says.

'Leaving? What do you mean?'

'I've got a job.'

'About time. Where?'

'Panama,' he says.

'Panama?'

'Come with me?'

She goes over to the window, shoves it open, and leans against the frame. A horse and a carriage clatter along the cobbles on the dark street below. 'When are you going?'

'Marie. I want you to leave Paris. Leave Victor. Come and live with me in Panama.'

CHAPTER 7

The air is cool against Marie's flushed face as she leans out of the window. Across the Montmartre rooftops, where it isn't still covered in scaffolding, the Sacre-Coeur's white stonework gleams in the moonlight.

'When are you going?' she asks.

'Tomorrow.'

'Tomorrow? Damn it, Gabe. Why didn't you tell me about this? How long have you known?'

'Does it matter?'

'Yes.'

'Not if you were to come with me. Join me in Panama, and you won't have to worry about Victor.' His fingers dig into the thin mattress, and he stands as if he has the pains of an old man.

'Why Panama?'

'Why else? Because of the canal.'

'You're mad.'

'I'm aware of the risks.'

'They don't call it the fever coast for nothing. People go there, and they die.'

'I'm going. I can make a difference there.' It's all arranged.

'You could make a difference anywhere. You can make a difference right here in Paris.' Marie rubs her hand across her face wiping away cold beads of sweat. Her watch reads fifteen minutes past eleven. She sighs. 'I need to go. I need to get home. You know I can't risk him getting back before me again, not this late. Oh god, what if he hasn't gone?'

'Fuck him.'

49

'I'd rather fuck you.'

'Then let's all the way to Panama. We could be on a boat tomorrow. We could be fucking all the way to the other side of the world.'

She goes over to the table, takes her coat off the chair and grabs her satchel. 'You're ridiculous, Gabe. Rash. Bloody impulsive.'

'You'd have me stay here like a pet forever, wouldn't you?'

'Don't be silly. You could be a doctor in Paris. You'd get a nice house.'

'And then what? You'd leave him and live with me?'

She walks over to the door and opens it.

'You're goddamned selfish, Marie.'

'Maybe I am. But maybe it's for reasons you could never understand. Goodbye, Gabe,' she says and leaves.

Gabriel lives in a simple loft apartment in Madame Durand's hotel on Rue des Martyrs, where six other trainee doctors and two artists lodge on each floor below. Marie feels her way down the rickety dark stairs and is glad not to encounter anyone.

She closes the front door behind her and starts up the street towards Boulevard de Clichy. The gas lamps are spaced far apart along the road, and shadows lie between each one. As she walks, she thinks about the thief Victor had struck the night before. The huddled buildings loom over her. Voices talk. Footsteps pass. Shoulders and elbows bump against her. Eyes peer from beneath top hats and hoods. Someone hawks phlegm. Tobacco odour lingers like smog, blown from glowing pipes. Cats growl, darting past like ghouls. Window shutters slam, and voices shout at each other behind the glass. A horse canters along the cobbles. Somebody runs. She pauses outside a bistro where a man inside barks like a

50

dog and a woman laughs. Glass shatters. Someone shouts. She walks on.

The footsteps come up behind her, and a hand grabs her shoulder. She jumps.

'Marie?'

'Gabe!'

They hug.

'I don't know what to say,' he says.

'Neither do I.'

'This could never last, not like this.' He cups her cheek.

'I know,' she says, and they kiss.

'Do you have to go tomorrow?'

'Tomorrow. In a month? Does it matter? Will things be different?'

'We could talk—'

'I have a life to lead,' he says.

'But if you could wait.'

'Waiting would kill what we have.'

In the dark street, they kiss and hold each other.

When they arrive at Marie's home on rue de l'Élysée, the street is well-lit, so she lets go of Gabriel's hand.

Approaching the front door, she can see manure on the cobbles outside her home. A horse and carriage have been there to collect Victor to take him out for the night. The house is in darkness.

On the step, Gabriel leans in to kiss her, but she pulls away. 'Are you mad? Not here.'

'Well, I guess this is it then.'

'Gabe, did you mean what you said?'

'When?'

'The other day. You said—'

'Yes. I do.'

'I did. I mean, I do too.' She unlocks her front door and enters. 'Goodbye, Gabe.'

'My train leaves Gare du Nord for Le Havre at six,' he says.

She nods, closes her front door and locks it behind her. 'For god sake Marie,' she says to herself. She rests her forehead against the door. An oil lamp burns on a side table in the entrance hall. Victor's coat isn't on the hook. She hangs her coat beside the empty one, unlaces her boots, and puts them on the rack. All the while she does this, her mind is telling her to leave and go with Gabriel. What's keeping you here with a man like Victor, a man you don't love? Why keep spying for America? She thinks about the house and her lifestyle. Is it worth it? There's a thought pulling and tugging her back towards the door to open it and go and leave with Gabriel. 'Six in the morning,' she whispers to herself, staring at the flame in the oil lamp.

Rather than light the gas lamps, she carries the oil lamp up two flights of stairs and into her bedroom. She changes into her nightclothes and dressing gown, sits on the edge of her bed with her head in her hands and thinks about leaving. Maybe she could go, and the world would think she'd gone missing? Victor, Maxwell Steiner, they'd presume she was dead. What would I do if Gabe wanted to return to Paris, she thinks.

When she goes down the stairs to their parlour on the first floor, she sees that the door to Victor's office is ajar. She hadn't noticed it being open on the way up. She puts her hand on the door and listens. Nothing. She opens the door. 'Victor?' she whispers. A lamp is lit inside. There is no reply. She goes inside, and he is not there. She sighs. She turns to leave. The Egyptian statue lies on the desk among a mess

52

of documents, plans, maps, contracts and deeds she'd seen earlier in his briefcase. She heads over and sifts through it, and finds the map. Her red fingerprint is on it. She winces. Although it says Panama on the map, the isthmus differs from other maps, she's seen of the country. It is bluer. There's more water.

She picks up the statue. It's the same as the one she'd seen the day before. But it is different. There are no scuff marks on this one. She turns it over in her hand. She remembers what Victor said about them being used to contain the plans. She tries twisting it in various places until she discovers it's the sun disc that turns. She twists it off. Inside, she can see a rolled-up piece of paper. She tries tapping it out, but it has no effect. She slides in her little finger and eases it out. She uncurls it. There are technical drawings of locks and dams. On the map on the table, swathes of land are flooded. Her eyes widen. 'This might just save the whole dig,' she says.

She goes into the parlour carrying the oil lamp and goes straight over to the bookcase. She runs her finger across the spines until she finds an atlas. She drags it off the shelf, hauls it under her arm and turns back to Victor's office.

'It's a little late to be only coming back now, don't you think?' Victor says, his voice coming from the shadows in the corner of the room.

CHAPTER 8

Marie drops the atlas onto the parlour floor. 'Victor! Jesus. You made me jump.'

In the dark corner of the room, Victor sits in an armchair. 'Where have you been?' he asks.

'At the Académie,' she says, putting the lamp onto a table.

'Till this hour?'

Bending down and picking up the atlas, she smiles and tries to let it filter into her voice. 'Why are you sitting in the dark?'

'It wasn't dark when I came home.'

He takes a glass from a side table and knocks back the cognac. Then he throws the glass against the wall.

Her spine straightens. Victor stands.

'I asked, where have you been?'

Marie hesitates.

Victor stalks over to her.

'I stayed late at the Académie.'

'Then it will stop.'

'No! You can't.'

'I forbid you to go anymore.'

'You can't do that.'

'Can't I? And it's not the only thing that's going to stop.'

He puts his face up against hers.

'I know your little secret,' he says.

Marie edges backwards.

'Don't think your sneaking around has gone unnoticed.'

She clutches the atlas to her chest.

'I know about the doctor and you. Or should I say the spy

and you?'

'What?' She almost laughs with relief. 'You think Gabriel's a spy?'

'Then why have you been giving him information about my dealings?'

'I haven't, I—'

Victor slaps her across the face.

Anger rises inside her. She stands up straight. She wants to hurt him. 'You're mad. He hasn't been spying on you. I haven't been passing on information about you. I've simply been fucking him.'

He rips the atlas from her hands and punches her in the stomach. She doubles over, staggering back.

'I fully expected you to be a whore. After all, I'm under no illusion. I know my money attracted you,' Victor says.

Marie holds her stomach. 'Yet it's okay to sleep with a different prostitute whenever you like.'

Victor slaps her with the back of his hand again.

She turns back to him, and her lip bleeds. 'You'd better go out, Victor. They're waiting for you.'

He punches her in the stomach again, and she drops to her knees this time.

'You're the only whore I'll be having tonight.' He takes off his coat and drops it onto the floor. Then he unfastens his cufflinks and rolls up his shirt sleeves.

She edges back from him. He grabs her throat and slams her down onto the floor. He stands over her and unbuttons his waistcoat. She kicks his bad leg. He falls to his knees, but before she can escape, he grabs her, and his hands wrap around her neck.

Marie claws at his wrists. She digs her fingernails into his forearms.

He squeezes her throat. Orbs float in her vision, and her face feels like it will burst.

Then her hand hits on something in his coat on the floor beside her; the pistol he carries for protection. She fumbles through the layers of his coat until she finds the pocket. She finds the handle, drags it out of the pocket and shoves the muzzle into his stomach.

It doesn't stop him. He squeezes Marie's throat harder.

Bang.

Victor flinches. His arms lock straight as they bear his weight, but his hands remain around her throat. He squeezes tighter and tighter until Marie's vision fades, and she passes out.

Madame Durand stands in the dark entrance hall of her lodging house with her fists planted on her wide hips. 'You told her then?'

'Yes,' Gabriel says as he sulks past.

'And, what happened?'

'I don't want to talk about it.'

'Your plan was stupid. Didn't I tell you? You boys, with all your life experience, you think you know better than old Camille?' But no, you wouldn't listen.

'Ah, shut up. I'm not in the mood.'

'And where do you think you're sloping off to, eh?'

'My train leaves in the morning. I need sleep.'

'You can sleep all the way to Panama. Get down those stairs, you love sick fool.' She grabs his wrist and pulls him back down. 'Everybody is at La Renaissance,' she says, shoving him towards the front door. 'So don't think you're leaving Paris without us having the chance to bid you good riddance.'

She hooks her arm through his as they walk down the street.

'It'll be a good new start for you in Panama,' she says.

'I know.'

'Get yourself a nice nurse. They all adore you, doctors, anyway. And don't bother with mistresses. You're the type that falls in love too easily.'

'Okay. Okay. But Marie was different.'

Madame Durand stands in front of him in the dark. 'Listen to you.'

'What?'

She grabs the back of his head. Her grog-blossomed face leans in, and she pushes her lips onto his. With her other hand, she gropes his crotch. 'There! Feel that stirring? Marie Blanchet's not the only woman that can have that effect, no?'

Gabriel staggers back.

'Another woman's touch after a break-up is always awkward,' she says, and she punches him on the shoulder and then hooks her arm back through his again. 'Get yourself a girl tonight,' she says, pulling him along. 'Fuck her up a wall down an alley. Whatever you do, don't be afraid to live your life as soon as possible.'

The bistro in the basement of hotel La Renaissance is the kind of establishment Madame Durand would run, were her own hotel big enough to house one. Laughter, singing and shouting travels out of the bistro. When their friends and fellow lodgers see them enter, they cheer, and Gabriel can't help but smile.

'Monsieur Dufour,' Madame Durand shouts to the owner. 'Bring us absinthe. We have some catching up to do.'

Marie opens her eyes. Her throat aches. She coughs, and it

57

hurts. She turns over.

Victor lies on his side facing her. He is wide-eyed, open-mouthed, and his tongue sticks out. She pushes him, and he rolls onto his back. She sits on her knees and stares at him, remembering what had happened. Her fingers are in his blood on the carpet. She retches several times and then vomits.

She crawls over to the chair where Victor had been sitting, and she takes a glass from the side table. She pours his cognac into it from the decanter and winces as she drinks.

The glass in her blood-stained hand is as still as Victor. She puts it back onto the side table. Neither hand shakes.

In the bathroom, pale-faced, messy-haired, her neck raw and sore, Marie stares at herself in the mirror. She tries taking her wedding ring off but she can't pull it off over her swollen fingers.

She holds her still hands under the flowing tap water until the blood has washed away and the skin on her fingers is wrinkled. The ring still wont come off.

Eventually, she goes up the stairs and into their bedroom. In the wardrobe, she finds a bag, then opens it on her bed, and stuffs some clothes inside. Then she removes some clothes and replaces them with others she thinks will be more suited for travel.

After packing, she goes down the stairs and pauses again in the doorway to Victor's study. She glances at the documents on the desk, then goes over to the safe built into the wall that is thankfully open. She removes her passport and a wallet containing several hundred francs and puts them into her bag. She turns back to the desk and sits down. She sifts through the paperwork, dividing what will be helpful and what isn't into two piles. She reads the proposal; to make a test dam, which, if it proves to be successful, would be adopted universally on the construction of the Panama Canal. She knows this would save the failing operation, which had become a national scandal. She puts the maps and plans from the Egyptian statue back inside it and then screws the head back on. She puts some other plans into a folder and pushes the other remaining documents into the safe, which she locks. She takes the folder and the statue and goes to go downstairs. She pauses on the landing. Victor lies in the parlour.

She goes in and kneels beside him. She thinks she should feel sorry for him, but she doesn't. She can't. The world is a better place without him. Then she wonders if she ever really knew him. It dawns on her that maybe she should have died instead. Was she any better? I'm a liar, a cheat, a spy. What for? Perhaps I am just a whore. Her shoulders slump and her head drops, and she cries.

At the front door, she puts on her boots and slides the folder of documents along with the statue of Tefnut into her rucksack of art materials. She checks her watch; it's one a.m., then she extinguishes the oil lamp and leaves their home.

The American embassy in Paris isn't far from Marie and Victor's home, where Marie decides to go. Marie locks the front door and hurries down Rue de l'Elysée. At the bottom of her street is the Jardin des Champs Élysées. Beneath the orderly trees at one a.m., she struggles to see. She follows the straight path. The clean gravel crunches beneath her feet. She heads towards the sound of the steady fountain and steers for the street lamps on Place de la Concorde. A lone horse and carriage rattle across the square. She waits at the park's iron gate until it goes past. The American Embassy sits across the square, and two men lean against a guard's hut. Marie retrieves the statue of Tefnut and hides the rucksack under a thick bush. It is clear up and down the street. She runs over to the gates.

'Hello, excuse me,' she says.

One of the guards adjusts his rifle on his shoulder and rubs his hands together as he struts over. 'How much do you charge then, lovely?'

'What?' Marie asks.

'Charge,' he says.

'I'm here to see the ambassador. I need to see him immediately.'

'Are you? Crazy woman! It's late. Go away.'

'Wait a minute,' the second guard says. 'I recognise you. You've been here before. You're here to see the ambassador?'

'Yes, I'm here to see Max.'

The two guards grin at each other. 'Max, you say? She's here to see the ambassador. Alright, you can come on in.' They open the gate and gesture her in.

One of them leads her along the short path to the front of the embassy, where he knocks on the door. After a short while, a man peers through a window and opens the door. 'What is this?' he asks.

'She's here for the—'

'I need to see the ambassador,' Marie says.

'What on earth are you doing bringing this woman to the house?'

'She's here to see the ambassador,' the guard says and winks.

'I need to see Maxwell Steiner immediately.'

'And who the devil are you?'

'I have intelligence I need to give to him.'

60

'What's going on?' Maxwell Steiner says from inside the house. Marie pushes past the man at the door, and the guard fumbles his rifle off his shoulder. Everyone protests. They try to grab her as she goes towards the ambassador.

'Wait!' Steiner says. 'It's okay, I know her, leave her, let go.'

The two men hesitate until Steiner raises his eyebrows, and they release her.

'Leave her with me. She's fine.'

'Are you sure, Sir?'

'Of course, I am. Come with me, Marie.'

Maxwell Steiner leads Marie into a room, closing the door behind them. Dim light flickers from the gas lamps hanging on the walls between full bookcases.

'Last night, when I invited you to come and talk to us, I wasn't expecting you to call in this late the next day. Take a seat.' He gestures at two high-backed chairs next to the fireplace. Marie drops her bag on the floor next to one of the chairs.

'You look like you're dressed for a journey. Do you want a drink first?' Maxwell asks.

'Victor's dead,' Marie says.

'Say again?'

'I've killed Victor.' Marie sits on the edge of the chair and holds her head in her hands.

'Jesus,' he says. He pours bourbon into the two glasses. He knocks one back, and then he fills the glass again. He goes over to Marie and holds one out to her. She doesn't lift her head from her hands. He puts the drink on a table beside her. Sitting opposite, he leans back into the chair and pulls his dressing gown over his knee. 'Want to tell me what happened?'

Marie shakes her head.

'Well, you're going to.'

Marie puts her hands on her knees. 'He tried to rape me. He tried to kill me. Now, he's the one that's dead.'

'Why?' he asks.

'What do you mean, why?'

'Why did he attack you? Did Victor find out why you married him?'

'No.'

'Then what caused him to attack you?'

Marie breaks eye contact. She decides not to tell him Victor suspected Gabriel was a spy she was passing on information to.

'Let me guess,' Maxwell says. 'He found out about the young doctor?'

She says nothing.

'Yeah, that's right,' he says, sipping his drink. 'You French, you can't help yourselves.'

Marie picks up the drink and downs it. She winces. Her throat hurts when she swallows.

'Are you sure Victor never knew you were spying on him for us? Could he have told anyone?'

Marie shakes her head. 'Don't worry, he had no idea.'

'I'm sure you had no idea he knew about your boyfriend.'

'Believe me, I would've been dead if he knew I was spying on his business.'

'So how did he find out about the doctor then?'

'I don't know. Victor didn't give me the courtesy of telling me before he started trying to throttle me.'

'So, why have you come here?'

'What do you mean, why have I come here? I work for you. I need protection. I've just killed the man I married for

62

you. You need to get me out of France. I need to get back to America.'

'We didn't ask you to kill him. That wasn't your mission. You were supposed to be getting information on his business dealings. You were supposed to be getting us information on the Panama Canal. Anyone would think you took being a sleeper agent too bloody literally.'

'Victor kept me separate from his business in every way. You know this.'

'It must've been over a year ago when you last visited us. Let me guess. When we last saw you, that was before you got with the doctor.'

'Would you stop going on about Gabe.'

'Well, if you'd spent your time more wisely—'

'I've got information for you. Are you happy?'

'It depends on what it is.'

Marie opens her bag and slams the statue of Tefnut onto the table.

'You did get it,' he says.

'No. I told you what happened to that one. It's at the bottom of the Seine. Victor had one. He came back with it yesterday. Victor had started financing the canal. After all these years of saying they'd never succeed, he started investing when it failed.

Maxwell puts the drink on the table and leans forwards. 'That's out of character. Why? Tell me you found out why?'

'They've finally abandoned the plans to cut through the land. Instead, they will use dams to flood large areas and create locks. Victor is funding a test dam. If it's successful, they'll adopt that system.'

'Bastards. That's bad news for us, alright,' Maxwell says. 'That would save their whole operation. We need to own

63

that canal. Whoever owns that canal controls the world's shipping.'

'I couldn't give a damn. I've given you the information. Now get me out of France.'

Maxwell shakes his head as he leans back into the chair. 'It's not that simple, Marie. You know we can't help you. If it was to get out that we're spying on them because we want the canal, they'd never give it up. Every Frenchman in the country would give his last damn franc to make it happen. No. You have the perfect cover.'

'The perfect cover for you, not for me. I need help.'

'Where are these documents? Are they inside?' he asks, pointing at the statue.

'I'm not a fool. I won't hand their plans over just so you don't have to help me.'

'Now, don't be like that.' He sits and stares at his drink, running his finger around the rim of the glass. 'Listen, Marie, the way I see it is this, you've got two options. Number one. Go on the run. Go and get lost in the world. Or number two, continue to work for us.'

'What do you mean work?' Marie asks. 'Victor's dead. How can I work for you?'

'Presuming you know where this dam is, sabotage it for us.'

'Sabotage? How on earth can I?'

'I'm guessing you never killed a man before today? You figured out how to do that.'

Marie glares at him.

He says: 'This dam's a test, correct?'

'Yes,' Marie says. 'That's what the documents said.'

'Well, I'm thinking. If the test fails and the dam doesn't work, they'll abandon the whole project. Then we can move in and take over as planned. Needless to say,' he says. 'Whichever path you take, like when you first joined us, you're on your own.'

'You're scared I'll talk?'

'What? And tell whomever you're a spy? You're not that silly. If they don't cut your head off for murdering Victor, they'll do it for that.'

'Two years, Max. Two years I was married to that bastard and spied on him for you. What have I got to show for it?'

He laughs.

'It's no laughing matter. I've got nothing,' she says. 'America owes me.'

'You knew what the deal was Marie. You knew we wouldn't pay you anything. With Victor, you wanted for nothing. You had a better life with him than if we'd paid you.'

'But I can't just walk into a bank and withdraw his money now. I haven't even got a roof over my head anymore.'

'Yeah, well, we didn't want him dead.'

Marie looks at the fireplace. 'If I was to do this, what do I get in return?'

'What do you want?'

'Freedom. I want a house and some land. I want citizenship. And I'm going to need money.'

He leans forwards and shakes his head. 'We could get anyone to sabotage the dam for us for a fraction of the cost.'

'Yes, I'm sure you could. But you don't know where they've built the dam.'

He leans back in his chair and claps his hands together. 'Well, well Marie, you must've learnt something about negotiation from the old dog after all. It's a shame he didn't teach you how to blow things up. Yeah,' he says. 'You'll need help. Your old mentor—'

'Wait, no. Stop right there, I'm not—'

'Charlie Blaine would be perfect. The only trouble is that he's distanced himself from us. We miss his usefulness. We want him back in the fold.'

'I'm not working with Charlie. Add that to my list of conditions.'

'Charlie Blaine will teach you the skills you need.'

'After what I did to him? Charlie won't come near me. He hates me.'

'How else will you trek through a jungle and destroy a dam without killing yourself? Do the job with Charlie's help, and you'll get what you want.'

'You're sadistic. I can't work with Charlie.'

'You don't have many choices for a woman that's just killed her husband.'

'We might've been married, but he wasn't my husband.' She shakes her head. 'How will I get what I've asked for? I'm not coming back to France to get it.'

He gets up and goes over to a side cabinet that has a globe on top of it. He spins it around and stops at the Caribbean. He taps on an island. 'Martinique. Any operation in Panama goes through there. Yes, we'll conduct our business through Martinique.'

Marie walks over to him. 'What does that mean?'

'Charlie will know. All you need to know is that once your mission is done, return to Martinique and your reward will await you.'

'I don't know where Charlie is.'

Maxwell writes down an address. 'Memorise it, then destroy it. He's in a village outside of Arles.' He slides it across the surface of the cabinet, and she takes it.

'What did he do? Why isn't he working for you anymore?'

The ambassador shakes his head. 'Why don't you ask him when you find him. Tell him you're in trouble. I'm sure he'll come running.'

Marie walks down the path to the gate. The two guards say nothing to her. They keep their heads down, unlock the gate and let her out.

She heads over to the park, finds the documents under the bush where she'd hidden them, and then checks her watch. It is two fifteen in the morning as Marie considers her options. She knows running away is her best hope of not getting caught. If she goes far away without any affiliation, she knows she has a good chance of getting away with it. She thinks about what she might do: she could travel to another country and find a rich husband to support her. However, this isn't the life she wants again. She decides she will be with Gabriel or forge a life without anyone, and Maxwell's proposition is the best chance. But right there and then, she needs to see Gabriel, if only for one last time. Besides, she thinks, both options lead to Panama.

CHAPTER 9

At the bottom of Rue de Martyrs, the bell atop Notre Dame de Lorette rings three times. The six trainee doctors, and the women they have acquired either that night or in the recent past, follow Madame Durand as if she is the Pied Piper. She plants her hands on her hips when she sees Marie sitting on her doorstep with her two bags.

'So you're going to Panama then?' Madame Durand asks.

'How could I leave him,' says Marie.

'What's wrong with your voice? You been drinking?'

'Nothing's wrong,' Marie says.

'Gabriel, there's someone here for you.'

Gabriel stumbles through the crowd. He spots Marie. He runs over to her, and they embrace. He reeks of alcohol and smoke. He kisses her, and she buries her head into his shoulder and hugs him.

Madame Durand saunters over to the woman Gabriel had met in La Renaissance.

'What's going on,' the woman asks, 'who's that?'

'Alas, my dear, it's nothing for you to worry about. Who are we to stand in the way of true love, eh?'

'I don't understand. Who's that woman?'

'Why don't you have a think about it while you walk home, my dear?'

'But I—'

'Listen to me. I know that over the last couple of hours, you'd imagined your life as the wife of a doctor. I'm sure you would've given him the best night of his life to achieve such an aim. But it's not happening.' Madame Durand strokes the woman's cheek. 'If you still have the need to fuck somebody tonight...'

The woman pulls away. 'I'm not that way inclined.'

'Then, fuck off.' Madame Durand plants her fists on her hips and steps into the woman so that their bodies touch. The woman steps back. She opens her mouth to say something and then wisely walks away.

When Madame Durand returns to her front door, Marie is helping Gabriel stay upright. The other lodgers are patting them on the back and making a lot of excited noise about their reunion.

Hugo, the group's joker, shouts, 'Love conquers all,' and the others laugh.

Michel starts chanting, 'Panama. Panama,' and the others join in until he falls over, and they laugh at him.

Across the street, window shutters smack against the wall. A middle-aged woman with wild grey hair shouts, 'Shut up with your noise, you drunken fools.'

'Hey,' Madame Durand shouts back. 'Shut up your own mouth Martinez and get back inside your stinking hovel.'

The woman leans out of the window and thrusts out two fingers before she grabs the shutters and slams them closed.

Madame Durand turns to Marie, as she unlocks the front door. 'You'd better get him sobered up. You only have a few hours until your train leaves.'

Gabriel lies on the bed, snoring. Madame Durand pushes the curtain back and leans against the doorframe. Gabriel rents two rooms from Madame Durand in her loft. Despite being colder in winter and warmer in the summer, he'd taken this room when it became available because Marie liked the view from the window. Madame Durand shakes her head on remembering this. Then she runs her finger down the bare crumbling plaster. 'Just my luck that they rent from me before getting a doctor's wage. I've been too kind to these boys. I'll have to start charging them more. This whole place is going to fall down.'

Marie strokes her neck.

'Don't let him sleep any longer than an hour,' Madame Durand says. 'That should be enough to rejuvenate him. Then you'll have to get to the station.' She goes to leave but stops and walks over to the sink instead, where she collects a couple of glasses and a half-empty bottle of wine. Then she sits down opposite Marie at the table. 'These trainee doctors are all the same. I'm amazed they hold a scalpel steady in the morning. It's a good job they're working on cadavers and criminals, no?'

Madame Durand finds a partially smoked cigar inside a concealed pocket in the folds of her skirt. She plants it between her teeth. From off the table, she lifts a bottle with a candle stabbed into it and lights the cigar off the flame. 'I must say, I'm surprised.'

'Really, why?'

'You're giving up a lot. A good home, security, status. You're braver than I thought.'

'Well...' Marie takes a deep breath. 'Maybe it's not all it's cracked up to be.

'I don't know. I imagine many would endure a man like Victor for such a life.'

'Would you?'

'I'm sure he'd be the one enduring me.' Madame Durand takes a long drag on the cigar and then blows out a smoke ring. 'What about your art?'

'There'll be a lot of scenes to capture in Panama.'

Madame Durand holds the cigar between her teeth and pours wine into the two glasses.

Marie is still stroking her neck.

'Are you alright?'

'It'll heal.'

'Why tell him?'

'I didn't.' Marie drags the glass across the table. She gulps half of the wine and grits her teeth at the vinegar-like taste. Then she finishes the rest of it.

Madame Durand takes another drag on the cigar, then tips half of the wine from her glass into Marie's.

'What did he do?'

'He tried to kill me.' Marie unties the scarf from her neck and unbuttons the high collar of her jacket. She leans towards the light from the candle. The skin on her neck is inflamed and bruised.

Madame Durand tuts. 'Marie,' she says and shakes her head. 'How on earth did you survive?'

'I killed him.'

Madame Durand takes the cigar from her mouth. 'You're being serious.'

Marie nods.

'Then it's no more a fate than he deserves.'

They drink in silence, and Gabriel's snores carry from the bedroom. Madame Durand leans across the table. 'How?'

'I—'

'No! Maybe it's best I don't know what happened. If the police come to ask—'

'Police?'

'If they find out about you and Gabriel, they'll come here. If I don't know, I'll have nothing to hide. Listen to me. What have you done with the body?'

'He's still there.'

'Will he be found?'

'Yes.'

'Shit. When?'

'This morning. When our maid arrives.'

Madame Durand takes a deep breath. 'What time does she come?'

'At six. To prepare our breakfast.'

Madame Durand raises her eyebrows. 'Your breakfasts?'

Marie nods.

'Hmm. I suppose that's good.'

'How?'

'Because your train leaves for Le Havre at six.' Madame Durand finishes her wine. 'How do you feel?'

Marie scratches a cut in the table's surface. 'I don't know.'

'You're very calm.'

Marie stares at her hand. It remains still. 'I am. I just feel… numb.'

'Who knows how we'd react, eh?'

'I was thinking of confessing.'

'What? Are you deranged?'

'I'll lose everything if not. I'll tell them what happened. I'll show them the scars. It's a crime of passion, no?'

Madame Durand shakes her head. 'You're so naïve, child. He might've gotten off with such a plea if he'd killed you. Do you really think you will? Has any woman in your position?'

'Some…'

'He had many friends high up, no? Judges. Politicians?'

Marie nods.

'So as to warn their wives and mistresses, they'd make sure you faced the guillotine.'

Marie's eyes widen.

72

'That's your reality, I'm afraid,' Madame Durand says. 'Better to be on the other side of the world than in France now.'

'I don't know,' Marie says. 'I don't know what to do. I've got nothing. I've no means of supporting myself.'

'Gabriel will look after you.'

Marie sighs. 'I'm tired of being looked after.'

Gabriel snores.

'Why have you never found a man and settled down?'

'I could've, many years ago now,' Madame Durand says as she stares at the cigar's burning end. 'I got myself into a situation where I didn't need anyone looking after me. I sacrificed a lot, though. I could've led a very different life.'

'Do you ever regret it?'

'Regret not having somebody control my life?' Madame Durand smiles. 'Listen. If you do love him. If you want to be with Gabe, then don't ever tell him what happened,' Madame Durand places her hand on top of Marie's. 'If he knows you didn't choose him, he'll resent you, and this will all be in vain.'

At dawn, five steaming locomotives wait like sleeping dragons lined up in the vast hall of Gare du Nord. Carriage after carriage stretches back beneath the vaulted, iron roof. The time is a quarter to six, and the train to Le Havre is due to depart from platform four on the hour. Madame Durand, who pushes through the crowds, leads Marie and Gabriel through the station. But whenever Marie sees policemen or gendarme, she squeezes Gabriel's hand. None pay them any attention.

Beside the carriage, Marie and Madame Durand hug, and she whispers into Marie's ear. 'I shall tell everyone that you left him at the station. I'll call you many an obscene name. I'll tell them you got on a train to Marseille alone.'

'No, not Marseille, Lyon or somewhere like that.'

'If the police do come, if they find out about you and Gabe, at least it'll sound believable if that's what everyone thinks.'

'Thank you. You're a true friend.'

The women separate.

'Take care of Gabriel,' Madame Durand says. 'Make sure he doesn't get eaten by a tiger.'

'We're going to Panama, not India,' Gabriel says, taking Madame Durand by the shoulders and kissing her on each cheek. 'Still, it's much more likely to be a snake or something just as awful.'

'Go, get on the train. I've had enough of your youthful love, and now I have a room to rent, no? So unless you wish to stay and pay me double the money, then be gone.'

Gabriel climbs aboard the train carrying their bags, followed by Marie. Madame Durand closes the door, and Marie leans out of the open window. 'Enjoy your new life. Live urgently, as if each day is your last.'

Madame Durand leaves, pushing through the crowds, gesturing and reprimanding anyone too slow in moving out of her way.

Above the platform, the clock reads five minutes to six.

CHAPTER 10

In Père Lachaise Cemetery, Inspector Mathis Legrand kneels at his late wife's grave and places a single rose onto the simple headstone. Then he closes his eyes and pictures her. When he's finished, he picks some moss from the chiselled letters of her name. His finger lingers on the letter Y and his head bows. 'I'm sorry, Yvette,' he says, then walks away.

Legrand's mentor, Inspector Jéan Foceau, is waiting nearby, a spectacled man past retirement age. He sits perched on an ossuary, enjoying the first rays of the morning sun warming his face.

Legrand walks past, Foceau climbs down, and they walk silently along the tree-lined path through the cemetery.

At the gates, Foceau flicks the end of his cigarette into the road. 'Bonnevay told me yesterday they're closing the case on the Lac Daumesnil drowning.'

Legrand stops and turns to Foceau. 'Seriously?'

Foceau nods.

'Do you tell me these things to piss me off?'

Foceau smiles.

'Bonnevay's fucking useless,' Legrand says. 'They're all fucking useless. That girl was murdered. How can they drop the case?'

'Nothing to go on,' Foceau says. 'No leads.'

Legrand sucks his teeth. 'No leads if you can't be bothered digging them out.'

'If that annoys you, you don't want to know what he is bragging about.'

Legrand pulls a box of cigarettes out of his coat pocket,

sticks one between his lips and lights it. 'What?'

'DuVille's going to promote him.'

Legrand throws the cigarette onto the floor. 'To hell he is!'

The door bangs off the wall. Legrand storms into Chief Inspector DuVille's office. DuVille, a huge man with a shiny, bald head and a moustache curling at the ends, sits behind his desk. He had once been a beat officer who instilled fear into the criminals of Paris. Sat across the desk is a current beat officer, Marnier, who looks like he'd be scared of the city's criminals.

'Get out,' Legrand says to Marnier as he stalks over to the desk and leans over it towards DuVille.

When Marnier doesn't move, Legrand thumps on the desk and glares back at him.

Marnier gets up and leaves.

'This intrusion better be worth it,' DuVille says.

'Is it true?' Legrand asks.

'About?'

'That fucking cunt.'

DuVille closes his eyes and tilts his head back. 'Bonnevay! Get in here.'

The two men stare at each other until Bonnevay opens the door and strolls into the office.

'You've got a loud mouth Bonnevay,' DuVille says. 'And it's cost you.'

'Me?'

'Do you know who that officer was with me before?'

Bonnevay tilts his head from side to side. He isn't sure, but he isn't going to commit to an answer either way. 'I've seen him around.'

DuVille points at Legrand. 'Do you know?'

76

'Marnier,' Legrand says.

'You're right.' DuVille stands. 'This morning, Marnier responded to a maid who'd found her master dead in his house.'

'Who?'

'Victor Blanchet.'

Bonnevay whistles.

'And the killer?' Legrand asks.

DuVille spreads his arms out wide. 'I don't know. That's your job.'

'I'll find you his killer,' Legrand says. 'But I'm not working with him.'

'I'm not asking you to. Think of this as your interview. The first one to discover who killed Victor Blanchet becomes my deputy.'

Bonnevay laughs.

'What's so funny, Inspector?' asks DuVille.

Bonnevay glowers. 'That today, of all days, my fellow inspector here might finally get a chance to make up for his past mistakes.'

Legrand swings his right fist into Bonnevay's face.

'Hey, cut it out. Enough!' DuVille shouts.

Legrand rubs his knuckles. Bonnevay straightens himself and tilts his head back as he pinches his nose to stop the blood streaming out.

'You asked for that, Bonnevay,' DuVille says. 'But I won't tolerate action like that, Legrand. You're not in the foreign legion now.'

'My apologies if I offended you,' Bonnevay says. 'I didn't mean to—'

'Stick it.'

'I said enough. Men. Your careers depend on results.'

77

DuVille's office door bangs against the wall as Legrand storms out. He winks at Foceau and Marnier, who are standing talking. 'Come on, quick, we haven't much time,' Legrand says.

Steam billows from the engine. The train rushes past the backs of tenement buildings on its way out of Paris. Gabriel lies on the seat in their private compartment nursing his hangover. Marie sits opposite, a slither of charcoal hovering over the drawing pad on her knee. She is relieved to be leaving Paris.

'I bet you're glad I upgraded us now.'

Gabriel opens an eye. 'It's fine, just this once, but I don't want us to live off his money.'

'Don't think of it as his. It's my money now.'

'I don't want us to live off your money either.'

'What's yours is mine, Gabe.' Marie smiles. She sketches the hard angular lines of his profile with speed and accuracy that pleases her. It is good to do something normal to keep her mind off Victor. She sketches Gabriel's profile, his strong neck, and his jutting Adam's apple. She draws the collar of his cotton shirt and shows more of his chest than is visible. She draws with broad, thrusting stabs that threaten to tear the paper. Then she stops drawing and stares at his body. She puts the drawing pad and the charcoal on the seat beside her. She pulls the layers of her dress up to her shins.

'Do you remember what you said we could do all the way to Panama?'

Gabriel opens an eye. He sees her black stockings and sits up, alert like a cat that's just seen a mouse. 'In here?'

'We're on our way, aren't we?'

'But what if someone comes....'

78

She pulls her skirt higher.

He launches himself across the narrow gap and falls upon her. She freezes beneath his weight. Victor stares down at her and not Gabriel. Somebody knocks on the door. Gabriel scrambles back into his seat. They stare at each other. Then he laughs as he leans over and pulls her dress down, breaking her trance. 'Come in,' he says.

The door slides open, and the conductor, a short man in a navy uniform, steps in. 'Good morning Madame, Monsieur.' He raises one of his grey, bushy eyebrows at Gabriel. 'May I see your tickets, please?'

Gabriel points his finger at the bag on the rack above him. 'Give me a minute.' But it is Marie who stands. She takes the load from the rack, drops it into Gabriel's lap, and then sits back down. Gabriel winces. He finds the tickets, and the inspector punches a hole in each.

Marie asks the inspector, 'I don't suppose you know what time our ship leaves?'

The inspector is pleased to assist. 'Yes, of course. What is your final destination?'

'Panama,' Marie says.

He takes a notebook from his breast pocket and thumbs the pages. 'There are two ships, Mademoiselle, the Africane and the Liberty. Which one is yours?'

'The Liberty,' Gabriel says.

'Ah, let me see, yes. The Liberty sets sail at four forty-five this afternoon.'

'What time?' Marie asks.

'Four forty-five. Is there anything else I can help you with?'

'We're fine, thanks,' Gabriel says. When the ticket inspector closes the door, Gabriel puts his hands on Marie's knees. The carriage darkens as the train passes through a canyon of

79

warehouses. He pulls her knees apart, kneels between them, and leans towards her. Marie pushes him away.

'Why's it leaving so late?' she asks.

'I don't know. I think they said something to do with the spring tides and the size of the ship.'

'I'm hungry,' she says. 'Shall we get something from the buffet car?'

Gabriel scratches his head. 'I thought we were going to...' He sits back on the seat opposite her.

Marie stands and wobbles as the carriage crosses some points. 'Come on, let's get something.'

A waiter leads Marie and Gabriel through the buffet cart as the train winds through the countryside along the banks of the tree-lined Seine. Marie's eyes dart around the carriage. Seated at tables, the women wear delicate silk dresses, and the men wear suits and top hats. They are underdressed compared to everyone else. She leans towards Gabriel and whispers, 'We should've stayed in the cabin.'

'Why? It's you that suddenly developed an appetite. What's wrong?'

'Nothing. It's nothing,' she says, satisfied that all the people in the carriage are strangers. She picks a table furthest from the cocktail bar and pushes Gabriel out of the way to take the chair so her back is to everyone.

After the waiter returned with coffee and pastries, Gabriel couldn't bear to eat.

'Just how much did you drink last night?' she asks.

'I thought I wasn't going to see you again.'

'Well then, I'll take the severity of your hangover as a compliment.' She slices a croissant in half and spreads raspberry jam upon it. He winces as she pushes the plate across the table to him. 'It'll make you feel better,' she says.

'Doctors orders?'

'You should know. Eat up.'

As Marie pours coffee from a cafetière and Gabriel nibbles the croissant, a woman with a flash of grey hair walks into the buffet cart. 'Marie, where do I know that woman from?'

Marie turns, and the two women recognise each other. It is Madame Gage. Her husband, wearing a black suit and a top hat, sits at a table. She says something to him, and he glances in their direction, then picks up a newspaper. Madame Gage walks over and tilts her head. 'What a surprise to see you here, of all places.'

'Madame Gage,' Marie says as the other woman bends down, and they kiss each other on the cheek.

The older woman points at Gabriel. 'You were at the salon,' she says.

'This is my brother, Gabe.'

Gabriel's face scrunches up. 'Yes, I'm her brother. Madame,' he says.

'Oh, I didn't realise you had a brother.'

'What on earth are you doing here?' Marie asks.

'I could ask you the same thing.'

'I'm sure it's not as interesting as where you're headed.'

Madame Gage smiles. 'My husband has been called to dine with the French consul in London.'

Gabriel's face scrunches up again. 'Actually—'

Marie kicks his leg under the table. 'Actually, we're just headed to visit our parents.'

'Ah, yes,' Madame Gage says, 'you were right.'

'See, what did I say?'

'Anyway, I should rejoin my husband.'

'Indeed. Have a safe journey.'

'Say, I hope Victor is well?'

'Victor?'

'Your husband.'

'I didn't realise you were on first-name terms?'

'Well, he was quite the presence at the Baron's salon the other night. You made quite a stir in the papers yourself. Anyway, goodbye.'

Madame Gage smirks and goes over to sit with her husband.

'Say, what's all that about being your brother?'

'Do you think she believed me?' Marie glances back over her shoulder. Madame Gage is seated with her back to them, talking at her husband, who continues reading his newspaper.

'I don't know. What does it matter?'

'I... It's our business, Gabe. It's nothing to do with her. The least she knows, the better.'

'Well, I'm sure she'll find out soon enough,' Gabriel says.

'Yes. I'm sure she will.'

'Say, what's all that about you and the papers?'

'I don't know.'

After they get the waiter's attention, he delivers them a selection of newspapers.

Marie turns straight to the society pages. She reads the most prominent headline on the page, Scandal overshadows Baron's salon. She scans the first paragraph. Then she folds the newspaper.

'What is it? What does it say?' Gabriel asks.

'Nothing, don't...'

Gabriel opens it anyway.

The train slows to a stop at Vernouillet station. Gabriel folds the newspaper and slaps it onto the table. The other diners stare at them. Marie puts her hand on his.

'It's ridiculous. I can't believe they can print something like that. You looked incredible in that dress.'

She shakes her head. 'I don't care. He made me wear it anyway.'

They sit in silence and eat breakfast in the buffet cart. Marie stares at her reflection as it appears and disappears in the window. It is eight-thirty when they finish.

Marie's silver watch strap sticks to her wrist. She loosens it and pushes it up and down. It reminds her of a handcuff. She releases the clasp on the bracelet, slides the watch off over her hand, and then places it on the table.

She tries to take the wedding ring off, but she still can't pull it off her finger.

When they get up to leave, as the train races through the lush fields of Normandy, Marie is relieved to see Madame Gage has already left the buffet cart. They are about to leave when Gabriel spots the watch on the table. 'You nearly forgot this,' he says, handing it to her.

She doesn't take it. 'I don't want it,' she says.

'You can't just leave it here. It must cost a fortune.'

'It does.'

'Well then, here you go.'

'You keep it,' she says.

'Why don't you want it?'

Marie shakes her head. 'It reminds me of him.'

CHAPTER 11

In the parlour on the first floor of the Blanchet residence on Rue de l'Elysee, Inspector Foceau sits in the chair and picks up the decanter. He removes the stopper and sniffs the contents. Inspector Legrand rubs his forehead. He crouches beside the body.

Officer Marnier appears in the doorway. 'Sir, the press are here.'

'Show them up.'

'Really?'

Legrand glares at the officer. He goes and does as he's told.

Legrand uses a pencil to lift the deceased's finger. Beneath it, in the stomach, is a dark wound full of congealed blood. He got some of it on the end of the pencil. The journalist and a photographer climb the stairs and come into the parlour. Legrand wipes the end of the pencil on the dead man's shirt and then walks over to them. Legrand puts his hand over the lens as the photographer lifts his camera.

The journalist says, 'Well Mathis, what gives?'

'Murder.'

'I can see that. I mean, letting us up here. That's not your style. What's your game?'

The journalist takes a notebook out of his pocket and roots around for a pen. Legrand gives him the pencil.

'What's going on then?' the journalist asks.

'How soon can you get this in print?' asks Legrand.

'The longer we stand here talking, the longer it'll take.'

'How long?'

'In Paris?' The journalist checks his watch. 'The next edition's not till midday.'

'I'm not talking about editions. Can't you run a cover?'

'Come on, this isn't anything big.'

'I'm sure your competitors will think differently. Marnier, show these boys out.'

The police officer steps towards them from the door.

'Now hang on. Alright. I'll see what I can do.'

'And you'll wire it too.'

'Now, come on.'

'All the travel hubs. Port towns, and I want it in train stations that lead on somewhere.'

'You've got a lead, haven't you?'

Legrand shakes his head. 'No.'

'You have. I can see it in your eyes,' the journalist says, then he bites on the end of the pencil.

Legrand smiles. 'I don't. We're starting this cold, but I want whoever did this to see your headlines. I want them to get scared. I want them to see the guillotine glinting every time they see the sun reflecting off a window.'

'Or the guillotine ratcheting,' the photographer says, 'when they hear the—'

Legrand and the journalist glare at him. 'You just stick to taking pictures, leave the words to me, eh. Go on then, give it to me.'

'Gunshot to the stomach,' Legrand says. 'But don't print that.'

'Don't print that?' The journalist spreads his hands. Then he raises his eyebrows. 'Signs of a struggle?'

'There's a glass smashed over there. Expensive cognac down the wall.'

'You don't throw expensive cognac down a wall if someone isn't coming at you.'

Legrand sways his head from side to side. 'You can if you can afford to buy it in the first place.'

'Who is he anyway?'

'Oh, you'll like this. Go and have a look.'

The journalist walks over and crouches at the side of the body. 'Victor Blanchet! This is his place?'

'Yes.'

'Do you want paying for this or something? Is that your angle?'

Legrand stares at him.

'No.' The journalist wags the pencil. 'The great Mathis Legrand wouldn't stoop that low.'

Legrand's jaw tenses.

The journalist clicks his fingers. 'Madame, mademoiselle Blanchet. What's her name? Maria.'

'Marie.'

'Yeah, that's the one.'

'What about her?' Legrand asks.

'The dress. She caused quite a scandal the other night at the Baron's salon. By all accounts, she was—'

'Alright, cool yourself. I read the social pages.'

'You do? What happened to her? Where's her body?'

'Not here.'

'You think she's got something to do with this?'

'Where else would she be than here?' Legrand points at him. 'Don't you dare make out like she's a suspect, though.'

'Is she?'

'My options are open. I don't want you blurting out I said she's in the frame, then we get a ransom note.'

'A kidnapping?'

'You guys made news of her dressed like she was. The next day this. I told you I'm keeping my options open.'

The journalist puts his hands on his hips. 'We just report the facts. Her disappearing's got nothing to do with us.'

Legrand grits his teeth. 'Keep it simple. You've got a high-profile murder. You just scratch my back with those covers, and I'll let you dine out on this for weeks.'

'I need some more details. What shall I say about her?'

'She's missing.'

The journalist writes that down.

Legrand continues, 'In fact, we're concerned for her. We want to know she's safe. Chances are she's just gone out of town because your stories have embarrassed her.'

'Who tipped you guys off?'

'Their maid.'

'She not a suspect?'

'Everyone's a suspect.'

'But she didn't do it?'

Legrand says nothing.

'I mean, she could've done?' the journalist asks. 'Victor here sent his wife away. But he's still all wound up from seeing her in a dress like that, so he tries it on with the maid.'

'And she just happens to be carrying a gun with her?'

'So it is a bullet wound then?'

'Do you have to ask me that? Open your eyes.'

'Do you have the weapon?'

Legrand says nothing.

'Come on, Mathis, stop playing hot and cold with me,' the journalist says.

Inspector Foceau sits in the chair, amused by the journalist's discomfort. He says: 'You've got plenty. You've got more than what anyone else has. Now get your photo and get writing your story.'

The photographer places his tripod over Victor Blanchet.

He aims the lens down and focuses up a birds-eye view. The powder catches, and there's a flash.

'It's a shame,' says the journalist.

'What's a shame? Don't tell me you care for a man like him?'

'No, of course not.'

'Then what?'

'That it's not her lying there. She'd sell more—'

'Get out of here.' Legrand grabs the journalist's collar and pushes him towards the door. 'And make sure those damn covers get out in the next hour or two.'

The photographer keeps his head low and doesn't make eye contact with Legrand as he passes. When they've gone, Officer Marnier comes over to Legrand.

'I hate those bastards.'

'He serves his purpose.'

'Are you done with the body, sir?' Marnier asks.

'Yeah. I'm done. Let's see what the coroner has to say.'

'Is he to be displayed at the morgue?'

'Yeah, of course. Say for the first day at least. Hang around in the viewing gallery. Watch if anyone acts suspicious.'

'Suspicious, sir? In the morgue? Have you been?'

'Of course, I have.'

'But everybody acts weirdly there.'

'Keep an eye on the ones that stare. I'm talking for longer than a minute. You expect the starers if it's a young woman with her breasts on show. Not for a guy like him.'

The police officer sighs. 'Yes, Sir. I'll arrange for his transportation now.'

CHAPTER 12

Marie refuses to get out when the train stops in Rouen for half an hour. Gabriel stretches his legs on the platform and, when he returns, enthuses about seeing the famed cathedral through a window. 'I don't need to see it,' Marie says. 'I've already seen Claude's paintings of it. Several of them.'

At midday, the train arrives in Le Havre. Marie takes her time leaving the carriage as she doesn't wish to see Madame Gage again. They make their way from the platform and into the station hall, where there is a cafe, tobacconists, waiting rooms and a ticket kiosk. It is a lot smaller than Gare du Nord, and Marie is relieved to feel like she is far away from Paris.

Marie heads for the station doors, but Gabriel puts his suitcase down. 'Wait here. I'll go and find us a carriage.'

Before she can protest, he heads across the station concourse. As Marie sits on a bench, a boy runs past her carrying a bundle of the latest edition front pages. He goes over to an older boy selling newspapers outside the waiting room. The two boys argue with each other. Then the youngest boy inserts the newspapers into the new covers. The older boy takes one, holds it above his head and shouts. 'Latest news! Murder in Paris. Wealthy businessman shot in his home!'

Marie's eyes widen. She twists around.

'Murder in Paris. Police search for killer,' he says, reading the headline filling the front page.

Her breathing is shallow and fast. How could they have got the news out already?

'Police search for Paris killer!'

It can't be me, she thinks.

Marie stands. She picks up her two bags, grabs Gabriel's suitcase, and heads out of the station. She keeps walking towards the road, lost in her thoughts, telling herself that the newspapers must refer to another murder. She is about to step before a tram when a black-gloved hand grabs her arm. She spins around. The man wears a bicorne. He is a gendarme.

'What are you doing?' he asks.

Marie pulls her arm from his grip.

'You should be more careful. You would've got flattened.'

She says nothing. She edges away from him.

'You just watch yourself. I don't want to be dealing with a death. I'm about to finish my shift.'

Marie nods, and then she turns back towards the station. Gabriel stands at one of the doors and spots her.

'What are you doing out here?' he asks.

'I just—'

'You're in shock. That's what it is. It's hitting you now, what you've done.'

'What have I done?'

His brow creases. 'That you've left Victor. Come on, let's get in the calèche.' Gabriel leads her to the calèche that waits for them. He helps her get in, unlike Victor would have. As it moves off, he puts his hand on hers. 'Listen. If you can't talk about it now, that's fine. But I hate seeing you suffer like this.'

She nods and squeezes his fingers, then slips her hand away.

'You still want to leave with me, don't you?' he asks.

'Of course, I do. I want to get on that ship more than anything. I want to get on it now, Gabe. Let's go. Let's try and

90

get on it now, please?'

'I thought we could go and explore the town and maybe eat.'

'Can't we eat on the ship?'

'I'm sure there's an art gallery.'

'You're adorable, Gabe. But you've finally got me to run away with you, and you're trying to keep me here?' She puts her hand on his knee and rubs a short way up his thigh. 'I thought you'd want to get me in that cabin of yours?'

'Shit,' he says.

'What's wrong?'

'We haven't thought this through at all, have we?'

'What?'

'Running away like this. I never thought you'd come with me in a million years.'

'You're worrying me now.'

'I'll be the only one going to Panama.'

She frowns, and he smiles.

'Unless,' he says. 'We can get you a ticket.'

The calèche pulls through the dock gates and stops behind a row of other carriages. The lovers get out, and Gabriel pays the driver.

'He said it's that ship there.' Gabriel points to the furthest of three ships docked in the port; two passenger ships and a cargo ship.

'Couldn't he have taken us to the gangplank?' Marie asks.

'I guess it's too busy to turn around or something.'

They go past the first passenger ship belching black smoke from its funnels. The sails are drawn up on the masts, where a couple of sailors attend to the ropes. Streams of people ascend three gangplanks; one that goes onto the deck and two that go into the belly of the ship.

At the next quay along, a train carriage floats in the air as a crane lifts it onto the cargo ship. Crates and containers, sacks and barrels are piled high the boat's length as merchant sailors and dockers scurry onto and off the vessel.

Gabriel smiles at the sight. 'Get used to that,' he says.

'Used to what?'

'They're like worker ants, don't you think? The jungle's full of them, apparently. They're a real problem in the hospitals.'

'You're selling it to me, Gabe, you really are.'

He smiles nervously.

The Liberty is at the end of the quay. A horde of people stands at the foot of the gangplank. Nobody is boarding, and many people shout and throw their hands in the air. Marie stops a man who is heading away from the ship. 'What's happening?'

'Would you believe it? It's a disgrace,' he says. He pulls at the corner of his moustache. 'We're going to have to stay in town another night.'

'Why?' Gabriel asks.

'Because they're bloody incompetents, that's why,' he says and hurries on his way.

Marie and Gabriel share a nervous glance.

'What do you think it is, Gabe?'

'I don't know.' He shrugs his shoulders. 'Let's go and see.'

There aren't any police officers or gendarmerie, so Marie follows Gabriel. They push through the crowd to one of the ship's officials at the foot of the gangplank.

'What's going on? Can't we board?' Gabriel asks.

The man sighs and rolls his eyes. In a monotonous voice, he says, 'I regret to inform you that there'll be a delay in the ship's departure of approximately one day as we wait

92

to repair the number two engine that has developed a fault with several of its pistons—'

'Alright, alright,' Gabriel says. 'What do we do?'

'Come back tomorrow. The ship's new departure time is hopefully three-thirty p.m.'

'No,' Marie says. 'Can't we get on the ship now and wait in our cabin?'

'You have a cabin?'

Gabriel gives an embarrassed laugh. 'Not quite.' He turns to Marie and rubs the back of his neck. 'I'm travelling steerage.'

Marie's mouth drops open.

'In fact, we need to get another ticket for Marie.'

The man takes a deep breath and rolls his eyes. 'Come with me,' he says.

CHAPTER 13

That afternoon, Inspector Legrand smokes and stares out of the window from the police station office. He thinks about the restaurant in Montparnasse, across town, where he and his wife used to go on special occasions. They would sit at the table in the window with his hand on top of hers while the chef cooked their steaks. Her fingers interlocked with his. Her long hair was pinned up. Her sapphire earrings reflected the candlelight. She would touch the earrings, reassuring herself she hadn't lost them.

She would turn to see when someone entered the restaurant, squeezing his hand if she recognised an artist or a writer. The restaurant would fill with artists dining with patrons, animated like shadow puppets against the candlelight. The sound was a cacophony of creative voices and ideas, bold, excited, the swell of hope.

He remembered these moments as if they had happened yesterday and not five years ago. He would meet his wife at the Pont des Arts. She'd lean against the iron railing beside a street lamp, admiring Notre Dame on the Île de la Cité. The setting autumn sun would backlight her auburn hair.

'Are you up to this today?' Foceau asks.

Legrand draws a deep breath of smoke from the cigarette. Then he obliterates the stub into an ashtray. 'I'm not going to let Bonnevay get a lead on us.'

Foceau nods and pats him on the shoulder. 'Go on then. Your turn.'

Legrand studies the woman who'd come in with information about the murder that was now front page news. 'What did she say?'

'Come on. Let's play our little game and see if what she tells you matches what she told me.'

The woman strokes at one of her blonde plaits and gazes around the office. As Legrand approaches her, she acts too coy about holding eye contact. He sits opposite her at the table and asks, 'Are you a time waster?'

She drops the act and holds his gaze. 'No,' she says. 'I'm not.'

'Alright.' He puts a cigarette between his lips and offers her one. She shakes her head, and he lights his cigarette. 'Tell me what you told Inspector Foceau.'

'I think I've seen that woman.'

Legrand says nothing. He stares at her and keeps a blank expression on his face.

She frowns. 'I did see that woman. You know. The one they're talking about in the papers. The one that killed her husband.'

'Nobody said any wife killed anyone's husband. Did Inspector Foceau say that?'

'No. The newspaper did.'

'No, it doesn't.'

'Well, it implied it,' she says.

'Forget the speculation. So you say you saw her. Where? Doing what?'

'I met a man in La Renaissance.'

'Which is?'

'A bar. He was a doctor, just qualified.'

'Where?'

'The bar or the doctor?'

'Both,' he said.

'Montmartre. I went back to his house with him, but a

woman was waiting for him. She looked like one of those rich women.'

'On account of what?'

'The way she looked.'

'You'd send a woman to the guillotine based on her appearance?'

'Yes. Well, no. But I remember her name was Marie. The doctor's landlady said that this woman had left her husband for him and told me to go and not cause a scene.'

'So you're sore you didn't get to spend the night with the doctor? Okay, Mademoiselle, I think we're done.'

'What? Done? Is that it?'

'Foceau's got your details, right?'

'Yes.'

'Then that's it.'

The woman takes her clutch bag from the table. She throws her nose high into the air and leaves.

Legrand stalks back through the hall over to Foceau.

'What are you doing to me?' Legrand asks.

'She's a nasty, vengeful girl,' Foceau says.

'That about sums it up. Why do you think it's a lead?'

'Because she says the doctor was off to Panama.'

'She didn't mention Panama to me.'

'Details, Mathis,' Foceau says. 'If you can't think straight to get the details off the witnesses, then you should leave it for today.'

'And go home and sit on my own? Thinking. Remembering?' He shakes his head. 'No.'

'Then focus, my friend. Give me a theory.'

Legrand pinches the bridge of his nose and closes his eyes. 'Marie Blanchet had a lover, this doctor. She killed her husband so she could run off to Panama with him.' He opens his

96

eyes. 'Did she give you an address?'

Inspector Foceau raises his eyebrows. 'Fancy a walk?' he asks.

Legrand and Foceau stroll across Paris to Montmartre. Legrand wants to take a carriage, but Foceau insists on walking because it is sunny. After half an hour, they arrive at the bottom of Rue de Martyrs and walk up the street. About a quarter of the way up the road, opposite a tobacconist and a cafe, is number nineteen, a tall and narrow building five stories high. A sign in one of the windows reads vacant room, enquire within. Legrand opens the door and goes in. Off the corridor, there is an open door, which he knocks on. Nothing. He knocks again. Somebody moves inside. Floorboards creak. A tall woman ambles out. She pats her greying dark hair back into shape then she covers a yawn with the back of her hand.

'Yes?' She plants her hands on her hips. 'One of you want a room?'

'I do,' Legrand says.

Madame Durand keeps her eyes on Foceau, watching his reaction. He gives none.

'Are you the landlady?' Legrand asks.

'I am.'

'Can I see it?'

She looks Legrand up and down. 'Sure, let me get the key.'

She goes back into her room. The two men linger in the hall until she comes out again. 'This way.'

Foceau and Legrand follow her up the creaking stairs to the top floor. She opens the door and lets them in.

'Are you two a couple?' she asks.

Foceau laughs.

97

'Well, it's thirty francs a week. Each.'

'Each?' says Legrand. 'Did your last tenants pay double for the room?'

'Thirty francs ain't bad,' Foceau says. 'The place has got some nice art.' He walks over to the painting hanging on the wall, a crane lily surrounded by lush foliage. 'Really nice. Who did it?'

'One of my lodgers.'

'Oh yeah, what's her name?'

Madame Durand opens her mouth and closes it. Then she says, 'He left.'

'Yesterday? This morning?' Legrand asks.

'Alright, who are you two? Do you want this place or not?'

Legrand goes over to Foceau and the painting. He traces his finger on the signature, M. Blanchet. A trace of paint sticks to his finger. 'Still fresh. It's a Blanchet, if I'm not mistaken?' Legrand says.

'A Blanchet? Well, they'll be in demand soon,' Foceau says.

Madame Durand remains in the doorway. The room key is still in the lock. As they turn to confront her, Madame Durand steps back onto the landing, swings the door shut and locks it.

'Well, that's never happened before,' Foceau says.

Legrand goes over and bangs on the door. 'Open it now, or I'll break it down.'

'Who are you?' she asks.

Legrand kicks the door.

'Hey. Take it easy,' Foceau says and waves Legrand out of the way. 'We're detectives,' he says to the door.

'Let me see your papers.'

Foceau takes his identity paper from his pocket and slides it under the door. She snatches it and reads it. It's legitimate.

98

She curses, and then she turns the key.

Legrand pulls it open. 'We should arrest you for false imprisonment,' he says.

'What's the matter, claustrophobic?'

'Not as much as you'll be when locked up in a cell.'

She scoffs and holds the identity paper out to Foceau.

'It's our fault. We should've told you,' Foceau says. 'Come, take a seat.'

Madame Durand walks back into the apartment, and Legrand slams the door behind her.

'You want to buy me a new door, eh? Who do you think you are, kicking my door and slamming it?'

'I'm the man you're going to start giving some answers to.'

'Or what?'

'Or I'll knock them out of you.'

She smiles and shakes her head as she approaches the table and sits down. 'I guess you want her?'

'We are trying to find Marie Blanchet,' Foceau says.

Madame Durand spits on the floor. 'Don't you say her name in my house.'

'Do you know where she is?' Legrand asks.

'In a ditch for all I care.'

'Why? What's she done?' Legrand asks.

'You tell me. Or don't you read the papers?'

'The newspapers haven't said she's done anything,' Legrand says. 'We're trying to ascertain she's alive.'

'Oh, she's alive alright.'

'Where is she?'

Madame Durand shakes her head. 'I don't know. She got on a train to Lyon.'

'Lyon?'

'When?' Legrand asks.

'This morning.'

'And this doctor? Is he with her?'

'No, he's well rid of her.'

'What's his name?'

'Gabriel Bertrand.'

'Tell us what happened. From the beginning.'

Madame Durand sighs. The two glasses and the empty bottle of wine she'd shared with Marie sit on the table. She thinks about the conversation and what Marie's husband had done to her. 'Gabriel,' she says, 'he's a lovely boy, but he's stupid. About a year ago, he was with his friend Michel who was buying art supplies from a shop on Rue des Plantes. It was there he met Marie Blanchet. He flirted with her, and that would've been that. But because Michel mixed in the same art circles as her, Marie and Gabriel met again. The two of them hadn't stopped fucking since. You should see the state of my wall.' She scowls and thumbs back towards the bedroom. Foceau sits with his legs crossed, wearing a content smile. Legrand sits with his hands together on the table.

'Go on,' Legrand says.

'What? You want me to tell you how they damaged the wall.'

'You know what I mean,' Legrand says.

'Well, that's how they continued for a year. She was his mistress, doing what a mistress does. The only thing is he falls for her. She never intended to leave her husband until he told her he was going to Panama.'

'When was that?'

'Last night.'

Legrand and Foceau study each other.

'Why wait to tell her at the last minute that he's going.'

'He thought it would shock her into a rash decision. That she'd leave with him. I guess it worked because we'd all gone out to celebrate him leaving, and when we came home, she was waiting on the step. She told me she left her husband because he'd throttled her. Her neck was all bruised. I guess that's why she shot him.'

'It would seem that way,' Foceau says.

'The next morning, I went with them to the station. She was going to go with him, but she'd gone all quiet. The next thing you know is she's saying she's sorry and that she can't go with him. She says she's going to Lyon—'

'Anybody else see this happen?' Legrand asks.

'Have you seen how busy Gare du Nord is in the morning? Says she's going to Lyon, and then she's gone. Poor lad was distraught. Best place for him is Panama, in my opinion far from her.'

'Did you not think to come and tell us?' Legrand says.

'I'm a busy woman.'

'Madame Durand would have gotten round to it, Mathis. When does his boat leave for Panama?'

'What time is it?'

Foceau checks his pocket watch. 'Just gone two thirty.'

'Lunchtime he says. I guess he's gone.'

'Is there anyone here we could speak to who was with you last night?'

'Sure.'

Legrand and Foceau interview some lodgers, including Gabriel's friend Michel DuPont. When they got all they could get out of the witnesses, they tell Madame Durand they'd likely return. Then, they go off down Rue de Martyrs.

'It would seem that Madame Durand's story checks out,' Foceau says as they both start smoking.

'Details. That's what you told me. It matches up until they'd gone to the station,' Legrand says. 'Only she witnessed that little drama play out.'

'So what do you think?'

'You mean, what do I know? I know that she's covering for them,' says Legrand.

'Why?'

'Because she knows how Victor Blanchet died. Our newspaper report doesn't mention he was shot. There's only one way she would know that.'

CHAPTER 14

In Le Havre town later that evening, Marie sits on their room's balcony. She drums her fingers on the two new sets of boarding documents on the table. Gabriel had sulked since she'd used Victor's money to upgrade them to a cabin.

The sky is ablaze with sunset. The silhouetted seagulls cry and swoop down onto the street below when a woman throws vegetable peelings out of her window opposite. Patrons in the bistro below sing and shout the drunker they get. The aroma of meat cooked in redolent cheap wine makes Marie hungry. She closes her eyes and imagines she is in Gabriel's room, back at Madame Durand's and not on the run.

Gabriel pushes the curtains aside. He leans on the balcony with his back to her. He lights a cigarette and flicks the match into the street below. He takes a few drags and then leans over the balcony, intrigued by what causes a woman to shriek outside the bistro.

'Do you want to go down and get something?' he asks.

'Maybe we should stay up here.' Marie's hand rests on the tickets.

'It won't always be like this. I'll be on a decent wage in Panama, and they'll supply accommodation and—'

'It's not that Gabe, it's....'

'I'm not saying it won't be tough. But I'll work hard and make a reputation for myself, you'll see.'

'I know. I'm sure you will.'

'And then we can come back to France.'

She rubs her temples. 'I'd rather we just stayed there.'

'No, that's the last thing you'll want. I don't want that. Why should we hide? We'll go back to Paris, and we'll show them. I'll be the famous doctor that saved the lives of thousands of people building France's greatest engineering feat. You'll be a celebrated artist, having done whatever it is you do. We'll attend dinner parties and be the toast of Paris, you'll see.'

'That's a nice thought.'

'I can't wait to see Victor's face when he sees us together.'

'Gabe!' Her hand drops from her temple and bangs on the table. They stare at each other. Then he throws the cigarette onto the street.

'I'm going for a drink,' he says, then heads back through the curtains and into the room. He slams the door behind him and stomps off down the corridor.

Marie turns to the heavens. 'For Christ's sake Marie. Pull yourself together,' she tells herself, but all she can picture is Victor's dead face.

The next day, rain drizzles from grey clouds as they arrive by carriage at the port. The Liberty is the only ship still docked. Beyond it, she can see the sea and fishing boats. A crowd stands on the quay again, and Marie is relieved to see people ascending the gangplank. Midway through the crowd, Marie spots two gendarmes standing with the ship's officials checking boarding papers.

'Gabe.'

'What's the matter?'

The gendarmes watch the crowd.

'I can't, I—'

'What? You don't want to come?'

'Shhh. No. Just come over here with me for a moment.'

They walk away from the crowd. Passengers board the ship via only one gangplank.

'Is it normal to have gendarmes checking the tickets like that?'

'Um, what?'

'Is it normal?'

'I don't know. You're the one that's been out of the country before,' he says.

She rubs her temples.

'What does it matter anyway?' he asks.

She bites her thumbnail.

One of the gendarmes takes the rifle off his shoulder, sticks the muzzle on the floor and leans his hip against the butt.

'They're probably just keeping the peace. It was a bit rowdy down here yesterday.' Gabriel starts walking back to the crowd.

She doesn't move.

'Come on,' Gabriel says.

She steps towards him and then stops. She shakes her head.

'Don't do this, Marie,' he says. 'We're so close.'

She drops her bag.

'Please, Marie. We've come this far. Not now, not here.'

'I can't get on that ship, Gabe.'

He rakes his fingers through his hair. 'Why not?'

A family walks past them, and the two toddlers are holding hands. It reminds Marie of being young with her sister. 'My sister,' she says, 'Capucine's not well.'

He frowns.

'When I got home last night, I'd received a telegram from her husband. She's not well, Gabe.'

'What's wrong with her?'

Marie stares at the cobbles. A single poppy grows between the cracks. 'Scarlett Fever. I can't leave without seeing her.'

His shoulders deflated. 'But—'

'What if we don't come back?' she asks. 'What if she dies? She's my sister Gabe. I've got to see her.'

'I'll come with you then,' he says. 'We'll sail out another day.'

'No. You've got to take this opportunity.' She touches his chest.

'I want you, though.'

'I know. I want you too. Believe me. I want to be in Panama with you and far from France and Victor.'

'You won't come.'

'I will, Gabe. I promise you I will.' He turns away from her. 'Listen to me. As soon as she's better, I'll join you.'

He shakes his head. 'I guess this is really it then?'

She takes a deep breath. 'I will. I promise, Gabe. I'll find you in Panama.'

'How?'

'I'll search every hospital.'

He feigns a smile and lets go of her hand. She kisses him, and then he walks towards the crowd with his head down and shoulders his way through. When she glances at the gendarmes, they point at her and talk to each other. Then, they walk along the quay's edge, still watching her.

'Merde,' she says under her breath. She kneels and picks up her bag. When she stands, the pair are on their tiptoes, examining the crowd. When they spot her again, they push their way through the people.

Marie walks faster.

When they are about to break through the crowd, she runs. They blow two shrill blasts on a whistle. She ignores them. She veers towards a steam engine tugging cargo along the quay and disappears into the steam.

Gabriel climbs the gangplank. He stops and watches the commotion. The steam train screeches to a stop. The gendarmes stand scratching their heads. The driver leans out and shrugs.

Marie is gone. She hadn't even waited to wave him goodbye. He sighs. Was the story about her sister real? She'd never mentioned a sister before. And he had noticed, she still wore her wedding ring.

CHAPTER 15

Marie leaves the port city of Le Havre at once, intending to travel to Marseille, where she and Victor have a second home. The quickest route to the Mediterranean coast is by train, which would require returning to Paris. She believes that route to be too dangerous, so she buys a map and plots her own route by road.

That day she travels to Rennes by stagecoach. There, she sends a telegram to her former mentor, Charlie Blaine, asking him to meet her at noon in a week outside Notre Dame de la Garde in Marseille. She keeps the message cryptic, telling him she is in trouble, and she hopes he'll be intrigued enough to find out why.

Afterwards, she rents a room in a half-timbered inn, and for most of that night, she sits in the window in her room. She twists the wedding ring around on her finger while she gazes at the Vilaine river; black and smooth like a mirror, the water reflects the lights from the buildings lining it. Then the ring slides off her finger. It takes a second for her to realise what has happened. She looks at it in her hand. It is a small token of the life she shared with Victor. She reminisces about the moments of their marriage that were real and even happy. Though it was built on a lie she'd lived it for several years. It had been real. She's not sure she even knows what real is anymore though. She cries, and all throughout that night, when somebody goes along the corridor or makes a noise in a neighbouring room, she jumps.

After falling asleep late, Marie wakes early the next day. She takes her necklace off, puts it and the ring she'd held all night into a pocket in her bag, and then heads for the stagecoach. She is the first onto it. Around mid-morning, the carriage wheels get stuck in deep ruts and puddles as it crawls past mizzle-drenched fields. The sun never breaks through the clouds at all that day, and when she gets to La Rochelle it is too late to get another stagecoach to Nantes.

On the third day of travelling south, Marie takes yet another stagecoach. A young man boards, reeking of stale liquor. He says hello and then falls asleep before they leave. Marie opens the window to let in some fresh air.

A woman wearing a shawl gets on, says good morning, and sits beside Marie. She smells of oranges. Pith sticks under her nails.

Marie smiles and turns to the window and doesn't invite small talk.

'It's a much sunnier day than yesterday, don't you think?'

'Yes,' Marie says.

'Where are you headed? Are you staying in La Rochelle?'

'No,' Marie says.

'I'm going to visit my son there,' the old woman says.

Marie stares out the window, and the woman bites at the pith under her nails.

Near the village of Chauché, a man wearing a suit and a top hat pulls himself into the carriage and sits opposite Marie. As the horses pull off, he stares at her and licks his lips. Despite tucking her legs beneath her seat, he ensures his knees or calves touch hers. Out of the window, the trees are losing their verdancy as autumn arrives.

After an hour or two of bumping along the dirt road, Marie's head keeps dropping, waking her up. The hungover man and the woman are asleep. The suited man places his hand on her knee. Victor sits opposite. Marie stamps the heel of her boot down onto his foot. He yells, and as he reaches down to nurse his foot, Marie raises her knee to meet the bridge of his nose.

The hungover man continues snoring. The woman startles awake. 'What is it? Are we there?'

Marie says nothing.

The man mutters to himself and massages his nose.

Out of the window, the bountiful wheat fields sway in the breeze as an army of countryfolk harvests.

In La Rochelle, ships sail to Panama from the port, the next one in two days. She doesn't know what to do. She'd set her mind on travelling to Marseille because she could get money and clothing from their house. There, she could forge a new passport with a new name. But going to Marseille meant meeting Charlie, and meeting him meant blowing up the dam. She knows such a mission increases her chance of being caught. It would be easy to run away and be kept by Gabriel, but that option was also not without risk. Would they bother to track him down on the other side of the world to see if she was with him? Blowing up the dam for the Americans meant gaining immunity and an opportunity to support herself.

She rents a room in Hotel La Marine on the quay at Le Vieux Port. That night, moonlight illuminates the room. But as the clouds pass before the moon, the room plunges into darkness. Lying on the bed, she decides to leave for Panama and join Gabriel. Better to be poor and a kept woman but free the rest of her life than be caught before she can start any kind of new life. She will convince Gabriel to leave Panama, and they will be free somewhere in the Americas. Because of the endless days spent sitting in a carriage and not being active, it takes her a long while to fall asleep, but when she does, she dreams Victor is making love to her and enjoys it.

The following day Marie wakes. She realises where she is. She remembers what she did. Her bag is open, and some of her clothes are on the floor. She stares at the bag. She could sense someone had been in the room. She feels under the duvet to see if she's sleepwalked and brought the wallet over without realising but knows she hasn't. There is nothing but the thin mattress. She curses. The door is closed. She throws off the duvet and scrambles across the floor to her bag. Sifting through the clothes, searching for the long leather wallet and her money, she finds the wallet, but the money is gone.

CHAPTER 16

Marie punches the floor. Her rucksack sits at the side of the bed. She crawls over, pulls out a couple of sketchbooks, and finds the two hundred francs she's kept separated in case of such an eventuality. 'You fool,' she says to herself. 'I should've separated half.'

Marie dresses, collects her belongings and goes downstairs. The concierge is the same stout woman from when she'd checked in.

'Where is it?' Marie asks.

'What?'

'You know damn well what.'

The stout woman raises a bushy eyebrow.

'My money,' Marie says. 'Your eyes grew when you saw my wallet when I checked in.'

'I don't know what you're talking about.'

'You came into my room last night and took my money.'

'Oh, did you leave your door unlocked, m'dear?'

'No. I locked it.'

'You should always lock your door. I can't vouch for the honesty of the people that stay here.'

'It was locked.'

'Well, we could fetch the gendarme if you want.'

'I know—'

'I don't appreciate being called a thief,' the stout woman says. 'Maybe you should leave.'

Marie tries to push her out of the way, but she resists and punches Marie in the face with surprising strength, and she falls onto the floor, clutching her cheek.

'Get out of here now,' the woman shouts. Marie grabs her bags and leaves.

The embarrassment of being naive and floored by an old woman's punch hurts Marie more than the punch did. Walking the streets of La Rochelle, Marie knows she must go to Marseille. She hopes the money she has left is enough to get her there.

She follows the Atlantic coast south, using another stage-coach. In Bordeaux, she finds a newspaper and discovers that Victor's murder is no longer a front-page story but a column describes how the police are baffled by Marie's disappearance. The journalist speculates that until spoken to, Marie must be considered a suspect. With a deep feeling of paranoia, Marie goes immediately to an apothecary and buys a bottle of C.Damschinsky's blonde liquid hair-dye.

From Bordeaux, she catches a train inland to Toulouse. Midway through this leg of the journey, as the train stops in Gare d'Agen for half an hour, she gets out. It hasn't changed since she was last there all those years ago. A bright yellow cafe, ticket office, and waiting room sit on the single plat-form. She smiles and heads inside.

'Now, what can I get for you today Madame?' the owner asks. She stares at him. He is older than Marie remembers him. His moustache has turned grey, and he's lost weight.

'A coffee, please.'

He places a cup on the counter and pours coffee into it with a hand, now shakier than before.

'This place hasn't changed one bit,' she says.

'Ah, you've been here before?'

'About fifteen years ago. Is your wife here? I'd very much like to see her again.'

His head bows, and he wipes his hands on a towel tucked into his apron. 'You knew Marcella?'

'I knew you both once, but only briefly.'

He's confused.

'You offered me a roof for the night. I was at the station and missed the last train to Paris.'

'And you ended up staying with us for a week. Your grandfather had died.'

'Yes, how do you remember?'

'Marie, isn't it?'

'Yes.' Tears are in her eyes.

'Marcella always wanted to know what happened to the young girl from Saint-Puy.'

'Well, here I am.'

'I'm afraid Marcella died five years ago.'

Marie puts her hand on top of his. 'I'm so sorry.'

'No matter. Life is for the living. I've learnt not to dwell on what happened.' He smiles. 'Tell me about you. You're not the wild Occitanie country girl you once was.'

Marie laughs. 'Well, that's what a boarding school education does to you.'

'And now? Are you married?'

'No. I'm an artist.'

'Really? Well...' he says. 'Are you going back to where it was?'

'Saint-Puy. I wish. I'm going to the Côte d'Azur to paint.'

While he serves customers at the counter, they reminisce about her stay, and she avoids any questions he asks regarding her life since.

She finishes her coffee when the bell rings on the platform signalling the train will leave in five minutes. They smile at each other, then he holds his arms out, and they kiss each other on the cheek.

'Won't you stay a night?'

'I'm afraid I might never leave if I was to.'

She journeys on. In Toulouse, she stays a night in Porte de L'Hotel Felzins and decides to dye her hair. Standing before a bowl of water, Marie takes the green bottle out of the box and reads the label, which says it is free from all substances which might have an injurious effect. She weighs up the risk and decides the least she looks like the infamous wife of Victor Blanchet the better. So she applies the dye. It transforms her so much that the hotel's owner cannot recognise her, and she avoids paying for the night she spends there.

That morning, while eating a breakfast of bread and water, Marie counts the money she has left. At the rate she's been spending it, she knows she won't afford transport, food and a place to sleep each night for the remainder of her journey to Marseille.

After breakfast, she decides to steal a horse and ride to her destination instead.

'Why isn't my husband's horse ready?' Marie asks the boy in the stables of the hotel. The boy gets up from lying in the hay. 'It should be ready by now like I asked,' she continues. 'I want to go riding on it.'

The boy frowns. 'Which one?'

Marie walks through the stables sizing up the horses.

'This one,' she says, pointing to a lithe brown mare.

'But that's—'

'Correct. It's not saddled.'

The boy bows his head.

'Do I have to tell your master?'

He gets a saddle.

'I don't want a lady's saddle.'

He takes it back and gets a male riding saddle. After he straps it on the horse, Marie rides away from the hotel's stables unchallenged.

Despite it wanting to break into a gallop and despite Marie wanting to let it, she paces the horse, keeping it at a trot, so as not to wear it out. With the autumn sun baking the road firmly, they manage to ride the whole day, and both woman and horse are exhausted when they reach Carcassonne that night. She finds lodgings in the old town within the walls of the castle. She drinks two bottles of wine that night until she is sick and passes out. She dreams of Gabriel and his friend Marcel Dupont in La Renaissance, and at some point, Marcel becomes Victor, and the two men drink and joke.

In Paris, Inspector Legrand turns off the gas lamp and pushes his chair under his desk. He is walking down the corridor when Chief Inspector DuVille calls out to him.

'Come in, sit down.' DuVille says. He is sitting at his desk reading through some documents. Legrand sits.

'We've had a witness statement come through. The wife of a diplomat, one Madame...' DuVille flicks back through the pages of the document and finds the name. 'Gage. She has seen our chief suspect, Marie Blanchet, on a train to Le Havre.'

Legrand stands. 'Le Havre? They're headed for Panama.'

'Sit down.'

Legrand's eyes narrow. He reluctantly sits. 'When was this?'

'The same morning, we found out about the murder.'

'So why are we only finding out now?'

'She didn't hear about the murder until she was in London.

116

She thought it would aid our investigation if she told us she'd seen Marie Blanchet leaving Paris on a train.'

'Can she be sure it was her?'

'Yes. They apparently study together at Académie Julian.'

'The art school?'

'Indeed. Marie was with a man who was introduced as her brother.'

'Her lover more like.' Legrand gets up from the chair again. 'I told you that landlady was lying. Listen, I need to go. They'll have fled to Panama. If I leave now, I can catch up with them.'

'I want you to go to Marseille.'

Legrand frowns. 'Marseille? But they've gone to Panama.'

'You're not going to Panama,' Chief Inspector DuVille says.

'What? But that's where they'll have gone. We can't let them escape.'

'They could've gone anywhere from Le Havre. Besides, it's possible Panama was just a ruse.'

'But it's the best lead we have.'

'Which is why Bonnevay has gone.'

Legrand swears and kicks the chair, which bangs against DuVille's desk. 'Are you serious? What about the goddamned first one to bring in the killer gets the job?'

'It still stands.'

'So you send him.'

'He got the telegram first and was eager to rush off like you without checking all the evidence.'

Legrand's temper slows, and he decides to listen.

'We've had a statement come through from the Le Havre gendarmerie.' DuVille picks up another piece of paper and hands it to Legrand. 'According to the boarding ledger Gabriel Bertrand has sailed. But there's no mention of a

Marie Blanchet having done so.'

'She would've boarded under a different name—'

'Read on.'

Legrand skims the report, which says that a woman fitting her description was seen running away from the ship. He thought about all the leads in the case. 'What's so special about Marseille?'

DuVille smiles. 'Victor Blanchet has a second house there.'

CHAPTER 17

Three days after leaving Carcassonne and staying in Béziers, Montpellier and Nimes, the high sun burns the back of Marie's neck. On the outskirts of the village of L'Estaque, she reluctantly sells the horse to a farmer, then walks the remaining couple of kilometres to her destination Marseille.

Along the coast road, Marie stops under the shade of some pine trees and sits on the brown needles on the floor. A murder of crows stands like statues on the pebble beach. The sea is smooth, like turquoise Murano glass melted to the shore. She wonders how far across that ocean Gabriel is and if he has spent the journey brooding. One of the crows flaps his wings, climbs into the air, and drops a shell onto the rocks. It swoops back down and pecks at the mollusc revealed inside the broken shell.

Soon after, she continues on and arrives in the terracotta-roofed city. She navigates her way through the tight streets. The forest of masts and funnels in the Vieux Port de Marseille sway. The boats and ships are packed as tight as a deck of playing cards. Their bows are pulled against the port wall, and their bowsprits point at the inns and hotels. Along the harbour, she walks in the shade of the unfurled sails being sewn, cleaned, or rigged, ready for sail.

A harbour master tells her she has missed a sailing to Panama by a day, but a packet boat is leaving for the isthmus the next day.

She goes to an art supply shop. Here she buys a new ribbon for the typewriter and some card that matches the hue and weight of the paper in her passport. She gets a photograph taken to replace the one in her passport of her with blonde hair, and she tells the photographer she'll collect it first thing in the morning.

Then, she buys a bottle of wine, a loaf of bread and some cheese and heads towards Parc Longchamp and to the house, number five on Boulevard Cassini.

She holds her key in her pocket. The tall, narrow building on the terrace is weathered but wears it well. Victor would've had the building, and the shutters painted immediately had he seen it like this. A couple passes by and lost in themselves, they pay her no attention. She goes up the steps, jabs the key into the lock and unlocks the door. She pushes the door open and goes inside, locks it behind her and slips the bolts across.

She leans back against the door. She breathes fast.

With the shutters closed on the windows, darkness fills the house. She decides to keep the front ones shut, so the house appears unoccupied. The rooms smell musty, and she feels her way through to the back of the house. A thin slit of light pierces the room through the join in the shutters. She opens them, lets in light, and then creates a new identity page in the passport. The name she types in to it is her maiden name, Marie Cadieux.

Inspector Legrand can't help himself. Despite it being half past nine when his train arrives from Paris into Gare de Marseille-Saint-Charles, he gets in a caleche and heads to the address he's scribbled into his notebook; number five, Boulevard Cassini.

The house is in darkness, and the shutters are closed. Some homes on the street also sit in darkness, but most have light spilling out from between their shutters. He approaches the door, crouches and peers through the keyhole. He can't see anything.

The caleche driver shuffles in his seat. The horse snorts.

Ripping off a corner of paper from his notebook, Legrand folds it and pushes it between the door and the frame. When he returns to the caleche, he orders the driver to take him to the nearest five-star hotel.

Marie stabs Victor in the face. It doesn't stop him from throttling her. He pulls the knife from his face and stabs her in the chest. Marie wakes. She is unsure of where she is. Thunder rumbles. Rain streams off the roof. She rubs her sore spine and sits upright in the chair. It is still dark. She has no idea what time it is because the clocks have stopped from not being wound. The oil lamp is on the floor, and the shadows of the furniture loom up the walls. She needs the toilet, so she picks up the lamp, and it almost goes out, but she manages to keep it lit.

The stairs creak as she climbs. She wipes the sweat from her brow when she gets to the landing. She'd forgotten how warm it was at night on the coast of the Mediterranean, even in autumn.

The church bells of Dominicaines de la Présentation toll seven times. Marie wakes. The blue sky fills the gap between the shutters.

She strides into Victor's office and finds the safe in the wall hidden behind her painting of Château d'If. Inside the safe is a pistol similar to the one she'd shot Victor with. She pushes it to the back and slides out a wallet. There are only three hundred and fifty francs, a gold bracelet, and a ruby necklace. She slams her fist against the wall. She isn't going

121

to risk having it stolen from her again, so she keeps it all in the safe.

A cool breeze slips off the Mediterranean and whips up through the streets of Marseille. The photographer's studio is closed, so she must wait an hour until he arrives and opens up. The first thing she does after getting her photograph is sit on a bench and put the new one into her passport.

Marie has a couple of hours until she is due to meet Charlie Blaine at Notre Dame de la Garde on the hilltop overlooking the city. She wonders whether or not he'll turn up. As she returns to her house and rounds the corner onto Boulevard Cassini, she sees a man standing on her doorstep. He turns and sees her too. Marie doesn't break her stride. She keeps walking up the street and past him, but she can feel him staring at her.

'Madame,' he says.

She stops and faces him.

'Yes?'

Rubbing his chin, his eyes dart across her face.

'Is there something I can help you with, Monsieur?'

'Do you have identification?'

'What? Why, who are you?'

'My name is Inspector Legrand.'

CHAPTER 18

Marie hands Inspector Legrand her passport from her bag, and she immediately regrets having typed her maiden name into it.

He puts a folded-up piece of paper between his teeth, inspects the passports, and looks at her.

'What is this all about?' she asks.

'Your name is Marie?'

'Yes. Marie Cadieux. It says it there.'

'And you were born when exactly.'

'Again, it says it right there. Just exactly who are you? You're scaring me. Give me back my passport.'

He looks at the passport again and then hands it to her. She takes it, but he holds onto it. His eyes narrow.

'Give it to me now. Who are you?'

'My name is Inspector Legrand.'

'I should go and report you for harrasment.'

He looks at her, deciding on what to do. 'Be on your way.'

He lets go of the passport.

She heads off up the street, and her whole body is shaking when she turns left onto Boulevard Jardin Zoologique. Across the boulevard, bordered by a tall wall is Parc Longchamp. She gets halfway down the boulevard when she glances over her shoulder. Inspector Legrand watches her from the junction she'd turned off. She keeps walking, and when she gets to an entrance to the park, he is following her.

In the park and out of his sight, Marie runs. Weaving her way through the sculpted gardens she arrives at the Palais Longchamp, which houses the Muséum d'histoire naturalle and the Musée des Beaux-Arts. Out of breath, she skirts the edge of the fountain, jogs up the stairs and goes through the colonnade. She stops to catch her breath against one of the white pillars, but urges herself across the reception hall, and into large rooms filled with stuffed wild animals.

Legrand arrives at the Palais Longchamp, but the blonde-haired woman he suspected has disappeared. He looks towards the Musée des Beaux-Arts, and knowing Marie Blanchet is an artist, he goes in there. He goes over to a security guard when he can't find her.

'Have you seen a blonde-haired woman come through here in a hurry?'

The security guard shakes his head. 'No. All I've seen is a rather nice redhead today. Why?'

'No reason, I'm just losing my mind. Say, where's the nearest police station?'

'Well, my old station would be the nearest. It's on La Canebière towards the harbour.'

'You were a policeman?'

'Thirty-two years.'

'Who's in charge there? What's he like?'

'Depends who's asking?'

'I'm an inspector from Paris.'

'Oh, he won't like that.'

'Well, I've got a house I want to get into. I'll do it with or without his help if need be.'

'Don't tell him what to do. Make him think he's come up with a solution, and you'll be okay. Oh, and tell him old Evra sent you.'

Legrand gave him a mock salute. 'Thanks.'

Marie takes the funicular railway up the steep slopes of Le Garde hill. The higher it climbs, the further she can see along the azure coastline beyond Marseille. Her mind races from her close call with Inspector Legrand. She wants to run far from Marseille but knows she'll be safe if she can just reach Charlie. She walks around Notre Dame de la Garde atop the hill's summit, paying no attention to the magnificent granite tower and dome. What if Charlie never received her telegram? What if he doesn't show up? At the entrance, a few people go in and out of the large basilica. She looks for Charlie Blaine, but he isn't here yet. She knows she is early.

She sits down on a bench. Then after not much time at all, she decides to stand. She paces and scratches at her satchel's leather strap. She heads into the basilica, and when she gets through the doors, she decides against it and heads back out.

A hand grabs her shoulder. 'Excuse me, Madame,' a voice says in French.

Marie pulls her shoulder free, and she spins around. The tension inside her evaporates, and she has to stop herself from hugging him. 'Charlie! Good god, you scared the life out of me.'

'Good,' he says, reverting to his gruff American-English accent. 'And don't think that makes us even, Frenchie.'

He places a cigarette in the corner of his mouth, and it points at the floor. He offers her one. She shakes her head, and they eye each other as he lights up. He has squinty eyes from having grown up on the harsh, sun-bleached plains of the American frontier, and he still dresses like he stepped off those plains yesterday.

'What you smirking at?' he asks. He frowns beneath the wide brim of his hat.

'It's good to see you again, Charlie,' she says.

'No, that's not it. Go on, say it.'

'What?'

He crosses his arms. 'You need my help.'

'I do need your help,' she says.

He grins.

'Well?' Marie asks.

'You must really need my help,' he says, pointing the cigarette at her. 'I'm the last person you would've come to.'

'Don't start, Charlie. You didn't have to meet me.'

Charlie grunts and looks away.

'Can we walk?' she asks.

'You drag me all the way up here just so we can walk back down? Sure, let's walk.'

They go down the white steps cut into the white rock. The sun is high, and she can feel her forehead burning. She leads them between the trees, where it is shady, and a lizard scuttles across the gravel path and into the scrub.

'So, you gonna tell me what this is all about? Dragging me away from my peace and quiet.'

'I bet you couldn't wait to meet me,' she says.

'I was just intrigued to see why the girl that needs no help suddenly needs help.'

'I take it you don't read the papers?'

'No. The world's worries aren't my concern any more.'

She takes a deep breath. 'I killed Victor.'

'What?' Charlie puts his hand on Marie's shoulder. 'You did what? Why? You're not that kind of agent.'

'He tried to kill me.'

'You weren't trained to kill anyone. You were trained to be devious and misleading. Not that you needed much training to be that.'

Marie rubs her head. 'He gave me no choice.'

126

'So, what do you expect me to do?'

'I've got a plan. I've got information.'

'Then give it to your employers then.'

'I did.'

'So where do I fit into all this?'

She touches his arm. 'They have a mission for us.'

Charlie pulls away from her as if she'd burnt him. 'No. I'm through with all that, with them. I take it they told you where to find me?'

'This is my one chance of getting out and making a life for myself.'

'Just run, Frenchie. Get out of here. Get out of the country. Find yourself a new man and start a new life.'

'No. I'm done with that. I want a life where I'm not reliant on or beholden to anyone.'

'Then just go.'

'How? A woman can't make a life for herself in this world with nothing.'

Charlie drops the cigarette butt and squashes it into the dry earth.

'Victor had just bought into the Panama dig,' she says.

'Bad timing.' Charlie says as he walks off down the path. 'The dig's in ruins. I thought he was supposed to be shrewd.'

'He was. He hadn't invested a franc in the whole venture up until recently. He bought into a plan that's going to save the dig.'

Charlie crosses his arms. 'How?'

She takes out a small leather-bound portfolio from her satchel. She pulls out the maps. 'It's not like Suez. Unlike the desert, there are areas where they simply can't cut through the land.'

Charlie takes the maps and the plans and strokes his stubble as he studies them. 'Of course.'

'DeLesseps has finally given in. He's agreed to a plan to flood the land instead. These plans show they're going to build locks and dams. The plans are by Eiffel himself. Do you see? I know Victor admired Eiffel. He once said he was the best engineer in the world.'

Charlie sits on one of the steps. After studying the plans for several minutes, he looks up. 'This could put them back on track. This could literally save their whole project.'

Marie pulls the papers away from him and stuffs them back into her satchel. 'They're building a test dam. If it's successful, they'll go ahead with the project. If not, then it's over.'

Charlie stands. 'Just like my countrymen want, so they can move in and take over.' He starts off down the hill again. 'I don't want to help them.'

'You don't have to do it for patriotic reasons.' She catches up with him. 'Listen, I've done a job, and I've got nothing to show for it—'

'Killing Victor wasn't your job.'

'And if he'd not tried to kill me, he'd still be alive. I want out, Charlie. I'm through with America, with France. What they're willing to pay for this job will set us both up for life.'

Charlie stops walking. He turns around and flicks his head in the air. 'Oh yeah? Just how much are they offering exactly?'

CHAPTER 19

On the afterdeck of SS La Touraine, Marie watches the dockers unhook the ropes off the bollards on the quay. Charlie leans against the rail and pushes some tobacco into a pipe. The ship is pulled from the dock wall, and Marie is relieved to watch the space between her and France grow. As Charlie chugs on his pipe and the ship's funnels belch black smoke above, Marie sees a man come running along the quay wall. She grips the taffrail. 'That's him,' she says. 'Charlie, look.'

Charlie squints in the man's direction and slowly takes the pipe from his mouth. 'Did he give you a name?'

'Legrand, I think it was.'

Charlie swears.

Inspector Legrand stops talking to the dockers, who shrug their shoulders and gesture at the ship. He spots Marie and Charlie.

'Can he stop the ship?' Marie asks.

Charlie opens his mouth. He frowns. 'I don't know, I don't think so.'

Legrand looks away from them and the ship. He seems to be studying the layout of the quay. Then he starts walking off.

'Where is he going?' Marie asks.

'How the hell should I know?' Charlie says, and he walks along the deck to see if he can see where Legrand is headed. Marie follows Charlie up some stairs.

'Do you think he's going to get the harbour master?' Marie asks.

Charlie doesn't answer. He takes some binoculars out of

129

his backpack and glasses the quayside. Then, between the masts and sails, he finds Legrand running along the wall.

By the time their ship approaches the port's entrance, Legrand has boarded the last ship docked; the closest one their ship will pass by the bow of. They watch as he runs along the deck and climbs stairs to the highest point on the ship. Their ship slips past with only a few metres separating the two vessels. Legrand keeps running. He bounds up some crates and jumps off the taffrail. Charlie's eyes are wide. Marie's mouth is agape.

'You gotta be kidding me,' Charlie says.

Legrand flies through the air. His arms are outstretched, and his legs kick beneath him. Marie and Charlie lean over to see where Legrand has landed. He has grabbed a rope on their ship and is already starting to climb up. Marie and Charlie run along the deck to where the rope is suspended. A couple of sailors are leant over talking to him as he climbs up. Charlie elbows them out of the way and reaches over, offering his hand to Legrand, who takes it. Charlie's friendly smile fades, and he punches Legrand in the face. Legrand manages to hold on, and it takes another punch to send the inspector falling into the sea as the ship sails out of the port.

Marie sees Legrand fall beneath the surface, and it takes a while before he comes back up, gasping for breath.

The sailors are pushing Charlie, questioning why he'd punched Legrand. Marie gets between them. She holds her hands up in surrender. 'It was my husband. He was trying to stop us from leaving. Please, he deserved it. He was horrible.'

The sailors melt under her pleading eyes, and then they merely glance overboard to see Legrand swimming back to the quay wall before they go back to their business.

Charlie shakes his head and rubs at his knuckles.

'Damn it,' Marie says. 'He knows where we're going now.'

'Only you would get inspector Mathis Legrand coming after you.'

'You know him?'

'Only by reputation. He was featured in a dossier of notable people to avoid causing trouble with in Paris.'

'Well, couldn't you have shot him or something?'

'This ain't the Wild West, Frenchie.' Charlie rubs his face and then looks at Marie. 'C'mon, we need to find our cabin.' The pair collect their bags from where they'd dropped them on the deck. 'Legrand's foreign legion,' Charlie explains. 'Well, ex foreign legion that is. Yeah... he's somewhat of a legend.'

'Are you scared of him or in love with him?'

Charlie scowls at her from under the brim of his hat.

'Me? No, I'm just worried. Worried for you.'

'Why, what's so special about him?'

Charlie leads her down some ladders inside the ship and speaks over his shoulder. 'The fact he's legion should be enough. Geez. The man was born in Morocco. At a fairly young age, he joined the legion. For most of the eighties, he fought in the Tonkin campaign and the Sino war. He's French through spilt blood. That's how he became a citizen of France.' A sign on the wall points towards where their cabin can be found. They walk down the narrow corridor. 'Legrand was shot in the leg during the Siege of Tuyên Quang. You French were outnumbered by the Chinese, but somehow you managed to hold the outpost at Quang for four or five months. This is us.' They walk into a parlour with a long table filling most of its length. At the far end is a boiler stove. Surrounding the room is about five doors. They find their cabin and unlock the door with their key. 'It's said that a legionnaire was caught in an explosion during the siege,' Charlie continued. 'He was catapulted into the enemy's parapets. That night Legrand went out alone and brought him back.'

'Why the hell is a bloody war hero chasing after me?'

She stands in the doorway and looks into the tiny cabin. A porthole lets in light above a small chest of drawers. Half of the room is taken up with a bunk bed. Marie sighs.

Charlie hauls his bags onto the top bunk.

'No. That's not happening,' Marie says. She pushes Charlie out of the way and throws her bags over his.

Charlie laughs. He takes his bag down, places it on the lower bunk and climbs in. The door had closed behind them. Marie sees how tiny the room is. It reminds her of a prison cell. She feels the colour drain from her face. She holds onto the bunk as the ship sways along with the floor beneath her. The last thing she sees is the round circle of blue sky through the porthole.

CHAPTER 20

Marie rouses when the ship still has Marseille in its sights. She is drowsy, and Charlie has her sleep off her exhaustion for the next twenty-four hours. When she finally wakes, the ship has slipped between the Balearic Isles and mainland Spain and is headed towards the Strait of Gibraltar. The next day, she eats and quickly regains her strength. Charlie says the shock of killing Victor and being on the run has finally caught up with her. As the ship goes out into the silver Atlantic, reflecting the moonlight, Marie's last sight of land is the twinkling lights of Tangier.

On the morning of her third day at sea, she opens her eyes to find Charlie awake and topless. In the years they'd been apart, his tanned back had acquired a long scar; a blade had scratched him from shoulder to waist. Pulling a series of contorted faces to make his skin taut, he clears greying stubble with his razor. Every now and again, he shakes the blade into a bowl of water on the small chest of drawers at the side of the bunks. In the mirror he'd propped against the port hole, he catches Marie watching him from the top bunk.

'Morning, Frenchie. Sleep well?'

She rubs her eyes. 'I'm getting used to it.'

'Good, then you'll have no excuses.'

'Excuses?'

'For your training. It starts today.'

Marie pushes herself up and leans on her elbows. 'What training?'

At the stern of the ship, Marie tilts her head to feel the warm northeasterly trade winds blowing off the Western Sahara. The SS La Touraine veers from following the Canary Current along the African Coast. The ship ventures into the Atlantic on a bearing along the North Equatorial Current towards Panama. Charlie takes his revolver out of his holster. 'Your ability to lie and manipulate will get you nowhere in the jungle.' He holds the gun out to her.

Marie tuts. She keeps her arms folded. 'That's why I brought you along.'

'Let's get one thing straight, Frenchie. Walking through the jungle ain't like taking a stroll through one of your fancy Parisian parks.'

'What are we going to do? Shoot our way through the undergrowth?'

Charlie grits his teeth. 'You come to me telling me you want to be independent, well I ain't carrying you. I've nursed you enough the last couple of days. We might just pull this job off if we work together. Here. Take it.'

She rolls her eyes and reaches for the gun but hesitates to take it.

'I can't—'

'Sure you can, here.'

Charlie pushes the gun into her hand. It is heavy, cold, and familiar.

'Why are you acting strange? You're not gonna pass out again?'

Marie swallows. 'No. Holding it reminds me of killing Victor.'

Charlie nods.

'Maybe it's best if you had it back. Here.' She offers him the gun.

Charlie puts his hands on his belt. 'Point it someplace else,

134

Frenchie.'

'Oh, sure.' She aims it at the floor instead of at Charlie and tilts the handle towards him.

He ignores it. 'How'd you feel when he attacked you? Tell me?'

Marie looks at her fingers curled around the handle and her finger resting on the trigger.

'What is it you're remembering?' he asks. 'Close your eyes, tell me.'

Marie sighs.

'Do it,' Charlie says gently.

Marie closes her eyes. She frowns. 'I can't—'

'Do you want to rely on men all your life?'

She twists her lips. Her frown furrows deeper. 'His hands around my neck.'

'Go on.'

'I can't.'

'Just keep your eyes closed. That's it. Now talk. Tell me what else you remember.'

'He's on top of me,' she says. 'I can't breathe. My head hurts. It feels like it's going to explode. I can't breathe. I feel helpless. I can't help myself. He's too strong. I can't move him. I'm just…helpless. Weak—'

Marie opens her eyes. She holds the gun pointed out in front of her. Away from its aim, Charlie was standing at Marie's side.

'You weren't weak, sister. You were strong. He's dead, and you're not. You had spirit. You will hold out long enough for you to survive. But remember how it felt just before you shot him? How helpless you felt. This,' Charlie says, pointing at the gun. 'This stopped you from being helpless. This kept you alive. This thing evens the odds. You did well shooting

Victor, but you might not be close enough to shoot someone in the belly next time. You need to learn how to shoot.'

Charlie walks over to a coil of rope attached at one end to a barrel and the other to the rail around the stern. In the sea below, the wake is white and fierce, and overhead the smoke from the funnels is thick and black.

'You ain't probably gonna hit it, but at least it'll give you something tangible to aim at.'

Charlie pulls on the knot attached to the railing, testing it, and then throws the barrel overboard into the sea.

'I won't be able to hit that—'

'Any shot is worth taking if there's a chance,' Charlie says.

Marie holds the gun in her left hand, closes one eye and looks down the gun. Then she swaps hands and her stance and looks down it again. She glances at Charlie. 'The barrel's bouncing around too much.'

'Which one...If it was a person, he'd have shot you already. Get!'

Marie frowns. She licks at her top lip. She points the revolver at the barrel. She squeezes the trigger. It goes all the way back, but nothing happens.

'Lesson one, you gotta cock the damn thing. Pull the hammer back.'

Marie cocks the revolver. She aims at the barrel bouncing in the wake. She pulls on the trigger. Bang. The gun ends up pointing somewhere into the sky.

'It's got some kick to it, ain't it? Try it again.'

Marie cocks the revolver and aims at the barrel.

'Look down the sights. Focus on them, not your target.'

'What, don't focus on the barrel?'

Charlie nods.

Aim. Squeeze. She feels the sway of the ship. The barrel

bobs about in the water. Instead of following it with her aim, she keeps her aim pointed in its general direction and waits for it to fall behind the sights. It does. It goes out of shot. She pauses, and it comes back into view. Bang. The bullet hits the barrel. Marie looks out at the target.

'Did I get it?'

Charlie's lips purse. His eyes narrow to slits. 'Yeah, you got it.'

'I got it!' Marie says and laughs.

'Stop waving that damn thing around, will ya?'

'Don't worry, it's not cocked.'

'Good. Now don't start thinking you're all that. Legrand ain't gonna give you that much time to shoot him.'

'He's going to come after me still? I'm going to have to shoot him? You want me to kill him?'

'If he's going to kill you, then yes. Jesus, you're helpless. Without it, you're weak. Give me the gun.' He takes the bullets out and then gives it back to her.

'Without the bullets, I can't shoot anything.'

'Pull it on a man first. You won't have to shoot. You'll have all the power you need. You gotta learn to be quick with it. Legrand's spent the best part of his life around guns. He'll be used to 'em.'

'How can I compete with that?'

'Well, he might not be a sharpshooter, but he'll be used to the feel. He'll be comfortable with one in hand. You gotta learn to hold it like it's one of your paintbrushes. Do you remember what it was like to draw and paint before you could?'

She nods.

'Feels like shooting does now to you, doesn't it? Except you don't have the hours to practice shooting like you did your art. Put this on.' Charlie removes his belt and holster, gives them to Marie and then goes and gets a deckchair. He unfolds it, places it on the deck, sits on it and puts his feet on the rail.

Marie puts the belt around her waist but it's too big. She pushes the strap through the loops and ties her scarf around it to secure it. The gun hangs at her hip.

'For the next hour,' Charlie says. 'Pull it, cock it and aim it at whatever I tell you.'

After half an hour, Marie can barely lift her arm into the air. Her bicep aches, and the tendons in her wrist are tight.

'Behind you, the bell, drop to your knee.' Marie falls to her knee. She drags the revolver from the holster and aims it toward the bell as she twists around.

'Too slow,' Charlie says.

Marie looks at the decking and winces.

'Turn it on me.'

'Gladly.' She turns back to Charlie, and he kicks the revolver out of her hand. He pulls another gun on her and cocks the trigger.

Marie collapses. 'That's ridiculous. At least give me a chance.'

'Do you think the world's gonna give you a chance?' He puts a hand on his chest and mimics her voice. 'Sorry, Inspector Legrand, please give me a chance to shoot you. No way. Danger ain't gonna wait for you to not be tired. What happens if we been trekking through the jungle all day and he comes up on you?'

'That's different. I won't have been swinging a gun about for the last hour."

'No, but you'll probably have been swinging a machete,

cutting through vines and branches.'

'But—'

'How much of a chance did Victor give you?'

Marie sighs. She thinks about it for a moment. Then she crawls over to the revolver, takes it and shoves it into the holster as she stands. 'What's the next target?'

The next day, Marie and Charlie stand in a doorway looking out at the wind and rain buffeting the deck. Marie rubs her sore bicep. Then she clenches her fingers. She leans out and squints at the mast Charlie points up at.

'That mast is about forty feet tall,' Charlie says. 'From your plans, it looks like the dam they've built in Panama is about the same height.'

Marie listens and nods.

'Well then, get to it,' Charlie says.

'Get to what?'

'Climb the damn thing.'

'Are you crazy? It's raining.'

'No shit.'

Marie doesn't move.

Charlie takes the pipe from his pocket. He begins scraping the tobacco from inside it with a pocket knife. After a short time, he says, 'You know, after Legrand became a citizen of France and got a job as an inspector in Paris, he got married. One night, he was late meeting his wife down by the Seine. So, she wanders off, thinking he'd meant to meet her somewhere else.' Charlie stuffs some tobacco into the pipe from a pouch. 'Well, she only goes and gets herself killed. A botched robbery, they say. The worst thing is the poor woman was pregnant. Well, Legrand nearly kills the suspect who made him late to meet her. He then brings in the man who killed her with a mere slither of life left in him. Just enough life to keep him alive to be tried and executed.' Charlie puts the pipe to his mouth and lights it with a match. 'Legrand took out the whole bloody gang this lad was a part of.' Charlie puffs on the pipe and then takes it out of his mouth. 'One by one, he brought them in. Each one barely alive, just enough so that they could be executed or thrown in prison.'

Marie says nothing. Charlie looks over at her. She is stony-faced and looking straight out into the driving rain.

'Anyway, ever since then, he's hated criminals,' Charlie says. 'Don't matter who they are or what they have done. Once he goes after them, he brings them in. It's actually quite funny, ain't it, don't you think? I mean, a man once in a legion full of criminals now hunts criminals down.'

'Sure,' Marie says. 'Hilariously funny.' She goes out into the rain and over to the foot of the mast. She grabs hold of the rope and begins to climb up. Every time the ship keels on a wave, she clings to the rigging, grits her teeth and closes her eyes. When she tries to look up to see how far she has left to climb before she reaches the top, the wind batters rain into her eyes. She takes it one rung at a time. As the rope bites into her skin, the saltwater spray in the air makes her wounds sting even more. By the end of that morning, Marie feels like she knows every fibre of that rigging.

CHAPTER 21

That afternoon as the ship continues to plough through the stormy Atlantic, Marie sits shivering in the parlour below deck. She pulls a blanket around herself and holds her palms to the stove.

A bespectacled man sitting reading at the long table puts his book down and studies her. He smiles when they make eye contact. 'I just have to enquire, Mademoiselle. I'm intrigued. What kind of endeavour are you and that fellow engaged in?'

The few people sitting around also look up from their knitting or reading.

'He's my teacher,' she says. 'We're going exploring.'

'Really?' the man says. 'Please, do tell us more.'

Marie smiles and shakes her head. 'I'm not sure I should.'

'Oh, please do,' a young woman says. 'It's so boring on here. What are you going to do?'

Marie pulls the blanket closer. Their eager faces stare at her.

I killed my husband, now I'm going to sabotage the Panama Canal. She wonders what they'd say if she said that. She wonders if they'd believe her.

Her mind races until she remembers one of Victor's books. She smiles at the thought.

'That smile suggests you're doing something exciting,' the man says.

She then knows it's the right story to tell.

'Do you know, this isn't the first time someone thought about connecting the Pacific to the Atlantic across Panama?

Hundreds of years ago, when Spain had a mighty fleet and sailed all over the world, King Alfonso had the same idea. You see, his armies were busy conquering the Americas and pillaging a great amount of gold from the Incas. The only trouble was that it was happening on the Pacific side of the continent. His gold-laden ships had to sail all the way down South America to Drake's Passage.' She drew a route with her finger in the air as if charting the eastern seaboard of South America. 'And then they had to travel back up again,' she says, charting a course up the western seaboard, 'before they could even cross the Atlantic.

'Well, those seas were treacherous and the King lost a hell of a lot of gold. So he came up with the idea of building a canal across Panama to transport it. But of course, they didn't have the technology to do something like that.'

'Some might say that is still the case,' the man says, and everybody laughs. They all look back to her to continue.

'Well, Panama being the narrowest point, the King would sail his gold down to Panama City, then his armies would make their slaves drag it across the isthmus to Colón, where he would reload it onto another ship and sail it back to Spain.' Marie leans forwards. 'The rivers, the jungles, the trails across the mountains were all just as treacherous as those seas. Panama has a lot of treasure just waiting to be found.'

The young woman's eyes are wide. 'You really think it's true?'

'Somebody I once knew,' Marie says, thinking of Victor, 'always said there was more money to be made from the lost treasure in Panama than there was from digging a trench of water.'

'You know where some is?' the man asks.

142

'Now that,' Marie says and smiles, 'is something I can't tell you.'

The next day, Charlie leads Marie down into the ship's bowels. The clanking noise grows louder, and the temperature increases the deeper they go. Charlie levers open a large door, and they are hit by a blast of desiccating heat that steals her breath. The room glows orange. Three men shovel coal from a tall heap into the massive flame-belching boiler.

'The boiler room,' Charlie says.

'I had no idea.'

'Well, this is where you're spending today.'

Marie's sore shoulders slump. 'And what's this supposed to teach me?'

'Not so much teach, more...acclimatise.'

'Acclimatise to what?'

'The jungle's hot.'

A man of solid muscle strolls over to them, his dark skin glistening with sweat. He looks down at Marie and winces. 'She ain't gonna last two minutes in here, Charlie.'

'Matthew here runs this operation. He'll show you what to do.'

'You expect me to work? In here?'

'You'll be hauling this here coal into the boiler o'er there, miss.'

Charlie grins. 'You won't be standing still in the jungle.'

'You're enjoying this, aren't you?'

'Frenchie, yes,' Charlie says as he chuckles to himself. 'I do believe I am.'

By day, Marie undertakes, with increasing gusto, whatever physical training scenario Charlie can create within the

143

confines of the ship. She is exhausted, but she is surprised at how her body adapts and can climb and run like it had ten years ago. At night Charlie teaches her how to navigate via the stars, and he also uses her art materials to draw plans and to show Marie how easy it is to crudely blow up something as large as a dam with dynamite. During her time aboard, she feels the apathy of a privileged, kept life slipping out of her, and she becomes less fearful of a future without cultured Parisian life. She falls asleep as soon as her head hits the pillow each night.

A week has passed since they boarded the SS La Touraine in Marseille. Marie leans against the taffrail. Her forehead rests on her forearms as she catches her breath. Her body aches, but she is smiling. She hadn't been this active since she'd lived with her grandpa when they used to go off into the Pyrenees and live off the land for weeks. He had taught her to be resourceful and self-sufficient. Only now does she realise how different she could've lived her life since his death. He had planted the seed of independence within her, but she had spent her life doing what others wanted.

'It's good to see land again,' Marie says. She stretches and looks out at the Virgin Islands to starboard.

Charlie leans with his back to the rail. He cleans out his pipe. 'The captain says we're a day from Colón.'

'Good. I can't wait to get to Panama now. I'm ready for it, Charlie.'

Charlie laughs. 'Ready?' He shakes his head. 'You've trained for a few days and think you're ready to take on the jungle and ex-foreign legion. You'll be lucky if you make it through this whole mission alive. If you do, then you'll be ready. Or broken.'

Marie frowns. 'Between the two of us, though, we'll

144

succeed.'

'You rely on people too much.'

'You never used to think like that, Charlie.'

'Yeah, well, things change.' Charlie started walking away. 'Lucky for me, I saw the error of my ways.'

'Where are you going? What about my training?'

Charlie waved his hand. 'I thought you were ready.' He sits on a bench. He pulls his hat down, so the brim shades his eyes.

Marie goes over to him and rests her hand on the revolver in the holster on her hip. 'What happened to you? Why did you retire?'

'Do you even have to ask?'

'Yes.'

'How about this,' Charlie says. 'If you beat your time, I'll tell you what happened.'

Marie smiles. She stands poised, ready to run. Charlie drags his pocket watch out. He holds five fingers up. He closes each finger. He points forwards. She runs. Marie completes one circuit of the ship. Then, she goes straight to the mast. He looks at the watch when she's climbed up the ladder out of sight. He raises his eyebrows. He sits forwards and watches her scurry up the rigging. At the top, she pulls the gun from her holster, and because they'd decided against using live bullets, she squeezes the trigger, and the hammer falls into an empty chamber. 'Bang, bang,' she mouths.

She climbs back down and jumps from the platform onto the decking in front of Charlie. She skids as she lands but rights herself and starts running again. When she's completed one more circuit of the ship, she skids onto her knees and pulls the gun on him. 'Bang, you're dead, Legrand.'

She collapses onto her back and laughs as she catches her

breath. When she pushes herself onto her elbows, she sees Charlie looking at her and smiling warmly.

'Maybe you might just pull this off,' he says.

'I beat my time?'

He shakes his head. 'I never thought you'd be up to this challenge.'

'I beat it, didn't I? Now you've got to tell me. Why did you retire?'

Charlie stands. 'You. Partially...'

She holds her hand for him to pull her up, but he turns and walks away. She scrambles to her feet. 'Listen, Charlie, what happened between us—'

'Forget it, Frenchie.'

'No. I just wanted to show you how good I was at the job.'

'Well, you certainly did that. I should thank you anyway. I joined this game because I was idealistic. I thought America could build a better world. You didn't think like that, though. You joined up to make your own life better.'

Marie bows her head.

'It's nothing to be ashamed of. I've done deeds far dirtier in the name of idealism. It was you that opened my eyes and made me begin to question why I was doing this.'

'You wouldn't just quit like that. What happened?'

'Cuban revolutionaries happened. They wanted to reclaim control of their country from Spain. America saw this as an opportunity to get Spain out of its backyard.'

'That's why you were sent to Spain?'

'I wasn't sent. I asked to go.'

'Why?'

'Why do you think? To get away from you and France. Well, it started off well enough. I managed to reclaim my sanity, at least. The job was pretty much the same as in

146

France. Be the man on the ground. Find out information. Record the state of the military, embed and facilitate sleeper agents like yourself. You know the drill. Command's orders became increasingly hostile, though. Sabotage and create accidents. Instigate insurgent groups. This one time, they ordered me to kill a captain, a guy that was seen as a rising star in the Spanish military. I don't have a problem killing an enemy, but this man wasn't an enemy yet. They wanted me to kill him based on what he might become, what he might do. Well, that didn't feel right to me. Still, I began to gather intelligence on him. I knew his routine. I knew when would be best to kill him. I knew how to do it, so it wouldn't create suspicion.'

'But you didn't do it?'

'No, I refused my orders.'

'What was it about him? What stopped you? What made you defy them?'

'As I watched him, I grew to see how much of a family man he was. He was always with his children. I couldn't deny them their father, so I resigned from my position. They denied me my pension and said it was only because of my record that I wouldn't face a court martial. Well, that was that. I was on my own. It's a damn sight better being free and looking out for myself than having masters like that. What are you smiling at?'

'And you say you're not idealistic.'

'Yeah, well,' he says. 'I heard the bastards sent someone else and got him anyway.'

Marie's smile fades. 'I meant what I said in Marseille, Charlie. I'm not doing this for America. I'm doing this for me. For a new life.'

Charlie frowns.

'I mean it, Charlie. I'm Victor's sole heir to his business empire. I'll get nothing, though.'

'That's because you killed him.'

'It was self-defence. But all his cronies would make sure I paid the price, not because of my guilt, but because they couldn't bear to see a woman take control of his wealth.'

'You know what I think? I think you're blowing this dam, sabotaging the whole French canal project just to stick one to the French patriarchy.'

Marie grins when she sees that Charlie is playing with her. 'Maybe you're right.'

Marie squints. She shields her eyes from the sunlight. There is Panama on the horizon. A dark line between the bleached sky and the glistening sea.

As the ship chugs closer, that thin band of land becomes foothills and mountains covered in jungle lined with white sand and mangrove thickets. Stood at the ship's bow, Marie smiles all the way into the port of Colón.

As the ship is pulled against the dock wall, Charlie approaches her. 'I thought I'd find you out here,' he says. 'Well, look at you.'

'What?'

'You, grinning from ear to ear.'

'I can't believe we're here.'

'So what are you waiting for? Come on, let's get our bags. We've been on this tub long enough.'

After getting off the ship, Marie and Charlie have their passports stamped, and no questions are asked of her. It is a hot day, almost the end of September, midday on a Saturday. They walk out of the port together and follow railway tracks that lead the short distance into the town.

'I didn't know what to expect, but it looks like the Wild West,' Marie says.

'What would you know of the Wild West?'

'I've seen pictures. Well, wouldn't you say?'

Charlie raises an eyebrow. 'No palm trees in Montana, that's for sure. Suppose most frontier town buildings look like this, though.'

Front Street is a narrow strip of dirt. It is barely wide enough for two horses pulling wagons to squeeze past each other. On one side of the street is a hodgepodge of wooden buildings, which are no more than two storeys high with rusted, corrugated tin roofs. Lined up, down the other side of the street, is a set of five train tracks and various sheds and shacks of all sizes.

'Right,' Charlie says. 'D'you know what to do?'

Marie smiles. 'Of course.'

'Okay, let's meet back here in an hour. Outside Maduro Juniors.' Charlie points at the small photographic studio they are outside, nestled between Lam and Lee's Chinese and Japanese Bazar and the Astor House Hotel. Charlie goes up the street and walks along the porches shaded by canopies. Marie watches him until she can't see him anymore.

She picks up her bags and goes over to the photographic studio. Inside, the photographer is adjusting the tie of a man in a suit about to have his portrait taken. She goes on along the porch to the Chinese and Japanese bazaar. Incense wafts out. It is dark inside, and an old woman sitting at the counter may be asleep or staring straight at her. She can't tell. The shop is piled high with a variety of trinkets and food.

As she carries on walking, a man stumbles out of the swing doors of the Astor House Hotel's saloon. He walks into the canopy, hanging down as if he hasn't seen it blocking his way. He tries to push himself underneath, but can't, so he staggers past Marie and he coughs at her. Arriving at the swing doors, she stands on her tiptoes and peers over. The ground floor is a saloon covered in tables and chairs with a bar at the back. She pushes through the doors and heads over to the bar.

'Excuse me—'

'Room or a drink Madame?' the bartender asks.

'You have rooms available?'

'Of course, we do. You can have it by the hour or by the day.'

'By the hour?'

'Yes, Madame.'

'Just the night will be fine, thank you.'

She hands over ten francs, and he slides her a key from beneath the bar.

'I don't suppose you can tell me where the hospital is?'

The bartender goes and serves whiskey to a man down the bar and shouts over to her. 'It's about ten minutes from here. Head along the street that runs along the coast from the docks. It's a cluster of about forty or so white wooden buildings next to the sea. You can't miss it.'

Marie savours the breeze from the Caribbean as she walks across one of the white wooden footbridges connecting the hospital buildings. Beneath her, the sea laps at the white sand. Music drifts from the small wooden staff administrators building. She hesitates from knocking on the door and listens to the scratchy quavering tune; Clare de Lune. Nearby, small groups of people, the relatives of patients, sit in the shadows beneath the palm trees. The door opens. Marie jumps. A gaunt but well-groomed man with grey hair stands in the doorway. He smiles and strokes the side of his hair.

'Madame,' he says. 'Are you looking for me?'

'I'm looking for a doctor.'

He shakes his head. 'Doctors... Beautiful women are always looking for doctors. Not administrators.' His lip quivers, then breaks into a smile. 'Come on in, please, take a seat,' he says, holding the door open. As she squeezes past him, he leans in so their bodies touch.

Marie places her rucksack on the floor and sits in the chair. 'His name is Gabriel Bertrand.'

The man nods. 'Aren't you just the contradiction, dressed like that but with a face so, so very beautiful.'

'I'm eager to find Gabriel. Do you know him? Have you seen him here?'

'Alas, no, I don't. The name sounds familiar,' he says, wagging a finger. 'But so many names and details pass through here. You seem really desperate to find him. I'll go and find his records.' He leaves through the door, and his footsteps drift down the corridor.

She wipes her brow on her rolled-up sleeve. The wooden shutters are pulled shut. Sunlight falls in rays through the slats. A fly buzzes in through a gap and flies an erratic route several times around the room. Then it goes out and off down the corridor.

There is a glass of water on his desk. Marie licks her dry lips.

He comes back up the corridor and into the room. 'Ah, I think I have Dr Bertrand's records right here.' He tilts a brown manila folder towards her. She goes to take it, but he moves it away. He sits on the edge of the desk beside her.

He takes some spectacles from the inside pocket of his blazer, puts them on and then starts sifting through the loose pages in the folder. Some are typed, and some are handwritten. She cranes her neck to see if she can read anything.

He looks up over the rim of his spectacles. He puts the folder on the table, leans forwards, and places his hand on her knee. 'Why is it you want to meet this doctor so much?'

She removes his hand.

'That's no concern of yours.'

'You see, it is. It's confidential. I don't know who you are. I don't even know if you like music.' He gets up, takes the folder with him, and goes to the gramophone by the window. The scratchy tune plays again. 'I need to get to know you.'

Her chair legs scrape against the terracotta tiles as she stands. 'Listen—'

He grabs her waist. She freezes. Victor stares back at her.

CHAPTER 23

She shuts her eyes and opens them. Victor has gone. Marie pushes the administrator back, and he doesn't resist. He just smiles and sifts through the papers again. 'Ah yes, Doctor Bertrand. He has been stationed in one of the hospitals of the line.'

'Of the line?'

'I have kindly given you something, now...'

Marie puts a hand on his chest. He grins. She gets down onto her knees. The man smiles and looks to the ceiling. She hides her grimace as she strokes down his leg. With her other hand, she reaches into her bag. His smile fades. He looks down at what is pushed into his crotch. She cocks the gun. He freezes. Rising up, she keeps the muzzle pointed at his groin.

'Where is Gabriel?' she asks.

'Paradise or Paraiso as it is called here. Doctor Bertrand has been stationed in a tiny hospital in the small town of Paraiso.'

'Where's that?'

'Let me show you.' He edges back from the gun and sighs with relief, but she keeps it trained on him. He goes around his desk and reaches for a drawer. Marie aims the revolver at his head. He holds up his hands. 'We are not all as well armed as you, Madame.'

He pulls a map from the drawer and opens it on the desk. 'It's on the other side of the isthmus, I'm afraid. There's not much there. But it's only about ten, fifteen kilometres or so as the crow flies from Panama City. Ah yes, here.'

Marie looks at the map. His finger rests on a green area.

'It's in the jungle?'

'If you're not in Colón or Panama City, you're in the jungle. It's the other side of the Gaillard cut. Does that mean anything to you?'

'Remind me.'

'They're trying to cut the canal through the Culebra mountain.'

'Cut through a mountain?'

'Yes, a hazardous and foolish endeavour.'

'I thought you said the hospital was small?'

'It is.'

'Well, shouldn't it be bigger if it's so dangerous?' Marie asks.

'It's an emergency hospital. Most people get patched up and transported to the main hospitals here in Colón or Panama City. But if you get injured, you're useless to the company.'

'Life's that cheap out here, isn't it?' she says.

He nods slowly. 'Yes, it is.'

Marie pulls the trigger. The hammer falls on the empty chamber with a click.

'Then just you remember that,' Marie says. She takes the glass of water and downs it. Then she swipes Gabriel's folder off the desk and leaves the building as the scratchy tune ends on the gramophone.

Marie is half an hour late to meet Charlie on Front Street. It is getting dark. He is standing outside Lam and Lee's bazaar talking to, she presumed, either Lam or Lee. She hangs back by the photographer's studio, looking at the tintype images pinned on a board until Charlie arrives. It is so long since she sketched a portrait, let alone painted one. She remembers drawing Gabriel when they were leaving Paris by train.

'Where you been?' he asks.

'Just staying out of trouble.'

'Is that why you decided to carry your gun?' He points at the holstered gun hanging off her hip.

'Trouble comes looking. I aim to be ready.'

'Taking control, huh?'

'Something like that. Where's the gear?'

'We collect it in the morning. Did you find us a place to stay?'

'Yes. Over there,' she says, pointing to the Astor Hotel.

Charlie raises his eyebrows. 'Colón's best brothel? You sure know how to pick 'em, Frenchie.'

Charlie places the pack down gently onto the floor in their room. Marie throws her bag onto the bed and crouches beside Charlie. 'Can I have a look at it?'

Charlie twists his lips. 'I suppose.'

He opens the pack and then the lid of the wooden box inside. The dynamite tubes are packed together so they can't rattle around in the box.

'It doesn't look much. Is there enough?'

'A lot goes a long way. It'll blow the rail tracks, the dam and then some.' Charlie frowns at her. 'I don't like that look.'

'What look?'

'That wild look. Intrigue or whatever it is.' He closes the lid on the box.

Marie shakes her head. She is about to answer, but there is banging against the wall of the adjoining room. They both look up at the wall it comes from. The muffled sounds of moaning starts like a chorus. They look at each other, and

Charlie smirks. Marie smiles. 'You're such a child.'

That night Charlie doesn't offer to sleep on the floor or in the chair, and she doesn't ask him to. They lie on the bed together with their backs to each other and a gap between them. Sweat runs off her forehead and tickles her temple. She opens her eyes because they don't even ache with tiredness. The window is open, and the incoming breeze stokes her temperature. Moaning and banging comes sporadically from the adjoining bedrooms and the ceiling above. She puts her forearm to her forehead and wipes away the constant sweat. She tries to imagine that Charlie isn't there, that she is alone in the room. His body is next to hers. She can feel his presence. Close. She remembers when the man in the hospital had grabbed her waist and how she'd seen Victor again. All of the times when Gabriel tried to kiss or hold her, his form had been taken over by the thought of Victor. But not now. How could she be so close to Charlie and not see Victor?

Charlie sleeps. She can tell by his steady breathing. She twists around, and there is barely a gap between them. She can feel the heat radiating off his bare tanned back. He turns onto his back brushing against her. She holds her breath. His eyes remain shut. Thank god he didn't wake and see me watching him sleep, she thinks. He twists his lips. He swallows. Then his lips part, and he starts breathing rhythmically again. She studies his face. Charlie's face. Not Victor's. She looks at his lips. Then she is drawn to his closed eyelids that flicker. His hand on his chest rises up and down with his breathing, and his other hand, closest to her, is at his side next to her groin. She wants him to move in his sleep and touch her. She edges closer to him, but he remains still. It

157

must be touch that triggers the visions of Victor, she thinks. She holds her hand out over his flat stomach. She lowers it slowly till there is barely a gap, and she can feel his hair against her palm. Charlie turns into her. Their bodies are pressed together. Her eyes go wide. Charlie's eyes open. It takes him a second or two to realise where he is. Then he grins.

'Sorry, Frenchie,' he says. Then he rolls back onto his side and puts his back to her. A few seconds later, he is breathing steadily again, and she knows he is back asleep. The tension falls out of her muscles. She bites her lower lip as she looks at his body in the grey moonlight. There is no Victor in bed with her, just Charlie.

CHAPTER 24

The following day, outside the blacksmiths and the stables, Marie strokes the horse's brown neck as she inspects its legs.

'She good enough for you, Frenchie?'

'She'll do.'

'Have you ever ridden before? Are you sure you can even ride?'

Marie puts her foot in the stirrup, holds onto the saddle and swings herself onto the horse. She clicks her tongue, pulls on the reins and steers her horse toward Charlie's steed. 'I can outride you, cowboy.'

'I keep telling you, this ain't the Wild West.'

'You keep telling yourself that, Charlie.'

'It's wilder than the Wild West out there, kid.' He twists around in the saddle and checks that the sack holding the box of dynamite is securely strapped down, then he clicks his tongue and gently digs in his heels, and the horse walks on.

As they follow the railway line out of Colón, their horses walk steadily. The hotels, shops and stores give way to tiny wooden homes, nothing more than huts with tin roofs, hundreds packed together and pressed against the train tracks.

'Won't a train come through?' Marie asks.

'Probably.'

'Then what will we do?'

Charlie sighs. 'Stand aside and let it pass. What else?'

The narrow corridor of red earth, with the train tracks running over it, is the only visible route into the tangle of greenery of the jungle. There isn't much space between the tracks and the women leaning on their porches who eye them passing by. Crippled amputees stare blankly through them as they pass. Marie and Charlie ride through the canyon of shacks which abruptly gives way to the jungle.

She stops at the threshold of the jungle.

'Now I miss the open expanse of the sea.'

Charlie swallows. 'I know what you mean.'

'When we're done with this, Steiner will give me a plot of land with a view.'

'You should've seen my view of the Med, Frenchie.'

She'd been through forests she thought were great in France. She remembers the days and nights spent camping wild in the Midi-Pyrénées with her grandfather. But in Panama, these vast shanty towns are tiny and insignificant compared to the jungle surrounding them.

The two iron rails bend together into the distance, disappearing into the trees. Twisting roots plunge into and out of the earth on either side of the tracks. Marie peers into the dark impenetrable understory. Damp ferns and saplings rise out of the detritus. Layer upon layer of leaves and vines block her view of the trunks of the massive trees. It is alive with the ticking and clacking of uncountable insects. Flies buzz. Frogs croak. Wings flap. Beaks chatter and warble. Branches snap. Monkeys screech. A forest with as many competing noises as the city she left behind. Two weeks ago. That is all. It seems like a lifetime ago.

The horses keep on. Marie sways in the saddle in time with the confident strut of the beast. It is as if they are connected like they'd melted together in this heat. Sweat glistens on the horse's neck. Marie feels sweat on her forehead. Sweat drips onto her own neck. Sweat runs down her spine. Sweat on the backs of her knees falls down her calves. Onwards. They reach the bend in the tracks, which is longer than it had looked. She can only see the rails curving through the rainforest behind and ahead.

There is no escape from the sun. It is high and seems to follow the train tracks with them. It feels just like the boiler room on the ship. It steals your breath and then pushes it back at you. But unlike the boiler room, there is no door to escape through. There is no sea breeze to make it better. Charlie rides ahead. She isn't going to congratulate him on being right. She would've needed to have spent the whole journey sleeping and living in that boiler room to have adequately acclimatised. She looks at Charlie. He sways with his horse's gait. The back of his shirt is drenched in sweat. Know it all, she thinks. You'd better be hating this too.

Onwards. Marie wonders how far they'd come. She can't be bothered looking at the map. Her eyes close, and she lets them, just for a moment. Her chin drops. Her eyes startle open. She looks at Charlie, he hadn't seen. She finds her canteen, unscrews the lid and pours the tepid water into her mouth. She doesn't feel any less tired. Any less refreshed.

Onwards. Something lands on her forearm. She splats the insect into mush and wipes the residue onto her skirt. Charlie had seen that. He smiles. Marie looks to the heavens. The tops of the trees sway in a breeze that doesn't penetrate the jungle. The sun beats down.

Onwards. The train track is no longer straight like it was coming out of Colón. Here it is shaped by the contours of the land. There is no telling visibly how much distance they have covered.

Onwards. Rounding the shoulder of another bend, the train tracks veer into the groin of another bend. They continue through the jungle canyon.

She hears it first in the iron tracks. A shimmering noise reverberates through them. Charlie steers his horse towards the forest, trampling into the fern as saplings bend or snap out of the way. He climbs down and holds onto the reins. Marie follows him in and does the same. She is surprised at how the dense forest accepts them. Then the mechanical roar approaches. The pistons thump. The coupling rods revolve. The staccato huffing of the steam as the black engine charges around the bend towards them. Steam hits them. It takes all her strength to hold onto her horse and stop it from bolting. When she looks back, she sees carriages. Faces in open windows. Hair moving in the breeze. Children. Women. Wealth. Then it is gone. Charlie hadn't even bothered to look. He is soothing the horse with his words. Holding the bridle. His face rests against the horse's, and he strokes its neck. Then, he leads it back out onto the tracks.

'There were families on that train,' Marie says. She looks down the tracks, but it has already gone.

Charlie climbs back onto the horse. 'Yeah, what of it?'

'It just surprised me, that's all.'

Charlie makes a clicking noise and his horse moves on.

Marie pulls herself up onto the saddle.

Onwards.

It is early afternoon. Another train had passed Marie and Charlie about an hour ago, heading in the same direction they were. They rode on until the train line had climbed to a ridge, and they could see across the canopy and the valley. Marie takes in the view and lets the breeze wash over her.

'Half a day and we're back seeing a view. You needn't have worried,' she says.

'Don't worry. You'll be back in the thick of it before long.' He waves his hand across the landscape. 'According to the plans, that's what they intend to flood,' Charlie says.

Marie shades her eyes. The jungle stretches as far as she can see. Quavering in the distance, the land rises up again, and beyond that, she can just about see the Atlantic Coast on the horizon. She shakes her head. 'I can't comprehend it. It's so vast.'

'Ain't it just.'

'Do you think it's possible to flood that much land?'

'If they can build a dam strong enough, then sure.' Charlie climbs off the horse. 'Here's where we sabotage the tracks.'

'Here?'

'Yes. It's perfect. If we do a good job, we can make it look natural, like part of the cliff fell away. The trick's gonna be not mangling the tracks. We don't want it to look like dynamite played a part.' Charlie finds a small stream and ties his horse to a nearby branch. Marie does the same. Charlie unfastens the pack of dynamite from the saddle and returns to the tracks.

'Charlie.'

'What now, Frenchie?' Charlie says without looking up. He lays out his tools like Gabriel would lay out his surgical instruments: Four sticks of dynamite side by side, pliers, a small shovel, a detonator, and wire. Charlie takes off his hat and scratches his damp hair. He puts the hat back on and turns to look at her because she's gone quiet.

She gazes off down the tracks towards the bend. 'They'll never see it until they're on top of it. Then it'll be too late.'

'There are over two hours until the next train comes through. That's plenty of time for us to warn them,' Charlie says.

Marie shakes her head. 'Wait. How do you mean, warn them?'

'Stop the train. What do you think?'

'No. We can't stop the train.'

Charlie frowns. 'This here,' Charlie says as he taps on one of the sleepers. 'After half an hour of my handy work, it ain't gonna be here any longer.'

'I know, but—'

'The engine, it's carriages, all the people in them are gonna go careering off this ridge,' Charlie says. 'Hell, this ridge won't even exist. And they're gonna go down, crashing right into that jungle.'

'How on earth have you made a career out of being a spy and a saboteur?' Marie says, putting her hands on her hips. 'We're here to do a job, Charlie. That job is to make France pull out of this project. A catastrophe like a train crash will help. Public confidence is already rock bottom on the whole thing—'

'Think about it, kid. Is that the type of person you are?'

She looks down into the jungle.

Charlie goes back to preparing the dynamite with blast fuses.

'It's too risky, making ourselves known like that.'

'So you'll just kill a load of innocent souls? You said yourself there were women and children on those trains.'

Marie turns her back on him. 'It's the line of work we do, Charlie.'

Charlie went over to her. He grabs her sleeve and pulls her around. 'He really changed you, didn't he?'

'Who?'

'Victor. You married him. Slept with him. Took his money. Lived his life by his rules, his way.' Charlie shakes his head.

164

'It's a damn shame.'

Marie swings a slap at his face. He goes to block her with his hand but realises he still holds a dynamite stick. She is so enraged that she doesn't see it. He doesn't stop her. She slaps him across the cheek. She curses him in French and hits him in the chest. He adjusts his footing and grabs her wrist. 'You're crazy. Look what I'm holding. Are you mad?'

He tries to show her the stick of dynamite, but Marie instinctively smacks his hand away. The dynamite flies through the air and over the ridge. Charlie grabs Marie. He pulls her down onto the floor. Boom. The deafening roar of the nitroglycerin exploding rips through the jungle. They hold onto each other. Their breathing is shallow and fast. Bodies against each other. The ground trembles from the explosion. Rocks and dirt fall onto them.

'What the hell do you think—'

Marie kisses him. It isn't Victor that kisses her back. It is Charlie. She pulls him towards her, and Charlie remains with her. She feels Charlie grow against her. Then she is on top of him. She doesn't take her eyes off him the whole time, lest he becomes Victor at the cruellest moment. But he doesn't. He remains as Charlie Blaine the entire time.

CHAPTER 25

After, Marie lies on her back beside the tracks as her senses recover. She feels the sun burning down on her again. She gets up and cleans herself in the stream, and when she returns, Charlie is drilling a hole into the ground with a weighted iron rod and a hammer.

'So you still intend to blow up the tracks here?'

'Yep.'

'I thought you might've changed your mind.'

'On account of what? That, just?'

'It would've, in the past.'

'Good job I got wise to you then,' he says.

'Just so long as you don't think it was for any other reason.'

'Don't worry, Frenchie, I know you're not the kind that falls in love.'

Once the holes were drilled into the dry earth around the train track on the ridge, they lower the sticks of dynamite down by the attached fuse wire. Then, they connect the fuses, and Charlie trails the wire back to a safe distance from which to detonate. Marie fetches the two horses. She ties them to nearby trees a little into the jungle forest. She hopes the wide trunks will provide some added protection from any debris.

She joins Charlie, lying on his belly behind a large fallen tree. Her elbows sink into the moss and bark. She looks back to where the jungle has been cleared for the train tracks. It is like a dry, sun-baked scab in the land.

'Here, take this,' Charlie says, handing her the detonator.

166

'When I started out, we used to do this the old-fashioned way and simply light the fuse with a match, now this little device does the job. It's not as fun, but at least you know if it hasn't triggered. The worst was when the fuse went out a couple of feet from the stick. Going over to sort it was the most terrifying thing you'll ever do. Here, attach it just there.'

Marie attaches the fuse cable to the detonator, following his direction. She holds the small detonator in her hand. Charlie gives her the handle.

'When you're ready,' he says. 'Put the handle in there, give it a twist to the right and boom. Job done.'

Marie places the handle into the detonator.

'Once we've stopped the train and told them, we'll be on our way,' he says. 'We'll blow the dam and be out of Panama before they know it.'

'Then what?' Marie asks.

Charlie swallows. 'Once the deal is done in Martinique, we'll go our separate ways.'

'New lives,' she says.

'Yes, new lives.'

Without breaking each other's stare, Marie twists the detonator. Nothing happens.

'I thought you said these things worked better?'

She twists it back and forth again.

The ground rolls up into the air. The explosion booms. A cloud rises. The ridge collapses. Earth, mud, and rock pitch into the air and fall back down. Marie hears a whooshing noise amongst all of this. She peeks over the tree trunk. A long piece of the train track flies towards them like a javelin. Marie grabs Charlie and pulls him down. Thud. It doesn't hit them, but it has landed close. As she looks up, the iron rail creaks and topples towards them. It hits the tree trunk and looms above. The horses are going crazy. They try to pull loose from where Marie has tied them. Their eyes are wide. They kick and fight against their reins. Most creatures have bolted from where they'd been doing whatever they did in the jungle. Birds launch into the air shaking the branches they take flight from. Monkeys screech as they dart off through the canopy. After the final rocks have finished raining onto the earth, Marie and Charlie climb from behind the log. They stare at the rail that could've flattened them. 'Well, that wasn't meant to happen,' Charlie says.

A cloud of smoke and dust billows from their creation, masking the destruction. They watch, with their mouths agape, as it slowly disperses. There is a crater, at least fifty metres wide, where the train line used to be. Mud and rocks still slide into the forest beneath the ridge as they approach it.

'It looks like a landslide,' Marie says.

'Yeah. Shame about the rails, though.' The tracks have bent on either side of the crater. Over on the other side, they spot a piece of rail that has been sent into the air like the one that had come close to hitting them. This one was jabbed into the earth like a spear. 'Damn it. Landslides don't flick iron rails into the air like matchsticks,' Charlie says.

The fire burns in the middle of the tracks. The brakes on the train squeal. Charlie jumps up and down, waving his arms.

'I should think the fire was enough to get their attention Charlie,' Marie says as she stands with a hand on her hip. The cattle catcher on the front of the steam engine stops within a few feet of hitting the fire. Through the steam, the driver looks out of the cab.

'What's going on? Is this a robbery?' The driver asks while

168

staying in the cab.

Marie rolls her eyes. 'We're saving your lives.'

'There's been a landslide around that bend.' Charlie says, pointing back around the tracks.

Along the carriages, people poke their heads out of the windows. The driver's eyebrows raise. He looks at the fireman in the cab, who shrugs his shoulders as they decide whether to believe the story.

'Come on, we'll show you,' Charlie says.

'We've waited long enough to tell them. We should get going.' Marie says.

'In a minute.'

Marie takes a deep breath. The driver climbs down. A passenger leans out of a carriage door and asks what is happening. 'There's been a landslide,' the driver shouts back. Then he follows Charlie and Marie around the bend until they reach the sabotaged tracks. The driver blows a low whistle and wipes his forehead with his neckerchief. He goes over to the crater's edge, puts his hand on the twisted rail and surveys the strewn sleepers. 'We'd have gone straight off.' He turns to Marie and Charlie. 'Who are you?'

'We're nobody,' Marie says.

'Explorers,' Charlie says. 'We're looking for lost gold.'

The train driver's forehead scrunches up. 'Gold?'

Marie closes her eyes. 'Godsake,' she mutters to herself.

'Listen, pal. We don't want nobody knowing we're out here. You see, there are other interested parties. If they knew where we were looking, they'd—'

'You're heroes. Yes. You're heroes. That's what you are. You've saved all our lives. We would've died.' The driver hugs Charlie, grabs Marie before she can back off, and hugs her too. When he lets go, she gasps for breath and staggers backwards. It was as if Victor himself had grabbed her.

The driver doesn't seem to notice her reaction. He ran back towards some passengers who had gotten off the train and had come to see why they were held up. He continues to describe Charlie and Marie as heroes. Marie is bent over. She coughs as if she is going to be sick. Charlie puts his hand on her back and a hand on her forearm. 'Are you okay, Frenchie?'

She nods. 'When he hugged me. Victor. It was as if Victor had grabbed me again.'

'Well, at least you didn't shoot him.'

Marie can't help but smile. Then she looks at his hand on her. 'When you touch me, I never see him. But I do when anyone else does.'

'Here. Look, this is what they saved us from,' the train driver says as he returns. A dozen passengers accompanying him look on in surprise at the crater where the ridge had been. They all thank them and express their disbelief. When the first one shakes Marie's hand, she looks at it. 'Just shake it,' Charlie tells her in English. 'Look into his eyes. See the man before you and not Victor.'

Marie takes the man's hand and shakes it. She concentrates on his features. He is smiling. He is young. Green-eyed. Thin lipped. He looks nothing like Victor. She tries to pull her hand away, but he clasps it, shaking it vigorously. He leans in. She closes her eyes. He kisses her on each cheek. Victor, her mind whispers. Then he lets go and shakes Charlie's hand instead. The next man comes to her. He is tall and thin and wearing a beige cotton suit. His bald, sweaty head glistens. 'Madame,' he says as he clasps her shoulders. He leans in and kisses her on each cheek. She concentrates on the weave of the fabric of his jacket. Victor would never have worn a suit like that. He goes away, and she exhales. She forces a smile as the next man thanks her. Victor grabs her neck and squeezes. She can't breathe. Pinpricks of pain flash across her skin.

'Alright, alright. We're thankful that you're grateful. But the heat and the excitement, it's getting a little overwhelming for the lady.'

Marie is sitting on the floor. She gulps for air and feels her chest loosen. Her eyes sting. She blinks. 'What happened, Charlie?'

'You just got a little overwhelmed,' Charlie says, helping her to her feet. Her legs feel weak.

'Why can't I stop feeling like this, Charlie?' Marie asks as they walk back to the train and where their horses are.

'You had a traumatic experience, kid.'

'But I can't control my own mind.'

'Give it time. You'll feel better.'

'No quip from you, Charlie? Now I know it must be serious.'

Charlie stops. He puts his hand on her cheek and looks into her eyes. For a beat, he doesn't say anything. His thumb strokes her cheek. 'Look. See? You're fine with me.' Then he drops his hand and looks away from her. 'You'll get over it. It'll just take time. Now come on, I think you were maybe right about drawing attention to ourselves.' Many people have gotten off the train and stand in the shadow of the carriages looking towards them. A few children run around and play at the edge of the jungle.

'You were right, Charlie. I don't know what I was thinking. They would've died.'

Charlie shakes his head. 'Don't worry. It's just self-preservation kicking in.'

'I know, but I'm not that kind of person. I hate what he's

171

made me.'

'It's just instinct, kid, and if ever there's a time in your life that you'll live on your instincts, it'll be now.'

'Well, it needs to change, Charlie. I need to change.' She looks out over Panama, spreading out before her to the horizon.

'Come on, let's get out of here,' Charlie says, and Marie nods in agreement.

CHAPTER 26

The next day, Inspector Legrand walks across the white, wooden footbridge. Underneath, the sea laps gently against the white sand. The administrator's door ahead is open, and he knocks on it before pushing it open.

There is nobody inside. There is a desk with a typewriter on it and some folders. Legrand opens one, and it is the records of a nurse from Lille.

'Hello. Is anybody here?'

'Just a minute,' a man calls from another room out back. Legrand goes over to the window. Beside it stands a table with a gramophone player on it. He lifts the needle and remembers how his wife loved listening to the music from such a machine.

'Ah, a music fan?'

'No,' Legrand says as he turns to face the man who enters the room. He is a gaunt old man with grey hair.

'My name is Legrand. I'm an inspector from Paris.'

The man raises a grey eyebrow and sits down behind his desk. 'Ah. What can I do for you? Please take a seat.'

Legrand remains standing. 'I'm told you are the person to ask about knowing where I might find a doctor Gabriel Bertrand who has been stationed in Panama.'

The man leans back in his chair. 'Well, well. An inspector, you say. Why are you after this man?'

'He might have information on a case I'm working on.'

'And you came all the way to Panama from Paris. Has to be some case?'

'It is. Do you know him?'

173

The man thinks for a moment. Then he nods. 'Dr Bertrand is in demand. You're the second person to come looking for him.'

Legrand is actually the third person, but he doesn't tell him about the other inspector from Paris who'd come seeking the doctor. He'd liked that other detective, Bonnevay. He hadn't liked the woman who'd come yesterday, and he doesn't particularly like the man before him, so he decides to honour the monetary incentive Bonnevay had given him to remain quiet about his asking.

'Why, who else has been asking after the doctor.'

'A woman. A very odd character. Very aggressive.'

'Why aggressive? Did she give a name?'

'Not that I remember. She came in here and started waving a gun around, believe it or not. Demanding to know where the doctor was stationed.'

'And you told her?

'I wasn't in any situation not to. She pointed a gun at me.'

'What did she look like?'

'I told you. Very odd. She wore a long dress, a shirt, and a gun belt like an American. She had blonde hair. Take all that away, and you might describe her as pretty.'

'And she didn't give you a name.'

'No. She just said she was looking for her fiancé, the doctor.'

'Her fiancé? You sure know how to drip-feed information. Listen, I've been held up on a ship for nearly two weeks, and I'm in a hurry. So just tell me straight from now on. Where's the doctor?'

'Paraiso,' the man says, letting the word roll off his tongue. 'Doctor Bertrand is stationed in the small hospital in Paraiso. May I ask why the Doctor is in so much demand?'

Legrand shakes his head. 'No, you may not.'

At Colòn train station, Legrand discovers the train line across the isthmus to Panama City is out of action due to a landslide. But it is the tale the station master tells him that intrigues him further; that of a man and a woman who had stopped the train from crashing into the landslide. The station master takes Legrand to see one of the train drivers tending to one of the stationary engines.

'I didn't see them myself,' the driver says. 'They were long gone by the time I arrived. It was Jean-Luc who stopped our train. They stopped his train, you see.'

'What do you know about them?' Legrand asks.

'Only what Jean-Luc told me. He kept calling them the heroes. A man and a woman. He said they were adventurers searching for Spanish gold left over from the days of the conquistadors. Sounds fishy to me.'

'Why?'

'I saw the landslide, and it looked like one for the most part. The tracks were all twisted up, and the sleepers were scattered as if they'd been chucked into the air. I'm no expert, but wouldn't it have just gotten swept away down the hill?'

'You think this couple did it?'

'I wouldn't say that,' the driver says. 'Why would they? If they did, why would they then stop the train? Say, do you think they were blasting to find this Spanish gold, and they happened to blow up the train tracks?'

Legrand has a distant look in his eyes as he shakes his head. 'No,' he says. 'I don't think so at all.'

175

Charlie and Marie had packed their camp early and ventured deeper into the jungle. As she rides her horse along the ancient, overgrown, cobbled trail, ducking beneath stray branches, she traces their route on one of Charlie's maps of Panama. 'I can't believe we're trekking along the Camino de Cruces,' Marie says, smiling.

'What do you know about the Camino de whatever it is?'

'I read about it in one of Victor's books about Panama.'

'So that's where you got that story from on the ship? What's so special about it?'

'There was a pirate called Henry Morgan. He gathered thousands of other pirates, practically every pirate in the Caribbean, and they came along this trail through the jungle.'

'Headed where?'

'Panama City.'

'Why?'

'Because that's where the Spanish took all the Inca gold they stole.'

'Gold, huh? Did they drop any?'

'I doubt it, would you?'

'Depends if we were being chased. Were they?'

'I don't know,' she says.

'Either way, ain't it funny that two mercenaries tread the same path hundreds of years later?'

Marie smiles. She fans herself with the map. 'What do you intend to do with your treasure Charlie?'

Charlie closes his eyes. 'I'm gonna get a little house on a beach beside the ocean. Here. Martinique. I don't know.

Somewhere in the Caribbean. Like the house, I had over-looking the Mediterranean.'

'What did you do there?'

'Not a lot.'

'Sounds boring,' Marie says.

'Yeah, well, I liked it.'

'Oh...' she smiles. 'It didn't take much to lure you away.'

Charlie huffs. 'I suppose you're gonna return to where I found you?'

'New York? I don't know. Maybe. Got my thoughts elsewhere.'

'You'll end up in New York. Can't do without your fancy life in the city, can ya? All those galleries and soirées.'

Marie doesn't answer.

Charlie looks over his shoulder. 'Well, where else are you thinking?'

'Somewhere with mountains, lakes, pine trees. Oregon, maybe Montana.'

'Out West? Those places are wild. Why do you wanna go somewhere like that?'

'I'll raise some livestock—'

'Livestock? Shit, girl, what do you know about livestock? Damned Buffalo Bill tours his show around Europe, and everyone wants to be a goddamned cowboy.'

'After my parents died, I grew up in the Pyrenees steppes on my grandfather's farm. I know cattle and mountains. If I'd been old enough, I would've taken the farm on instead of being sent to America.'

Charlie raises an eyebrow.

'We had a hundred Béarnaise cattle. His Vikings, he used to call them.'

'Why Vikings?'

177

'Because of their massive horns.'

'Who'd have thought. You. A farm girl.'

'We all have a past, Charlie.'

'Don't we just.' He climbs down from the saddle. 'I need a piss.'

While Charlie makes no effort to hide as he relieves himself on the side of the trail, Marie climbs off the horse and goes over to a stream. The water feels refreshing on her hands and wrists. She cups a handful and pours it over her neck. Then she washes her face. Over the babbling water, she thinks she hears something that sounds out of place in the jungle.

She listens.

Nothing.

She stands. She hears what sounds like crying.

'Hey, Frenchie, where you up to? Are you ready?' Charlie shouts.

She ignores him and listens for the crying noise.

She hears it again.

'Hey, Frenchie–'

'Just shut up for one second, Charlie. Did you hear that?'

Charlie comes over to her and scowls. 'Am I allowed to speak?'

'Yes.'

'Hear what?'

'That crying sound, listen.'

'It's probably a frog. If it's little, red, and all cute looking, don't go near 'em. They're damn poisonous.' The jungle's teeming with them,' he says, picking something from between his teeth.

'It wasn't a frog Charlie. It sounds like crying.'

'Then a bird.'

'There, listen.'

Marie starts off across the stream, climbing over the rocks. She hears the crying again and stops. 'Hello,' she shouts. 'Can you hear me?'

The only reply is moaning. She follows its direction and climbs up the bank on the other side.

'I'm not following after you, kid,' Charlie shouts from the opposite bank.

She ignores him and approaches a group of moss-covered rocks taller than her.

'Be careful it ain't a puma or something.'

Her eyes widen. She pulls out the gun from her holster and clicks back the hammer.

The moaning is coming from within the cluster of rocks. Marie climbs up the closest rock and looks down inside. A face stares up at her. A little indigenous girl. She is crying. Marie stalks forwards anticipating a cat leaping at her.

Then, she holsters the gun. 'Hello there, are you hurt?'

The girl is terrified.

'Are you stuck? Can you climb?' Marie holds her hand out to her. The girl flinches. Her leg is trapped in the rocks. 'Charlie! I need your help. Come quickly.'

Marie climbs down into the cluster of rocks. The girl screams. 'I'm going to help you,' Marie says, but she doubts the girl can understand her. The girl's leg is bleeding and swollen. Marie winces. It doesn't look like the rock had fallen onto her leg. More like she'd fallen inside and got stuck.

Charlie appears above. The girl cries louder.

'Your face scares her,' Marie says.

'Sorry, it's the one I was born with.'

Marie shushes the girl and strokes her long black hair. 'I think I'll be able to move the rock, but only enough to free her. When I do, pull her out.'

179

Charlie climbs onto his stomach and reaches down, but the girl won't lift her hands to him. Marie grabs her hands and holds them up to Charlie. 'Have you got her?'

'Sure, if she stops goddamned struggling.'

Marie reaches down and tests the rock. It moves. 'Are you ready, Charlie? Right. Three. Two. One. Now!' Marie pushes the rock, releasing the girl's leg. Charlie pulls her out. On top of the rock, the girl smacks Charlie around the face. Surprised, he lets go of his grip on her. The girl slides off the rock and tries to run, but she crumples to the floor instead, unable to put her weight on her leg.

'Where did she go?' Marie asks, climbing back up.

'The ungrateful brat slapped me,' Charlie says, stroking his cheek.

'I'm sure it's not the first time.'

The girl is on the floor, clutching at her injured leg. Marie climbs down and goes over, but the girl backs away. 'It's alright,' Marie says as she crouches and inspects the leg. Eventually, the girl lets Marie pick her up, and she wades back across the stream carrying her. She sets the girl beside the horse and finds some material from her bag.

'Now what are you going to do with her?' Charlie asks as Marie bandages the girl's leg.

'She can't have come far.'

'Try asking her where her village is then.'

'Where's your– she doesn't understand us, Charlie.' Marie looks at the girl and thinks about how to communicate with her. Marie gets the girl's attention and slowly turns around, pointing in various directions. Then Marie places her hands to the side of her head, closes her eyes and pretends to snore. The girl smiles through her sniffles. Marie points at the girl and then pretends to sleep again. Then, Marie points in various directions into the jungle. The girl lifts her hand and points downstream.

Marie smiles. 'There you go, Charlie. It's this way.'

Marie rides with the girl on her saddle, points at the geometric tattoos on her arm, and smiles. The girl smiles back. Every now and again, the girl directs them deeper into the forest, and somehow a trail materialises between the trees they follow. Charlie meticulously plots the route on his map, annotating it with notes or drawings of notable landmarks.

'This is a bad idea,' Charlie says. 'We're gonna get lost.'

'Don't worry.'

'Well, we don't know how friendly her folks will be. They'll probably kill us or—'

'Or be thankful that we returned their daughter safely.'

'I seen first-hand when our family moved out west as a kid what native tribes do. I got stories that would make your knees go weak, Frenchie. Savages they are.'

'What, your family? I could believe that.'

'Sure, laugh now, but you won't be laughing when they cook or wear us or something.'

'Shall we just leave her here to crawl back? Just think, Charlie, they might never have seen anybody from outside before.'

'That's what I'm afraid of. You saw her reaction. I saw a woman get her scalp cut from her living head once.'

'She might live in a castle made of gold for all you know,' Marie says.

'Hardly. Look at the state of her. She's not exactly dripping in gold, is she? No, she probably ran away because it was so bad.'

'Well, I guess we're about to find out,' Marie says. The

forest thins, and they ride out onto the banks of a river.

Charlie's hand drops to his gun. 'You better be loaded, Frenchie.'

Nearby, a couple of adolescent men are carving out a canoe from a log. They stop and look up in surprise when they see Marie, Charlie, and the girl ride past on their horses. Ahead are several open-air dwellings with thatched palm leaf roofs. They are sat on stilts at least six feet off the ground and scattered along the riverbank.

A bare-chested woman, wearing a bright skirt like the girl's and a cluster of coloured necklaces, shouts back towards the village at the top of her voice. The woman approaches Marie's horse and then stops. She speaks to the girl in their language. The girl says something back that sounds defiant. She remains on the horse, and Marie notices how she sits up a little prouder and straighter.

'Let's not go any further, kid.'

They stop. It isn't long before half the village comes running over to confront them.

'I know you were worried about becoming a monster and dooming those people on the train. But I sure as hell wish you'd waited a little longer to find compassion,' Charlie says.

The two parties stand a few metres apart. Bows are raised and arrows are aimed at Marie and Charlie.

CHAPTER 28

Charlie aims his gun back at the tribesmen. 'Don't let that kid out of your grasp. They won't shoot while she's with you,' Charlie says.

Two adolescents stand behind them, holding axes they'd been carving the canoe with. A man pushes through the crowd. Like the other men, he wears a loin cloth and nothing else. Tattooed lines cross his chest. He stands before Marie and says something to the girl. The girl argues back, and then she points to her leg. The man's demeanour shifts. He comes closer and holds out his hands to the girl. Marie lifts her down into his arms.

'What the hell are you doing? You just gave away our only bargaining chip. Great going, Frenchie.'

Marie throws her leg over the saddle and slides off the horse. Charlie's jaw nearly drops off. The arrows tense in the bows. The man crouches, listening to the girl, looking at her leg.

The girl points at Marie. The man stands. Charlie trains his gun on him, but Marie is in his line of sight.

'Marie, get outta the way.'

The man embraces Marie. Charlie, the tribe, the girl and Marie are all surprised.

Marie and Charlie climb up the ladder into the roundhouse. It is an open-air dwelling made of logs with no windows. Inside, it is sparse, strips of bark cover the floor, and the roof is made of palm leaves. The man climbs up after them, carrying the girl on his back. He takes her over to their beds which are also layers of palm leaves with some brightly woven fabric for blankets. Her mother follows, carrying a wooden bowl of water, and she begins bathing the girl's swollen foot and leg. The man turns to Marie and Charlie and beckons them to sit.

'Enerdo.' The man says, smiling and tapping his chest as he tells them his name.

'I'm Marie, and this is Charlie.'

He points at his wife. 'Feliciana,' he says. Then he points at the girl Marie had rescued. 'Cheché.'

Marie smiles and winks at the girl.

Enerdo points at Marie and Charlie. Then he puts his fingers to his mouth and chomps his teeth together before returning to the ladder.

'See, what did I tell you?' Charlie says. 'He's gonna eat us.'

Marie gets up, leans on the ledge that circles the hut, and looks out at the village. Enerdo goes over to the river. He speaks to some fishermen, and he is given some fish.

'Can you imagine living like this, Charlie?'

'Quite easily,' he says, looking at a couple of women pass by beneath.

'They've got everything they need. There's no need for grand society.' She picks up a nearby woven basket. 'Look at their art. It's all around them. Their tattoos, what they wear. It doesn't need to hang in a gallery. They live amongst it.'

'Come off it. I couldn't imagine you living like this.'

'I didn't say I wanted to.'

'Then stop romanticising it. I've never seen anyone want a life like what you wanted and go and get it the way you did.'

She looks away. 'I wanted a better life. Can you blame me? I paid the price. It wasn't all that, Charlie.'

'Get off it. You had everything you could wish for.'

'I didn't have you.'

They look at each other. 'You did, kid. You just didn't see it.'

'And what about now?'

'Now's just now. Enjoy it for what it is. If there's one thing you taught me, Frenchie, it's stupid to expect anything from the future.'

Marie pinches the bridge of her nose and closes her eyes, stemming the impending tears. 'You know, you're right. I never imagined two weeks ago that I'd be here. It's all very bizarre. But I'm glad.' She touches his hand as it rests on the ledge. 'It's nice to be with you again,' Marie says, then she goes to the ladder.

'Where you going?' Charlie asks.

'To see if I still remember.'

'Remember what?'

'What I used to be like when I was a wild country girl.'

Marie goes over to Enerdo, who has started preparing the fish. She smiles as she approaches him, but he looks confused and gestures for her to go back and sit inside the hut. She ignores him, picks up one of the fish from a basket, takes her pocket knife out and scrapes the scales from its body. Surprised, Enerdo watches her, then he smiles, nods, and continues to do the same. When the silver scales litter the floor, she cuts a line down the fish's belly and pulls out its guts, which they pile together on top of a log. When the five fish are prepared like this, Marie takes them over to the river, washes them inside and out, and then stacks them up inside a clean bowl.

While Marie does that, Enerdo starts a small fire to cook them on. He takes the fish, rubs some leaves over them, and then they both skewer them through the mouth and suspend them over the glowing charcoal. Marie sits on a rock and watches as he peels some plantains to cook. She looks out across the village as she takes some and copies what he does. The sun has dropped below the tree line, and the smoke from the fire catches the rays piercing the jungle. Charlie sits at the top of the ladder in the hut, watching her through the haze. It's the first time he's seen her content since they met in Marseille.

When the food is cooked, Marie and Enerdo return to the hut. Marie goes over to his daughter, Cheché, and gives her some food. She smiles, as does the girl's mother, who gestures her thanks and points at the girl's leg, which is bandaged with some of their brightly coloured woven fabric.

When she turns to Charlie, he shows Enerdo the map and sighs as he points his finger at the river. Enerdo just nods and smiles.

'How the hell is it you can rustle up a whole dinner with him, but I can't get him to tell me if this is their goddamned river,' he says, pointing at the map. 'Say, how did you know how to do all that?'

'I used to go fishing with my grandpa.' She holds the bowl towards him, and Charlie takes a fish and breaks some crispy meat from its side. 'What are you trying to show him anyway?' she asks.

'The river, look at it.'

'What am I supposed to be looking at?'

'Don't you start. Look at all those rocks. That's the river bed. It's drying up. There's not much water flowing through.' He points back down at the map. 'I reckon we're here, one of these tributaries. Which means our dam is causing even these little rivers to dry up.'

186

Marie's mouth drops open as she realises. She looked out at the village. 'That blasted canal,' she says. 'It's going to destroy all of this.'

Charlie nods. 'Who knows how many tribes are out there like this one.' He speaks with his mouth full. 'Just you wait till they flood the whole valley. Say, is this all you have? Haven't you got any more?' He tilts the carcass of the fish towards her.

Marie ignores him. Tears well in her eyes. She clenches her fist and drops it gently against the ledge. Charlie takes one of the plantains, frowns at it, sniffs it, takes a bite and raises his eyebrows in approval of the taste. 'These are good,' he says. 'You should try one.'

'I'm fine. I'm not hungry any more.'

It is light the next day when Marie lies staring up at the layers of palm leaves. The rain taps against the roof. She eventually stretches her aching muscles and twists her clothes into place that she'd slept in. The family are still asleep, the child lying between her parents.

Marie leans over and shakes Charlie. He wakes, looks at his pocket watch, scowls at her and turns back over. It is five a.m.

Marie climbs down the ladders and checks their horses tied beneath the house. They are calm as she strokes their necks, unties them, and leads them to the river. She lets them loose and watches as they graze on the banks. After a while, she goes to the river and crouches in the dry bed. She picks up a smooth, dry stone, turns it over in her hand, and steps over to the water's edge. The water is so different to the murky Seine, she thinks. It is so clear and pure.

Across the river, a spider monkey careers down from the branches. It clings to a vine with its hand and foot and sways from side to side. It looks at her with its little dark eyes as if it has never seen a human before. Then with a pull of the vine, it swings and disappears into the branches. She smiles. She decides she won't let this be destroyed by the dam. She tosses the smooth stone in. Bubbles rise up as it sinks into the clear depths.

Later, but still early that morning, dense mist fills the jungle giving it a ghostly pallor. It smells earthy and fresh. Marie and Charlie say goodbye to the family, ride out of the village, and head for the dam. If Charlie is correct, they are only about five kilometres away from it. But after an hour of riding, they haven't made it more than a mile along the overgrown trail. They must dismount and cut through the tangled vines and branches with their machetes. When Marie stops to drink, her hand shakes as she pulls the cork from her bottle. The water is tepid. She licks her dry lips but is still thirsty as she pushes the bottle back into the bag strapped to her saddle. Before continuing, she twists her arm and flexes her fingers to ease the ache. It doesn't relax. But she continues on hacking through the understory nonetheless.

By the time the day has passed into the afternoon, and despite the dense canopy above, Marie and Charlie are drenched as the rain pours off the leaves like it does from the gargoyles of Notre Dame cathedral. There is no way of steering their horses around these fountains. The leaves would always seem to buckle under the weight of the water and empty their hold just as they passed beneath.

A tarp is draped over the box of dynamite tied onto Charlie's saddle, and he keeps twisting around to look at it while mumbling his displeasure at the rain streaming off it.

They ride and stop and continue and hack for the rest of the day. They follow the trail that takes them away and then back to the river several times. Half a mile from the dam, as the rain drenches them into the late afternoon, they come across a cave.

'A good a place as any to stay, wouldn't you say?' Charlie takes his gun from his holster and aims it into the cave.

'What are you doing?'

'There's something inside,' he says, tilting his ear towards the cave. Charlie scowls at the howler monkeys as they live up to their name as they retreat from the nearby trees. 'There look,' Charlie says. He points his gun into the cave.

Marie flinches. A large black cat is watching them. It is hugging low to the ground. The horses sense its presence, and Marie has to squeeze her knees into the saddle to stop herself from being thrown off.

Charlie fires his gun off into the roof of the cave. The loud bang startles the cat, and it dashes off into the jungle.

Marie leans forwards, crossing her wrists on the pommel of her saddle. 'You should've shot it.'

'It's a puma.'

'I don't care what it was,' Marie says, patting her horse's neck.

'All those cats are shit-scared of anything.'

'Well, I don't fancy it coming back to us when we're asleep.'

'Then we'll build a fire. They're scared of those too.'

They unload the dynamite and their baggage from the saddles and store them inside the cave. The heavy rain eventually stops, but the mist and humidity remain. Since they are so close and can now travel lightly, they decide to go and see the dam.

It takes them an hour to follow the river and climb the slight gradient until they can see the dam between the trees. It looks taller than they'd expected. The dam spans a gorge that is roughly two hundred metres wide. In the middle of the dam, an overflow channel, the only source now feeding the river, streams off the top like a waterfall. Charlie smiles. 'This thing's gonna be a pretty sight when it comes tumbling down.'

They tie their horses to some trees near the dam's base. Then they climb up the scree banks beside the dam, grabbing onto roots and using vines and branches to haul themselves up in the wet mud. At the top, they can see the reservoir that had been created.

Charlie whistles in surprise.

'My god, that's a lot of water,' Marie says.

'Just imagine what the one at Gatún will be like. Remember that valley we saw from the train tracks. The whole thing flooded. I'm surprised.'

'I bet they're really proud of themselves.'

'Eiffel outdid himself this time. He's gone and saved the whole project.'

'No wonder Victor was willing to invest.'

'So how does it feel being the woman to destroy France's greatest engineering feat.'

Marie smiles. 'Is this what it feels like to have power?'

'You're asking the wrong man.'

'I wish Victor was here, looking smug, thinking all his money was safely invested in this and nothing could go wrong.'

'Never mind him. Think of all his cronies, all those men of substance, all those men who would've seen you dead for defending yourself. That's the difference for us Americans, Frenchie. We're allowed to defend ourselves.'

'I can just imagine the cigars dropping from their fat lips.'

Charlie turns and looks out at the jungle. 'Yeah, it's a shame nobody but us will see it go down. That whole valley we just climbed up ain't gonna know what hit it.'

Marie's smile fades as she thinks about what he says, then she turns to him. 'What about the village?'

Charlie swallows. He tilts his head to the side and goes to speak but says nothing.

'Will it be destroyed?' she asks.

'I don't know. It was pretty close to the river. Nah, it'll be okay. The river was wide there—'

'Not wide enough to contain all of this,' she says, waving her hand at the artificial lake. 'The whole village will be destroyed.'

'Don't worry about it. They're just stupid natives. If we hadn't saved that kid, I'm sure they would've eaten us.'

'How can you save a trainload of people in one breath but then condemn just as many people in another?'

'Because blowing the dam is what we're here to do, Frenchie. It's our goal. Our ultimate mission. We didn't have to blow those tracks. That was just a matter of making life difficult for them.'

'But we should at least warn Enerdo. He could get them to move,' Marie says.

'They didn't understand us. How are we going to tell them a flash flood is gonna wipe out their village?'

'We should at least try.'

Charlie throws his hands in the air and returns to the slope they'd climbed up. He stops and turns back to Marie. 'Why do you suddenly care anyway? It was only a couple of days ago that you were willing to let that trainload perish.'

'I wasn't thinking straight.'

'God, you're so frustrating, woman. Think of it this way. If this dam is successful, they'll build a bigger one. You saw the size of that valley. The whole thing will be flooded. Think how much life will be destroyed then. The forest, everything living in it. Every tribe you haven't yet come across.'

'That's the kind of justification Victor would've made, not you, Charlie.'

'Listen, Frenchie, I don't care. I'm not being dragged halfway across the world and not getting paid. This is happening whether you like it or not.'

Charlie points at the dark black clouds coming from the Pacific side of the isthmus. 'Look, let's not get caught in that. Let's get back to the cave.'

'Don't change the subject, Charlie.'

'I'm not. Can't you see it? That's a storm rolling in if ever I saw.'

'We can't not warn them, Charlie.'

'Listen. If you want to warn the tribe, then be my guest.'

'I'll never find them.'

'Sure you would. 'Your biggest problem, Marie, is that you never trust yourself,' Charlie says before sliding down the embankment back towards the forest.

CHAPTER 30

Marie sits outside the entrance of the cave on a large boulder with her knees drawn up to her chest. She stops picking the moss from the rock and looks up at the swaying canopy. It had gone dark as the storm clouds reached them. Thunder rumbles.

Beneath the rustling leaves and branches, frogs croak, monkeys screech, insects crawl, buzz and click, and their sounds intermingle with the noise from the myriad beaks that chirp, squawk and trill.

Thunder rumbles again. The noise reminds her of sitting on her grandfather's balcony, watching the lightning illuminate the clouds over the fields.

She continues picking moss from the boulder and looks along the river. Tree roots twist out of the exposed banks like gnarled fingers. She imagines the torrent racing down when the dam is blown up. She sighs, slides off the boulder and picks her way between the rocks towards Charlie, who is in the cave.

He glances over his shoulder as she approaches. His face has an expression of boyish wonder to it, and he says: 'Would you look at this.' She slows her stride, and her brow creases.

'Look,' he says. He moves around so Marie can see what captivates him.

The tarantula's body is as big as her fist, and its bony legs, as long as a pianist's fingers, feel their way between the rocks. Occasionally, Charlie blocks its path with the stick so that it darts back and forth but remains in roughly the same area.

Marie kneels down to get a closer look. Blonde hair covers

its brawny body.

'Is it poisonous?'

'No. But it bites.'

'Charlie, about what you said earlier.'

He huffs. He jabs the ground petulantly with the stick, blocking the spider's path.

'Charlie, did you mean what you said about the tribe?'

'In this line of work, for the mission to succeed, you gotta have a cold heart.'

'But—'

'But, things get in the way, and you must see past them.'

'You didn't, not with that Spanish General you told me about. You realised it was wrong and didn't continue the mission.'

'And like I said, he was killed anyway, and I was no better off.'

Thunder rumbles overhead, and the sound echoes inside the cave.

Marie puts her hands on her hips. 'I don't care what France or America want—'

'Damn right. To hell with their reasons. So remember why you're here. Remember what you did. You murdered a man and went on the run. D'you know, they won't stop till they find you. You're here because you can start a new life if you do this one job. If you back out now, if you don't follow through on this job for the Americans, you'll have no security, no diplomatic immunity. You'll be on the run, looking over your shoulder for the rest of your life.' He glances up at her before he continues to keep the spider in its place.

'What if we just disappeared Charlie? We could go anywhere and nobody would find us.'

He doesn't answer.

Marie turns away from him to look out into the jungle. The cave amplifies the sound of the thunder directly overhead— A fork of lightning strikes one of the giant ancient trees close to them. There is a flash of brilliant light. The loud crack hurts Marie's ears.

The top half of the tree crashes to the floor in front of the cave.

'Magnificent little creature, isn't it?' Charlie says, having not even bothered to look up at the blackened, split tree, billowing smoke and alight with flame.

'What?' Marie says. 'Didn't you just see that?'

Charlie says nothing. He stabs the point of the stick between the spider's body and the neck.

'Charlie! What are you—?'

The spider is rigid. Charlie twists the stick through its dead body and then lifts the skewered creature. It hangs limply upside down. As the stench of charred wood and the tang of the lightning, which smells like scorched metal, drifts into the cave, he raises an eyebrow at her. 'Dinner?' he asks.

The storm passes, and well into the evening, the rain eventually stops too. Charlie cooks the tarantula within one of the glowing fissures in the tree. Marie declines his invitation to eat some of the blackened meat and grimaces as he crunches his way through it leg by leg. When the evening light has a dark cornflower quality, Charlie finds some dry logs from inside the cave and makes a campfire using embers from the smouldering tree.

They camp outside the cave because there is nowhere to string the hammocks inside, and the only thing they can agree on is that it isn't wise to sleep on the floor with tarantulas. Charlie chooses a place away from the river. Marie strings their two hammocks to three nearby trees around the fire, but then Charlie takes his down and ties it to a couple of trunks on the other side of the fire, away from Marie's.

In the flickering glow of the campfire, he eventually stops sulking. They cook plantains in their green skins until they turn black on the glowing charcoal. While eating, they swap stories about what it was like for Charlie growing up on the frontiers of the American West and Marie growing up in the Midi-Pyrenees with her grandfather. As various flies and mosquitos buzz and glance at any piece of exposed skin, the pair eventually climb into their hammocks. Every time she is about to fall asleep, Marie hears noises in the surrounding trees. Finally, her eyelids grow heavy, and the fear of the puma returning cannot stop her from sleeping.

When Marie wakes from a dream about spiders crawling out of Victor's mouth, it feels like she is trapped in the hammock. She fights free, spins around and falls onto her hands and knees on the floor. She calms her breathing and realises it was a dream.

It is light. The branches and vines are still. The fire is a pile of grey ash. It's as if she is still in a dream. She looks towards Charlie. He is gone. His hammock is empty, and his horse is also gone.

'Bastard,' she says to herself. 'Bastard,' she says again when she discovers the box of dynamite has gone too.

Marie looks at the trail they'd taken to see the dam. 'Come on, you can do this,' she says. But she doesn't move. There doesn't appear to be a gap through the tangle of trees. What if I get lost? She thinks about the girl in the village. It's enough to give her courage. She climbs onto the horse and rides in the direction she thinks the dam is.

Marie arrives at the foot of the dam and finds Charlie's horse tied to a branch at the tree line. She climbs down from her saddle and ties the reins next to the other horse. Charlie's rucksack is on the floor, but the dynamite box and the detonating wire reel are gone. The end of the detonating wire is on the floor with a rock on top of it to stop it from shifting. The wire goes off up towards the dam through the ferns and grass. Next to the rock is the fist-sized detonator. Nearby is another rock the same size as the detonator. She kneels, picks both up, weighs them in her hands, and smiles as a plan formulates.

She follows the detonator wire to the dam and looks for Charlie, but she can't see him. She finds the first stick of dynamite. She eases it out of the hole Charlie has drilled into the dam. She stops. She hears the chink-chink sound as Charlie hits the hammer on the metal rod and drills into the dam.

She detaches the fuse wire from the blasting cap on the end of the stick of dynamite and lays it down on the floor. Then she goes on to the next one, does the same, and continues pulling out each stick until she gets to the channelled water flowing off the dam and passes behind it. Charlie is further along. He's shirtless and is hammering the iron rod three-quarters deep into the rock.

Marie goes back along the dam the way she has come, being careful to collect each stick of dynamite along the way and not tread on any. When she is back at the horses, she puts them into the sack Charlie had carried the box in and stows them between some rocks so neither they nor the horses might stumble upon them. Then, she heads back up to the dam. She can't hear Charlie hammering the drill over the sound of the water anymore. She pictures him picking out a stick and attaching the blasting fuse and the detonator wire.

She runs up the bank beside the dam, climbing by grabbing onto roots and pulling herself up by vines. Along the top of the dam, she runs towards the middle, and when she can see Charlie beneath, she shouts down at him. Charlie dives for cover, and Marie can't help but smile.

'Come out, Charlie Blaine, you can't hide. I've seen you down there.'

He steps back and looks up. 'What the hell are you doing? Get down from there.'

'No. The question is, what are you doing?'

'Get down before somebody sees you.'

'There's nobody here, Charlie. Do you see this?' She holds up the detonator. 'I'm going to throw it into the lake.'

Charlie points at her. 'Then I'll just detonate it manually.'

'Go ahead then.'

'Just you wait there.' He runs back along the bottom of the dam and clambers up the way Marie had. She puts the detonator in her satchel and takes out the rock. As soon as he gets to the top, she makes sure he is looking and launches the rock into the lake. Charlie presumes it's the detonator. He rushes towards the water's edge with his arms outstretched but then stops as it plunges into the water and falls beneath the surface.

Charlie goes over to her.

'You're a goddamned crazy woman.'

'I was down there asleep. What would you do, blow the dam and wash me away too?'

'You were far enough away from the river. Besides, you would've heard the blast and gotten away.'

'And then what?'

Charlie holds his hands to his head and looks at the lake. 'You hired me to do a job, Frenchie.'

'Yes, I did. I hired you to help me. I didn't say we were not going to blow the dam, just that I wanted that village moved first.'

'Couldn't you have done this without throwing the detonator into the water?'

Marie shook her head and smiled.

'Goddamn it, woman.'

'When we've moved the tribe on, warned them to stay away from the river, you can blow this whole construction to pieces.' Marie walks past him.

'Not before we've gone to Paraiso.'

Marie stops and turns to him. 'Paraiso. Why would we go to Paraiso?'

'Because it's the closest place we'll be able to steal a new detonator from,' Charlie says as he pushes past her.

They get halfway down the bank when they hear the terrible noise the horses make. Charlie and Marie look at each other. They know it is trouble.

CHAPTER 31

Charlie pulls his gun out and bounds down the remainder of the slope. When they get to the horses, one is still standing. It throws its head from side to side, trying to break free of the reins tied to the tree. The other horse is lying on the floor. Its eyes bulging. A puma bites its neck. The horse weakly kicks its legs.

Charlie runs towards the carnage, screaming. The puma bolts away. Charlie shoots at it. But the cat disappears into the undergrowth. Marie tries to calm the horse, still reined to the tree, but it isn't in the mood to be settled. Charlie kneels beside the injured horse. Its neck is a mess. Blood spurts from a vein. There is nothing he can do to save it. So he takes a deep breath and puts his gun to the horse's head. He pulls the trigger and puts the poor beast out of its misery. The sound startles Marie and the other horse, but she eventually calms it by stroking its nose, and Charlie sits on his haunches with his head bowed.

It is only when Marie and Charlie get back to the camp that they speak.

'How far is Paraiso then?'

'A few kilometres west,' Charlie says.

Marie stuffs her hammock into her bag, and they gather their gear and tie what they can to the saddle of the remaining horse. Charlie takes the box of dynamite and the fuse wire they'd recovered from the dam into the cave. Marie follows him in carrying the heavy drilling rod.

Charlie crouches and places the box between some rocks.

The reel of dynamite fuse wire rolls off, and he reaches down to pick it up from behind the rock. 'One less thing to carry—' Charlie screams in pain. As he spins around, something whips Marie. Charlie falls to the floor. She only sees what it is as he grabs it and rips it off his arm along with a chunk of flesh. The brown snake, with dark triangles running the length of its body, hits the dry dirt on the cave floor. It twists onto its yellow belly. Marie lifts the iron drilling rod and smashes it down on the snake. And again, and again.

Charlie is swearing and writhing around in agony. She helps him to his feet, and they both stumble out of the cave. Charlie drops to the floor.

'Cut it off quickly,' he says.

Marie's face contorts in horror. 'Cut it off?'

'The blood supply, damn it. Tourniquet it.'

A chunk of flesh is missing from his right forearm, where he's pulled the snake off while it still had its mouth attached.

Marie unties the knot of his bootlace and pulls it out of the eyelets. She then ties the lace around the top of his forearm beneath the elbow and pulls it tight.

Charlie lies back. He swears again and hits the floor with his good hand. Sweat streams off his forehead. His arm has already swelled around the bite.

She knows she must seal the wound to prevent it from getting infected. She is sure the venom will do enough damage, but she knows the jungle will only add to it if left open.

She goes to her satchel and pulls out her canteen of water, Charlie's bottle of bourbon, and the shirt she'd ripped up to cover the girl's injury. Then she dashes back over to Charlie and drops to her knees at his side. Ants have already crawled into the wound. She picks them out, and he winces. She pours water, diluting the blood, giving her a cleaner look.

'Stay awake, Charlie,' she says. She pops the cork out of the bottle of bourbon. He lifts his head to the sound, and his eyes grow expansive and hopeful. She doesn't offer him a drink; instead, she pours it onto the wound. He bares his teeth and lets his head thump back onto the floor.

She rips the shirt into several strips. Dressing the wound, she winds several layers of the fabric around Charlie's arm, and his blood stains the makeshift bandage. She reminds herself that no blood is flowing to the arm now. It is just the wound. With the remaining material, she improvises a sling and straps his arm high to his chest.

When finished, she falls back and breathes. She looks at the patches of blue sky between the trees. She thinks she should thank god but doesn't because why would she thank someone for being in this mess.

She hauls Charlie off the floor and sits him up against her. The humidity makes everything twice as hard to do. He winces.

'Well,' she says, 'This is a right mess if ever there was one.'

'If you hadn't smashed it into mush...' He grits his teeth and grimaces at the sight of the dead snake. 'Maybe you could've made it into a belt.'

She shakes her head in disbelief and smiles. 'How far is it to Paraiso?'

"Bout half a day,' he says, though his voice is barely audible. His eyes close with long, slow blinks. She tries to rouse him, but he remains drowsy. As she holds him against her, she sighs.

He breathes slowly.

She looks around at the disorienting, dense landscape. Through every gap between the trees, she can see more trees. It is layer upon layer of leaves, trunks, branches and vines. They are hours away from anywhere civilised.

She shakes his shoulders and calls his name. 'Charlie, I need to get you on the horse.' He drifts in and out of consciousness.

She puts her hand under his wet armpit and hauls him to a standing position. He must've still understood their dilemma and what she is trying to do because he finds the strength, with her help, to carry some of his weight. She pulls his arm around her shoulders like a scarf, and they stumble across to the horse, moving past the ash that was last night's fire. He loses consciousness again. She manages to drag him to the horse with his full weight resting on her, and they both collapse onto the floor at the beast's hooves.

Covered in sweat and blood, her hands rest in the dirt. 'Charlie, we can do this,' she shakes him. 'Charlie, wake up.'

His eyes flicker open, and he slurs: 'I'll have a whisky.'

She leaves him on the floor and gathers their possessions. She discovers the maps in his bag. She rouses him, and she pulls him to his feet once more. 'You need to get on the horse.'

He holds the saddle. His foot misses the stirrup, not once but twice. Marie grabs his foot and pushes it into the stirrup. 'Charlie, are you ready?'

He nods and grunts.

She puts her hands on his buttocks and pushes him up. Somehow he clambers onto the horse and slumps forwards in the saddle. The crook of his shoulder holds him against the horse's neck.

'Charlie. Which way do we go?'

She asks him again. Sweat trickles down her back as she awaits a response. He doesn't offer one. She picks up the map again, and as she studies it, it dawns on her that the route he had plotted in pencil the night before makes no sense. There are no landmarks that hint at which way to even start walking. It is simply a pencil line drawn on the map. She thinks it is possible to retrace their steps and maybe navigate them back to the Emberá's village instead. Though what would be the point? She needs to get him to Gabriel.

Her heart thumps. 'Think, Marie. How do I find my way to Gabe?' She closes her eyes. She imagines walking through the jungle, leading the horse and holding the map, a compass—

She hurries around the back of the horse. Charlie slips sideways from the saddle, but she pushes him back on. She roots around inside his bag and finds the compass. If she heads in the vague direction of Paraiso, she will find their way there.

She studies the map and the compass. She estimates that Paraiso is situated on a line roughly forty degrees, between north and east from their current location. She turns to face that direction. The foliage is dense. There is no path through it. So she reaches up to the sleeve attached to the saddle and withdraws the machete.

CHAPTER 32

Roots trip Marie. Massive tree trunks block her way, and the bark grazes her. Twigs scratch her. The mud sucks at her feet or sends her slipping and sliding into stems that slap her. Thin, barbed tendrils are tangled and entwined like fishing nets across her path. She believes the jungle wants to hold them until they decompose into nutrients in the soil that the trees can feed off.

Her arms rage with pain. Physically striking out against the jungle is cathartic, though, and it spurs her from branch to vine. After an hour of hacking and slashing with the machete, she stops. She pants. Mud and sweat are smeared across her face, and she looks like a wild creature born of their environment.

She resists the urge to panic; she longs to see a clearing, climb a hill, or hear the sound of a river or stream, not least because their water supply is running low. She sips water from her canteen, which is warm, then pours some between Charlie's cracked lips, and then she continues, hacking, cutting, stomping, sawing, kicking and snapping her way through the jungle. The sun hangs in the middle of the sky, and the rays pierce like stage spotlights through the ramified canopy.

Charlie slides sideways off the horse. Marie doesn't hear him land in the soft mud with a squelch because she is too focused on what she sees ahead. I must be going insane, she thinks. The jungle thins at last. The gaps between the trees grow, revealing a blue sky.

She stabs the machete into the mud and turns to drag the horse through where she's carved a path. Charlie is sprawled on the floor. She curses and wades through the humidity to kneel beside him. He is conscious again.

'How are you, Charlie?'

'Dandy,' he drawls. She places a hand on his damp forehead, but gauging his temperature is impossible.

A bird squeals nearby. It is the first sound of life beyond insects that she's heard for hours, and hope fills her. 'Just hold on here, Charlie.'

'Sure,' he says.

She retrieves his map and binoculars from the saddlebag and then plucks the machete out of the mud. She winds the fabric attached to the handle around her grazed knuckles and begins striking at the foliage again. Her muscles sting from having rested momentarily, and her fingers spasm and cramp.

She spends another five minutes slicing through the jungle and then stops. Water gushes nearby. Her spirits soar. It must be a river. Invigorated, she swings the machete with more force. The blue sky feels like it is in touching distance, but both dread and relief tug at her emotions. She stops hacking, pushes through the vines and saplings, and gasps for air. The jungle abruptly ends on the edge of a cliff that plunges at least a hundred feet into a raging river below.

The view is both liberating and soul-destroying. Marie's heart quickens as she gazes across a large swathe of Panama. The landscape undulates to the Pacific, and the ocean extends to the horizon. The jungle engulfs the land. A harpy eagle squeals as it swoops into the vast cloudless sky, and the thermal winds carry it hundreds of metres.

On the cliff's edge, she flexes her blistered toes that rub

against the insides of her sweaty boots. On the other side of the river, the bank is only ten metres higher than the water-line, and the trees are tall but still way below her vantage point. She imagines stepping across the river and walking across the canopy.

Marie takes the compass out of her pocket, and the needle sways and settles towards the north. She sees a shimmering smudge in the landscape forty degrees east across the ter-rain. She swings the binoculars up to her eyes, but the glass is dirty, so she rubs the muck and condensation away and sharpens the focus. Tin rooftops glint and waver in the heat haze.

She compares the curves of the hills with those drawn on the map and concludes that it must be the town of Paraiso. She finds where she thinks her position is, half a finger's width west from where Charlie's pencil line crosses the river. According to the map scale, that is about two or three kilometres away from the crossing and another five away from the town. Her pursed lips break into a smile, and she dares to hope she might just get them to safety, but it won't be easy.

Rather than hack through the undergrowth, Marie leads the horse along the clifftop ledge; a thin slither of dirt that runs between the jungle and the precipice. If the horse is startled or takes a wrong step, it will fall over the cliff and worse, throw Charlie into the torrent, never to be seen again.

They creep along, covering a greater distance in less time than they had travelled that entire day. Occasionally, she cuts a vine or kicks a fallen branch out of the way over the edge, but it is mostly an easy traverse despite the danger of the drop.

After half an hour of navigating this trail, she spots something she hoped she wouldn't see again, and she goes rigid. Another snake, green, thin and long, slithers towards them.

'Merde,' she whispers. The snake stops and lifts its head, and its cold, unsympathetic eyes glare at them. She doesn't know if it's a venomous snake like in the cave, and it doesn't matter because its mere presence is enough to make the horse fidgety. 'Charlie, right now would be good if you'd like to offer some advice.' She glances back at him, but he is unconscious again. Her jaw tenses. 'Sure Marie,' she says to herself. 'Ask a man with snakebite what to do about a snake.' She adjusts her grip on the machete and considers whether to throw the blade at the snake, but she figures the sharp edge will probably miss, and it will bounce off the floor instead and tumble over the cliff edge. Maybe I could shoot it. The revolver weighs heavily against her thigh. No, I'd never hit it. Not to mention the shot will startle the horse. So, after spending most of the day striking at vines, she feels confident that when the snake slithers towards them, she can successfully lash out at it with the machete.

The horse rocks its head from side to side and shuffles its hooves, sending dust and stones falling over the edge. She tugs on its reins and drags it closer to the fringe of the jungle and away from the drop. Charlie wobbles in the saddle. I should just pull him down now, she thinks. The snake remains as still as a piece of rope. Then, just as quickly as the snake appeared, it slinks back into the jungle.

Marie blows out the breath she hadn't realised she'd been holding, and after making sure Charlie wasn't going to fall, she calms the horse and then continues creeping along the ledge.

After traversing the precarious ledge for a couple of kilometres, Marie and Charlie arrive at a rope bridge. Each side of the river is now the exact height of at least fifty or so metres above the white rushing rapid below. Marie sighs as she leans against one of the stumps holding the bridge suspended to the cliff. How will she get Charlie and the horse across a rickety bridge like that? She cannot lead the horse across it with Charlie on its back. Could Charlie walk? He is still unconscious. Could I pull him across it? The span of the bridge is at least thirty metres. She recalls seeing someone brought to the hospital in Colón on a makeshift stretcher, trimmed branches with a sheet tied between them. She figures that if she placed him in the hammock, she could drag him across the bridge.

She pulls him off the horse and breaks his fall by having him slide into her rather than onto the sun-baked dirt path.

She removes one of the hammocks from the saddle bags, lays it out on the floor, and drags Charlie into it. She ties a knot in the bottom of the hammock around his boots, then walks around to his head, gathers the material above it, and lifts him up. He is a dead weight, and she is glad she'll only have to drag him across the bridge and no further.

First, Marie takes their bags across. The wooden slats are spaced close together and there is no danger of falling between them. Below, the water is loud and furious. Hurrying across, the bridge sways. Then having delivered the bags to the other side, she returns for Charlie.

The bridge sways more as they cross it. Charlie bumps up and down on the uneven slats as she drags him over them. He doesn't complain. Marie is relieved when they make it safely to the other side, and they lie beside each other in the dirt. After a short time, she sits up and looks back across the bridge to the horse. She sighs.

She's glad she'll only have to cross it one more time. She leads the horse to the bridge, but it pulls its head back as soon as it reaches the threshold. She shortens her hold on the reins, strokes the white flash of hair on the top of its head down to its nose and gazes into its brown eyes that grow wide. 'Come on now, do you think after we've come this far, I'm just going to leave you here?' She repeatedly backs the horse in order to position its hooves centrally on the slats and then teases it forward. Leading the horse along the clifftop ledge had been bad enough, but driving it across the bridge felt even more terrifying. The river continues raging beneath them. The bridge wobbles considerably more from the horse's weight than did with Charlie and Marie. She stands still and lets the motion settle, then she edges backwards, step by step. Her gaze fixes squarely on the horse's eyes. They cross the halfway point, and the bridge sways uncontrollably. The horse panics. Its hooves skate on the narrow wooden slats as if the bridge is covered with ice. The bridge rocks from side to side. Marie grabs onto one of the rope rails. The horse's eyes are wide and fearful, and its neigh is a panicked screech. One of its front hooves stomps down, and it misses the bridge. The horse falls. The bridge twists, and Marie falls too.

CHAPTER 33

Marie's arm wrenches as she holds on to the rope, and she dangles over the raging river. The horse hits the torrent and is swept away with its legs writhing above the surface. All she can do is reach out to it and watch in horror as it slams against the rocks.

The bridge remains intact and suspended to each side of the canyon. She grabs it with her other hand, easing some of the pain in her bicep, forearm and elbow. Eventually, she stops swinging like a pendulum.

The water roars beneath her. She pulls herself up the ropes, and when she can, she tries to swing her leg up onto the wooden slats. Her heel connects but slips off.

She tries again. The toe of her boot hooks onto where the ropes join the slats. Though her arms shudder and her palms and fingers burn against the rope, she pulls herself onto the bridge. She lies there panting and clinging to the slats. Further down the river, as it gushes around rocks breaking the surface, there is no sign of the horse.

'Come on, Marie, get off here,' she tells herself. Too afraid to stand and walk, she crawls along the swaying bridge, pulling herself with her blistered hands and fingers, slat by slat.

Back safey on the cliffside, she rolls onto her back and squints at the sky. The ground is firm and safe beneath her. The trail leads from the bridge into the jungle and eventually, if the maps are to be believed, to Paraiso. Then she looks at Charlie, and it dawns on her that her means of transporting an injured man across several more kilometres of unbearable terrain is gone. She grabs the machete and hits the floor with it as she screams in frustration.

'At least we didn't have to cut through the jungle,' Marie says as she kneels beside Charlie. 'But dragging your sorry backside along that road wasn't the easiest thing I've ever done.'

'I 'ppreciate it, Frenchie,' Charlie murmurs.

It has taken the whole afternoon to get to Paraiso. She had pulled Charlie in the hammock, slung over her shoulder, along the sun-baked mud trail that weaves through the jungle.

They sit on the dirt trail where it intersects with the train line. She drags the back of her wrist across her forehead, wiping away the sweat. Ahead is the small high street. People mill around going about their business.

'Nearly there, Charlie. Let's find this hospital.' She wraps the end of the hammock around her hand, slings it over her shoulder and drags Charlie behind her once more. The dusty high street has a hardware store, blacksmiths, an undertaker and a small saloon. Everyone she passes just looks at her. Nobody offers to help. She stops beside a man who leans against a hitching post. He chews on some tobacco and looks at Marie, then at Charlie, then back to Marie. 'They never said on the recruitment posters how many strange sights you'll see in Panama.' He speaks English, but with a strange accent Marie can't place. He arches his eyebrow and spits tobacco residue onto the floor.

'Where's the hospital?' she asks.

He thumbs off towards the end of the street. 'That way.'

Marie lifts her chin in recognition. Then she goes on, dragging Charlie behind her.

'Do you need a hand?' the man asks.

'No, I'm fine. I made it this far,' she says without looking

213

back at the man.

Marie pushes the gate open with her foot when she gets to the hospital. Then she leans her hip against it to keep it open. She drags Charlie through, and it bangs off his side. 'Why put a stupid gate at the entrance to a hospital,' she mutters.

The sky is darkening, and the brick-built building ahead is the only one with light coming from within. She heads towards it across the courtyard. She stops by the water pump when she hears shouting from the building.

She pumps some water onto Charlie's neckerchief and pats his face. 'We're here, Charlie.'

Charlie swallows.

'Just wait here. I'll get help.'

'Ain't goin' nowhere,' he manages to say.

Marie goes over to the brick building. On the steps that lead up to the door, a woman sits with her head in her hands. The woman doesn't look up. Marie goes past and arrives at the ajar door, and peers inside. A man is trying to get off the operating table. A young nurse is shaking her head.

'You must stay here,' she says.

Then, Gabriel rushes over to the operating table with a glass bottle.

CHAPTER 34

Gabriel has his back to Marie facing the man refusing to lie down on the operating table. 'Agwe,' Gabriel says. 'If I don't amputate, you'll die. See reason, man.'

Agwe and Marie's eyes both widen. Agwe shakes his head and pushes Gabriel. Gabriel pivots on his heels and uses his full weight to push Agwe down onto the table where he holds him.

'Come on, Aceline, quick. I can't hold him.'

The nurse, Sister Aceline, tries to pull a strap across Agwe's chest, but he pulls his arm free, and as he does so, he strikes the nurse across the face. Sister Aceline loses her balance and slips on the blood on the floor. She hits her head and knocks herself unconscious. A tray flips into the air. Scalpels, saws and knives clatter onto the floor. The glass bottle shatters. The last dregs of chloroform mingle into a pool of blood, and its sweet smell is more pungent than the stench of sweat, urine and vomit.

'Do you need a hand?' Marie asks.

Gabriel looks up at Marie in the doorway. It takes him a moment to recognise her. His mouth falls open. Marie is unrecognisable compared to how she looked in Paris. Her hair is now blonde from dyeing it. She wears a functional floor-length skirt, a drab, dirty sweat-stained, ripped shirt with her sleeves rolled up, and her gun belt draped around her waist. He shakes his head in disbelief. 'Marie?'

'I told you I'd come. Let me help.'

Gabriel takes a deep breath. 'Move her out of the way,' he says, gesturing at the unconscious nurse. He turns his attention back to Agwe, who he still holds down. 'Listen, if we do nothing, you'll die. Do you understand? This won't get better. Let me save you.'

Agwe's brow furrows. He bares his teeth as he wrestles with the pain. Then he nods.

'Do you know how sick I am of dragging people across this damn place?' Marie says while pulling Aceline out of the way.

Gabriel flashes her a look of confusion.

'Don't worry,' she says. 'What next?'

'Bite down on this,' Gabriel says, putting a stick into Agwe's mouth. 'Marie. Pick up the instruments.' Gabriel pulls the tourniquet tight around Agwe's thigh, causing the muscle to bulge.

Marie finds the scalpel in a pool of blood on the floor, with the other instruments Aceline had knocked over. She picks it up. Flies scatter into the air. She wipes the blade against her shirt sleeves that are rolled up to her elbow, then hands it to Gabriel.

Gabriel moves around the table. He places the blade against Agwe's dark skin, just above the knee, and then he sinks the blade into the flesh and slices. Agwe bites the stick. His scream is muffled. Muscles tense. His nostrils flare as he breathes through the pain.

Marie holds Agwe's gaze. She places her hand on his shoulder. Droplets of sweat run down her brow, trickle down her nose and fall onto his chest. The sodden strands of hair, which had fallen loose from her fishtail braid, clung to her flushed cheeks.

'Marie, the saw,' Gabriel says.

Marie finds it on the floor under the table and hands it to Gabriel. She holds Agwe's hand while his whole body tenses.

He squeezes her hand. She hears the serrated blade tug through the muscle.

Agwe's grip eases as he falls unconscious.

'What happened to him,' Marie asks.

'He's a digger on the canal. There was a landslide. An iron rail smashed into his leg.'

Gabriel saws. The table wobbles. The blade screeches against bone. 'His fibula is broken. His tibia is smashed to bits.'

'Couldn't it be set?'

Gabriel doesn't answer. Marie looks towards him as he breaks through the bone. She can see the blood pumping out of the stump. 'That clamp over there, pass it to me.'

Marie finds a hemostatic clamp on the floor. 'This?'

'Yes, quickly.'

She wipes it against her hip, smudging mud, blood and an ant or two. Gabriel stuck a finger and thumb into the muscle and parted it so that she could see the white vein, which had retracted and was spurting dark, pulsatile blood.

'Clamp it here, on this vein.'

'Me?'

'Yes, quickly.'

She plunges the clamp into the leg and locks it around the severed vein stopping the flow.

Gabriel slaps the back of his neck. A mosquito splatters on his palm, and he rubs it down his trouser leg before tying a knot in the vein Marie has clamped. More insects congregate in the theatre seeking out the metallic smell of blood.

'It smells like a butcher's in here.'

'Well, we're all made of the same stuff.' He sets to work on the leg and says, 'What are you doing here? I can't believe you came.'

217

'I told you I would.'

'I know you did, but... How's your sister?'

'My—' Marie remembers her lie. 'She's fine, thank you. Listen, Gabe. Charlie, my guide, he's outside. He's in a bad way. He was bitten by a snake in the jungle.'

Gabriel nods as he works. 'When?'

'Close to sunrise this morning.'

'What were you doing in the jungle at sunrise?'

'Camping.'

'Camping? You?' Gabriel laughs.

'It doesn't matter. Will he be okay?'

'I don't know. I'll need to see him. Was it venomous?'

'He's been drifting in and out of consciousness. I put a tourniquet on his arm.'

'You shouldn't have done that.'

'Charlie told me to.'

'Is he a doctor?'

Marie shakes her head. Gabriel cuts the flap of skin free at the back of the leg, finally separating it. Marie can't take her eyes off the limb when he puts it on a nearby table.

Sister Aceline stirs. 'See if she's okay, will you?' Gabriel says as he starts sewing the skin flap over the new stump.

The nurse pushes herself upright as Marie approaches and offers her a hand.

'How are you feeling? You took quite the fall.'

'I'm fine,' Sister Aceline says, swaying as she stands. She shakes her head. She goes to rub her temples but sees the blood on her hands. She goes over to Gabriel at the operating table and checks Agwe is breathing. 'How did it go?' she asks Gabriel.

'It's a good job I'm a medical genius,' he says, winking at the nurse. Then he looks furtively over at Marie.

Marie turns to the door and goes to leave.

'Where are you going?' he asks after her.

'I should check on Charlie.'

Gabriel nods. 'I won't be long.'

Marie goes outside. It is marginally cooler outside than in the stifling operating theatre. In the twilight, she looks at her blood-stained hands. She sighs and begins down a couple of steps.

'Is he alive?'

Marie nods at the woman still sitting on the steps. 'Yes. He survived. Gabriel's a good surgeon. He was top of his class in Paris.'

The woman stands and hugs Marie. 'Oh, thank god, praise be thank you. Thank you.'

Marie smiles and works herself free of the woman's embrace. 'Don't thank me, thank Gabe.'

Just then, the door opens, and the nurse comes out backwards. She turns around and is holding the severed limb on a tray. The woman on the step bursts into tears and drops to her knees. 'Well timed, Sister,' says Marie.

The nurse scowls at her as she goes past.

'He's alive. Be thankful,' Marie says, touching the woman on the shoulder.

'Lete,' Gabriel calls from the operating theatre. The woman enters, and Marie walks over to Charlie and kneels beside him.

'What kept you?' he asks.

'You're still with us then.'

'Don't get rid of me that easily.'

Marie stands and finds a bar of soap next to the water pump. She rubs it over the dried blood on her arms and then washes them under the pump. 'The doctor will be out soon.

219

I told you I'd get you here.'

Charlie says nothing. He is either asleep or unconscious again.

After a short while, Gabriel and Sister Aceline carry the patient out on a stretcher. Marie thinks that the nurse is strong for someone so slight and young. After all, the patient is still a muscular and heavy man, despite only having one leg. The woman Gabriel had called Lete follows behind them as they go across to the ward; a long wooden chalet. After transferring Agwe to the bed, Gabriel carries the stretcher out, and Sister Aceline follows carrying a bucket.

She fills the bucket at the water pump and goes to the operating theatre. 'Once it's cleaned up, we'll take your friend over,' Gabriel says, as he washes his arms and cups water over his head several times. He smooths his long blonde hair back. 'It's good to see you,' he says.

They stand apart.

'You too, Gabe.' It isn't the reunion she'd imagined they'd have.

'What's with the outfit? You're dressed like a young Madame Durand.'

Marie laughs. She looks down at herself. 'Well, it's more comfortable than that dress from the art salon.'

'Oh, I don't know, you had me captivated.'

'Really.'

'Of course.'

He steps towards her and awkwardly puts his hand on her shoulder. The door to the operating theatre slams, and Gabriel sighs.

'It's ready,' Sister Aceline says as she storms off.

'She's friendly.'

'Let's get your friend inside.'

CHAPTER 35

Gabriel and Marie place Charlie onto the stretcher and carry him into the operating theatre. There they transfer him onto the operating table. 'I've got to ask,' Gabriel says. 'Why do you have a gun? Is it his?'

'Pumas,' Marie says.

He raises an eyebrow. 'You're just one surprise after another.' He unties the tourniquet and cuts the sleeve off Charlie's shirt. He turns the arm over and removes the makeshift bandage. He scrunches his nose up at the wound. 'Charlie,' Gabriel says.

Charlie doesn't open his eyes.

Marie shakes his shoulders. 'Charlie,' she says. He opens his eyes.

'Can you feel this?' Gabriel asks as he pinches Charlie's fingers.

'Charlie, did you feel that?'

'Feel what? I...I need a drink.'

Gabriel taps up the arm with the handle of the scalpel. Charlie doesn't react. Gabriel prods the wound with it. Still no reaction. 'Well, there's clearly nerve damage. Probably lasting, well I suppose that's still to be seen.'

Gabriel cleans the wound, and Marie winces at how rough he is with it. 'Can't you be more gentle?'

'He can't feel it. It's best to get it cleaned.'

Gabriel squeezes the dirty, bloody water into a separate bowl. 'So then. How do you know him?'

'Charlie? Oh, he's...'

'He's what?'

'My guide, I told you.'

Sister Aceline walks into the operating theatre. She goes over to a cupboard and stocks it with bandages. 'Bring one of those here, would you?'

She brings one over to Gabriel and holds it out to him.

'Could you bandage this up,' he says, waggling his finger at Charlie's arm.

'Are you not doing anything?' Marie asks.

'He's had a dose alright, but he'd be dead if it was a pit viper. I'd say it was a fairly dry bite.'

'What do you mean, dry?'

'If the snake had killed and eaten something, like, say, a mouse not long before, then it wouldn't have had enough time to have reproduced its full dose of venom.'

Marie looks confused.

'You know, like, err, like how a man doesn't replenish his load very soon after he's—'

Marie holds up her hands. 'I get what you're saying, Gabe.'

Sister Aceline walks over to them. 'The bandage is done. If you don't need me, I shall check on Agwe.'

Gabriel scratches the top of his neck. 'Yes, please do so.'

Marie watches after the woman as she leaves. 'What is the matter with her?'

'Aceline? Oh, nothing.' He turns away and walks back over to Charlie.

'Don't give me that. Is she always that rude, or does she look at everyone the same way she looks at me?'

'I don't see that. I don't know what you mean.'

'You thought I wasn't coming. You thought you'd never see me again. I'm just surprised how quickly you got over me.'

'She's a nun.'

Marie raises her eyebrows, and Gabriel spends longer than

he needs to inspect the bandage. Marie is too tired to start feeling jealous.

'There's nothing more we can do for him tonight,' Gabriel says. 'We'll take him to the ward. Sister Andrea will watch over him.'

'Oh, another nun?'

'She'll let me know if he deteriorates overnight—'

'And if he does?'

'There's not a lot I can do. Listen, he's travelled with the venom in him all day and survived. At least now he can get some rest and let his body fight against it. Come on, let's get him over to the ward.'

They carry the stretcher across the courtyard, past the water pump and over to the ward. Inside, it is hot. The windows are open, but because the jungle surrounds the hospital on three sides, there is no flow of air coming in. The wood is whitewashed inside, making it look bright, even in the low glow of the paraffin lamps and the sunset.

There are five beds on each side of the room, and six have patients in them, including Agwe, who is conscious and sobbing with his forehead against his wife's. They carry Charlie over to the empty bed. A large, old woman with a winged cornette atop her head glides out to greet them. She looks Marie up and down, then her gaze remains on the holstered gun on Marie's hip. Sister Aceline follows her.

'Snakebite,' Charlie says to Sister Audrey.

'So I believe. On the arm.'

'Yes.'

'And is he likely to die?'

'Better bloody not,' Charlie murmurs.

'He's well enough to quip,' Sister Audrey says. The old woman helps them roll Charlie off the stretcher and onto the bed.

'Keep an eye on him. Let me know how he develops,' Gabriel says.

Gabriel goes over to Agwe and speaks with him. Marie kneels at the side of Charlie's bed. She holds his hand as he drifts off to sleep. 'What do we do now, Charlie?'

He breathes deeply as he sleeps. Marie taps her fingers on the mattress. She stares at the legs of the bed standing in bowls of water. She is too exhausted to recognise how strange it is.

Sister Audrey returns and looms over them. 'You'll have to leave. We can't have the patient's getting distracted.'

'What about her?' Marie asks, looking over at the amputee and his wife that Gabriel talks to.

'Though Lete is our cook, she will be leaving shortly.'

Marie stands and rests her hand on her belt. The nurse's eye is drawn to the gun again. 'Make sure he doesn't die.'

The old woman twists her lips and goes over to another patient, followed by Sister Aceline, who continues to scowl at Marie as she walks off.

Marie stands outside on the porch. She looks up at the stars and takes a deep breath before sighing. She closes her eyes and concentrates on her breathing. She feels like she can sleep right there standing up.

The door opens behind her, and she recognises Gabriel's footfall.

'Next, you'll tell me they won't let me sleep with you,' she says.

Gabriel stands beside her. 'Not even Sister Andrea could stop that from happening tonight.' He slips his hand around Marie's waist and pulls her into him. They kiss. She pulls away, feeling guilty towards Charlie.

'I still can't believe you're here,' Gabriel says.

'You don't hate me then? I wasn't sure what type of reception I would get.'

Gabriel takes her hand and leads her across the courtyard. 'I know it's dark, and we've walked like this a hundred times in Paris, but doesn't it feel different. I bet it's killing Victor you not going back to him.'

'Don't mention him Gabe. The future is all that matters now.'

'Of course.' Gabriel stops and grabs Marie around the waist. He picks her up and spins her around in the air.

'What are you doing?' she asks, laughing.

He puts her down and hugs her again.

'I've missed you, Gabe,' she says as they arrive at the porch of his small bohío. 'I've missed your joie de vivre.'

'Welcome home. It's not much, not what you are used to, but—'

'It's fine, Gabe.'

'Take a seat,' he says, gesturing for her to sit on a chair on the porch. He strikes a match and lights a storm lantern. 'I'll get you a drink and something to eat. Oh and get ready to tell me why you're blonde now,' he says, shaking his head in disbelief before disappearing inside. When he comes out again, carrying a glass of wine, a plate of bread and some sun-dried tomatoes, he finds her fast asleep in the chair. He leans against one of the posts that holds up the porch and looks at her as he eats the bread. He frowns. He still can't believe she is here.

CHAPTER 36

The next day, Marie wakes in bed with nothing on but her underwear. A thin cotton sheet covers her. It is hot, and the room is bright. Sitting up and looking around, it takes her a while to remember where she is. She lies back down, kicks the sheet off and stares up at the roof made of roughly cut wood. Sweat runs down the back of her neck beneath her hair. Gabriel must've let down her braid. She smiles at how much he cares for her.

Twisting off the side of the bed, Marie stretches her arms above her head, and they still ache. A jar of cream sits on the bedside table with a note that reads: For your hands. X. She flexes her fingers and winces and then applies cream to the cuts and sores.

She finds one of Gabriel's clean shirts in a pile of clothes and puts it on. Her skirt hangs over a chair, stiff and smeared with dried mud and jungle residue. It is as dirty as one of her cleaning rags covered in oil paints. She holds it up. 'Well, if that doesn't tell a story more than any painting I've ever done, I don't know what does.' She pulls the skirt on, along with a pair of Gabriel's socks and slides into her boots. Her feet are sore as they settle into the imprints in the soles, and she ties the laces.

The bohío is one large room. Marie walks away from the bed, brushing her fingertips along the worn fabric on the back of the lone armchair and looks at Gabriel's desk. It is empty except for a few well-used medical books and her gun belt and revolver. She removes the gun and checks the barrel. Bullets fill the chambers. She slides it back into the

226

holster, pulls the belt around her waist, and positions the gun on her hip. She slides the strap through the loops and once more ties her scarf to secure it.

She pulls the gauze curtain to one side and looks out. The jungle surrounds the small hospital.

On a table beside the stove is some bread under an upturned bowl. It is stale, but Marie breaks some off and hungrily eats it. It scratches her throat, and she finds a bottle of wine, pulls the cork stopper out of it with her teeth like her grandfather used to, and swallows the warm red liquid. The alcohol is sharp against her throat. She coughs, wipes her lips, pushes the fly screen open, and walks onto the porch.

The sun is already above the tree line and uncomfortably bright. The ward's windows and doors are open, and people move within. The operating theatre looks empty and unused since last night.

She goes over to the water pump and pumps some out, putting her mouth to the stream, gulping the water down, and rubbing some over her face.

Feeling refreshed, she strolls over to the ward. Sister Aceline tends to the patients, but there is no sign of Gabriel or the older nun, Sister Audrey.

'Have you seen Gabe?'

Sister Aceline shakes her head. 'Not today.'

Marie frowns, and then she looks over at Charlie. 'How's the patient this morning?'

'You mean this afternoon.'

'It's the afternoon?' Marie asks.

'He's no different to last night.'

Marie goes over to Charlie and sees that he is pale and clammy. He looks worse than he'd done the night before. Marie turns back to relay this to the nurse, but she's made her way to the end of the ward. She shakes Charlie on the shoulder. 'Charlie,' she says.

His eyes flicker open, and then they close. She takes the glass of water from the bedside table, plucks a fly out, and tilts the rim against his lips. His mouth opens, and he takes some water.

'Charlie, listen. You've got to pull through this, do you hear? I'm not dragging your behind across the jungle just so you can die on me now.' She puts the glass back on the bedside table. 'If I knew you were going to die, I could've just left you there and saved myself the trouble.'

Charlie coughs. The door opens at the end of the ward, and Gabriel comes in. He beckons Marie over to join him. She pats Charlie on the shoulder, 'Don't be sweet-talking the nurses, okay? They're nuns.'

Charlie grimaces in reply. She gets up and goes over to Gabriel, and he leads her outside. 'What's the matter,' she asks.

'Nothing,' he says. But she knows when something is bothering him. 'You're up? How do you feel? Your hands looked sore. How are they?'

He takes her hands in his and inspects them, turning them over. He strokes the sores on her fingers. 'How did they get like this?'

'I had to cut through the jungle?'

'Cut through the jungle?'

'Yes. With a machete.'

'Well at least you don't need that now, or the gun,' Gabriel says.

'Why?' she asks.

Gabriel shakes his head. 'Because you're here.' He laughs. 'Cutting through the jungle with a machete are words I never thought I'd hear you say.'

'Why not?' She pulls her hands away from his.

'Marie. Come on...'

'Why not? Don't you think I'm capable?'

'I'm sure you're capable of anything,' he says.

Marie studies him. He can't look at her, especially after saying that. He knows about Victor, she thinks. 'What do you mean by that?' she asks.

'Nothing. I just never imagined a sophisticated lady who lived across from the Elysee Palace would ever have reason to be cutting through the jungle.'

'Me in Paris. That wasn't me, Gabe. This is me. As I stand. This is what I used to be. This is what I am now.'

They don't say anything momentarily, and then Gabe turns back to her. 'Fine. But what about your art? You can't tell me that wasn't you.'

'It's probably the last thing I'll return to now.'

'No. You were good at it.'

Marie shakes her head. 'Maybe, one day.'

'No. Listen, I've got a confession.'

'What?'

'I brought one of your paintings with me. The one you did of the people by the river.'

Marie raises her eyebrows.

'Listen, I never thought I'd see you again. I thought you ditched me. Seeing that painting on my wall made me think of you every time.'

'I understand. You don't have to explain.'

'No, I do. Because you see, I sold it.'

Marie looks surprised at him. 'It sold?'

'Well, not quite. Wait here a minute.' Gabriel runs back across the courtyard to his bohío. Marie stands there. He

229

comes back out, clutching a piece of paper.

'This is yours. I gave the painting to an art dealer in Panama City. He sells art to the wealthy French families that have moved here because of the dig. This is the receipt. He said it was exquisite, those are his words, and he thought he could sell it quite easily.'

Marie hugs Gabriel.

'You're not upset?' Gabriel asks.

'A piece of my work actually sold, of course not.'

'See, I guess that makes you an artist. Look, there's no reason why you can't create more and sell them. Before you know it, you'll be back in Paris with your own exhibition.'

She sighs.

'What's wrong?'

Marie shakes her head.

She looks back towards the ward. 'I'm happy, and Charlie's in there on death's door. Have you looked at him today? He doesn't look any better. He looks worse than he did last night.'

'Well, he's had quite a dose of poison—'

'I thought you said he didn't have a strong dose?'

Gabriel holds up his hands. 'Who can tell? He's alive still. He either had a low dose, or he's really resilient. What would you say?'

'Damn it. He's resilient. If anyone would take on a snake, it's him. Is there anything you can do for him, Gabe?'

Gabriel looks away. 'It's really unfortunate.'

'He can't die, Gabe.'

'Who is he?'

'A friend.'

They look at each other. Gabriel scratches his forehead. He rolls his eyes. 'It's a long shot.'

'Any shot is worth taking if there's a chance,' she says, and she remembers Charlie saying it to her as she fired the gun at the barrel somewhere across the Atlantic.

'There's a chap in Panama City. I met him the other week when I visited the hospital there. He's doing some interesting research, but it's just research. There's no proof that it can save him.'

'Who is he? What's his research?'

'His name is Albert Calmette. He's an immunologist, a Navy man. He's been all over the globe researching various diseases and looking for cures. One of the things he's working on is venom antiserums.' Gabriel takes a box of cigarettes out of his pocket and lights one.

'What is it, Gabe?'

'Well, the thing about research is that it might work or it might not.'

'Like I said, any shot is worth it.'

'I don't think you understand. What I'm saying is...' He takes a drag on the cigarette. 'As much as it might save him or do nothing at all, it could kill him.'

Marie puts her hand on her hip. 'If he's going to die, he's going to die. If he's getting better by the time I come back, then we don't give it to him.'

Gabriel nods. 'Well then, here's to scientific progress and you being a true artist.'

231

Marie opens the train carriage window and then sits. She adjusts her posture on the wooden benches but can't get comfortable. She stares out at Paraiso while waiting for the train to pull off. She pushes the gun belt around her waist, so the hilt doesn't dig into her side as she sits. A woman sits on the bench opposite, stares at the gun, and pulls her young daughter closer. Marie smiles, but the woman doesn't smile back. Marie looks at the station. There isn't a platform. There's just a tiny ticket hall and a waiting room. She strums the corner of her ticket.

'Mama, why does she have a gun?'

Marie smiles. 'The jungle is dangerous,' she says. 'Just yesterday, I came face to face with a puma, so it's to protect me.'

'But you're not in the jungle. You're on a train.'

'Celine,' her mother says. 'Stop pestering the woman.'

Marie smiles. She continues strumming her ticket and looks out of the window again. She stops strumming. She feels sick. Adrenaline races through her thighs. She feels the urge to stand, to run, but she can't. Inspector Mathis Legrand, who she'd last seen in Marseille trying to board her ship, sits on a horse outside her window.

The mother and daughter opposite have started arguing about the young girl's behaviour.

Marie shushes them, but they pay her no attention. Their voices are getting louder, and the girl shrieks in defiance.

Marie kicks the mother's leg and puts the palm of her hand on the pommel of the gun. 'Shut up,' she whispers. The pair fall silent.

Legrand squints in the blazing sun. He looks at all of the people milling around.

Marie turns away from the window and leans her head into her hand to hide her face. The station master waves a flag and blows his whistle. The engine up front blows out a hiss of steam. The train jolts as the brakes release. The engine begins to chug.

Legrand rides his horse beside the carriage.

'Look at the horse, mama,' the young girl says as she crawls over her mother's lap to the window. The girl starts tapping on the glass.

'Can't you control—'

Legrand looks at the girl through the window. Marie holds her breath. The train picks up speed. The girl keeps tapping. Marie clasps the pommel of the gun. Steam passes by. The wheels clack against the rails.

Legrand steers his horse around and heads back towards the town.

Marie lets go of her breath. She looks through the windows down the carriage. She can't see him. He must've found out about her and Gabriel and then discovered Gabriel had been stationed in Paraiso and concluded that's where she was headed. When she turns back, the woman is frowning at her, and the child wipes her nose against the window, looking out at the jungle they have plunged into.

'I'm sorry I kicked you.'

'Are you okay?' The woman asks. 'Did you know that man? You went really pale when you saw him.'

Marie's breathing settles. 'Husband,' she says.

'Oh, I see.'

'No, I ran away from my husband. That man's been sent to find me.'

233

'You're not that woman from Paris, are you?'

'What woman?'

'The one that killed her husband. It's rumoured she's here in Panama.' The woman begins to smile and shake her head. 'I know it's not you, though. She was some kind of socialite. By all accounts, she wore risqué, daring dresses. I mean no offence.'

Marie leans forwards. 'Maybe I'm in disguise.'

The woman frowns. Then she laughs.

They sit quietly, and the girl eventually settles and plaits her doll's hair.

Eventually, Marie says, 'How might a woman leave Panama?'

'Where are you going?'

'I don't know, I've not thought it through yet.'

'Ships leave for California all the time. Do you not have a family you could go to?'

Marie shakes her head.

'Do you not have any money?'

'Not much.'

'You could sell that gun or rob a bank with it.'

Marie smiles. 'Yes, maybe I'll do just that.'

Marie looks out the window for the remainder of the journey as the train line breaks free of the jungle and the carriages rattle parallel to the canal dig. Vast swathes of the jungle are stripped back to the bare earth. A massive trench runs through the mud fields, and hundreds of men work the terraces looking as small as ants.

Inspector Legrand rides down the main street in Paraiso and arrives at the hospital gates. He climbs down off his horse. As he ties the reins to a hitching post, the horse drinks from the water trough. He goes over to the gate, looks through, and sees two nuns in winged cornettes crossing the courtyard.

He returns to the horse, unfastens his bag off the saddle, and slings it over his shoulder. Then he goes in. The nuns have disappeared, and the place looks deserted. He goes over to the largest of the buildings, climbs the steps, pushes the door open, and enters the ward. A doctor moves from bed to bed, assessing the patients. Legrand puts his bag onto the floor and leans against the door frame.

When the doctor sees him, he comes over.

'Can I help you, monsieur?'

'You're the doctor?'

Gabriel nods.

'Then I hope so. When you have a spare moment, that is.'

'Now is a good a time as any. Do you want to come through to my office?'

'Lead the way, doctor,' Legrand says. As he follows him through the ward, he looks at the patients in the beds, either cripples or on death's door with fever. The doctor opens the door and invites Legrand inside. They sit down on either side of a small desk. Gabriel opens a ledger and dips the nib of his pen in a bottle of Indian ink. 'What is your name?'

'Jean Pavard,' says Legrand.

'Well, Mr Pavard, what is wrong with you today?'

'I have terrible pains. It feels like I've been shot in the stomach.'

'Well, that's quite dramatic, if you don't mind me saying.'

Legrand shrugs his shoulders. 'It is what it feels like.'

'You've been shot before?'

Legrand nods.

'Well, in that case, I take it back. Do you mind getting onto the bed and unbuttoning your shirt?'

Legrand does as is asked of him. Gabriel examines Legrand's stomach, pushing and prodding. 'Is this where you were shot?'

'Yes.'

'And these are?' Gabriel points at a scar.

'From a sword.'

Gabriel raises an eyebrow. 'You're ex-army, navy?'

'Legion.'

Gabriel smiles. 'How long has it been hurting for?'

'A few days. It comes and goes.'

'I'm done. You can button your shirt.' Gabriel goes and sits back down and waits as Legrand dresses and sits.

'So, what is it?'

Gabriel holds up his hands. 'Everything felt fine. Nothing is out of place. Have you had any pain from your war wounds in the past?'

'No.'

'Have you been sick recently? Have your stools changed at all?'

Legrand shakes his head.

'It might be that you've stretched something inside yourself.'

'Maybe. It must be hard diagnosing symptoms you can't see.'

'Indeed,' Gabriel says. 'You know, there's a million ways this country can make you ill. It's much easier when a leg's hanging off, that's for sure.'

'You get many injuries like that?'

'Sure do. They get patched up here and then sent on to Panama City. Just last night, I had two.'

'Two? They survive?'

'Of course,' Gabriel says. 'I had to amputate the one. There

236

was nothing for it. His leg was a mess. His wife's our cook. I had to ensure he lived, or else she might poison us.'

Legrand laughs at his joke. 'What about the other?'

'Oh, a snakebite.'

Legrand winces. 'Nasty.'

'Here's where you tell me you've been bitten too?'

'No. And I plan to keep it that way.'

'I don't blame you.'

'Did he survive?'

'He's clinging on.'

'Not much you can do.'

'We're trying. In fact, my fiancée, well, she soon will be, has gone to Panama City. There's a doctor out there, ex-navy. He's developing some kind of anti-venom to counter the effects.'

'Incredible, isn't it. Modern medicine can achieve so much. Anyway,' Legrand says as he stands. 'I won't keep you any longer. How much do I owe you?'

Gabriel waves his offer away. 'Don't worry about it.' They shake hands and leave the office and walk through the ward. 'No, it's good to have a conversation that's not from a patient or a nun.'

'Or your intended fiancée, I'd imagine.'

'Oh no, she's just arrived, so everything's sweet while we get reacquainted.'

Legrand laughs at his joke again as they go outside. On the steps, Legrand turns to face Gabriel. 'Are you sure I can't pay you anything?'

'Honestly. If I'd been able to diagnose you, then maybe, but I'd feel like I was a fraud.'

'I like paying my way in life, doctor.'

'Listen, if you're staying local for a while, you can buy me a drink at the salon next time I'm in.'

'Alright. Rest assured, I will do. Thanks again, doctor.'

They shake hands once more, and Legrand goes on his way.

As Gabriel watches the man go through the gate, he scratches himself on the neck where he'd got bitten by a mosquito the night before. 'Nice guy,' he says to himself. Then he heads back into the ward.

CHAPTER 38

Marie had arrived in Panama City feeling determined to leave Panama yet torn about leaving Charlie. As she walks through the city she recognises the district of Casco Viejo from the descriptions and the beautiful illustrations in Victor's book on the pirates of Panama that she had read. This district was built after the pirate Henry Morgan had destroyed the old town. She walks through the narrow cobbled streets until she arrives at Plaza Catedral, exiting the square beside the bank. She rests her hand on the pommel of the holstered gun and looks up at the building.

She narrows her eyes. She looks around the square, dominated by the Spanish-styled baroque cathedral with two white towers encrusted with mother of pearl on either side of its three large wooden doors.

Marie wonders whether confession would bring her solace. She doubted it. Her grandfather had raised her not to believe in the church and its stories, designed only to control the will of people, he said.

Just as well. She doesn't think God will forgive her for killing Victor and, for now, leaving Charlie to die. Charlie. I can't leave him to die, she thinks. No, you've made up your mind. Legrand will arrest me if I return. Charlie would understand. Then she imagines the disappointed look on his face. She wished she wasn't the person he thought she was. I guess he know me too well, she thinks.

She storms across the square and heads beside the cathedral along Avenue Central. She follows the map and directions Gabriel had drawn for her, and eventually, she arrives at a tall white building with a balcony opposite the Amador Theatre.

She goes through the archway beneath the balcony and walks into a small courtyard filled with large palms in sub-stantial terracotta pots alongside various marble statues.

There is nobody around.

'Hello, is there anybody here?' Marie calls out. There is no reply. She tries one of the doors but finds it locked. She peers through the glass. Various paintings hang on the walls and are presented on easels. She moves from door to door around the courtyard looking inside, but she can't see her artwork. She wonders how it had even survived taken off its frame and rolled up in Gabriel's luggage.

Marie sighs. She sits on a bench, and while she waits for the dealer to return, she worries that the painting has not sold or, even if it had, it not making enough money for her to buy a ticket for passage on a ship to America.

After half an hour, the art dealer, a handsome young man dressed well with large sideburns, returns with a pristine young woman on his arm. From how they look at her, they must think she'd never been near a boutique. It feels like a lifetime ago since Marie wore the latest haute couture. At that moment she believes she would even wear the dress she wore to the art salon in order to feel cosmopolitan again.

The young man steps forwards. The woman lingers behind him. 'Can I help you?'

Marie stands. She readjusts the gun belt on her hip and rests her hand on the gun. Then, she realises what she must look like to the two people standing before her. She takes her hand off the weapon, spreads her fingers and holds her shooting hand at her side.

'Yes, I dearly hope so,' she says, turning to her rucksack on the bench. Marie pulls out the receipt Gabriel has given her. 'You've sold a piece of my art, at least. I'm hoping you have.'

He walks towards her. 'A piece of your art?' He takes the receipt. 'I don't believe we've met. At least, I think I would've remembered.' His eyebrows raise, conscious that he might've offended her. He looks down at the piece of paper. 'This is from the doctor based in err...'

'Paraiso, yes, doctor Gabriel Bertrand.'

'Ah. You are his partner? He says his partner created it.'

Marie nods.

'Well, he says you are quite the artist. Please, Esme, would you fetch us some drinks?' he asks, turning to the woman.

Her eyebrow raises. 'Of course. What would you like?'

'Oh, just water, please,' Marie says.

The art dealer unlocks a door, and she watches Esme in her beautiful dress slink inside. He turns back to Marie and puts his hand on his chest as he walks over. 'My name is Paul. I am very pleased to meet you,' he says, shaking Marie's hand. 'Please sit.'

They both sit on the marble bench. Marie adjusts her skirt. She pulls a strand of hair back behind her ear. It feels greasy. 'Your fiancée is very beautiful.'

'Yes, isn't she just.'

'Seeing her dressed like that makes me miss my wardrobe,' Marie says, brushing her skirt with her hand. A small cloud of dust billows off that she wasn't expecting. Marie sighs. 'It's been quite a journey from Paris.'

Esme walks out with two glasses filled with water and a slice of lemon and lime.

'Thank you,' Marie says, taking the glass from the young woman's clean, manicured hand. Paul takes the other glass without looking from Marie. With nowhere to sit and unwilling to be second to her beau's attention, Esme huffs and walks away.

'Of course, you're from Paris. The doctor thought you'd abandoned him, yet here you are. Where was it that he said you studied?'

'The Académie Julian.'

'Ah, but of course, Julian, yes. And it shows. Your brushwork is magnificent. Not to mention your use of colour.'

Marie smiles as she blushes. 'It means a lot to hear somebody say that about my work.'

'Well, I'm not the only person who thought so. Madame Pelletier, who is shrewd and has an exquisite collection bought it.'

'Really, she did?' Marie can't contain her smile. 'How much for?'

Paul leans into Marie, encouraging her to turn her ear towards his cupped hand. He whispers the price to her. Marie's mouth falls open.

'You sold a piece of my work for that much.'

He looks pleased with himself and nods. 'To be fair, I didn't have to do much selling, though I did need to reframe the canvas and make some minor touch-ups to the paintwork.'

'Of course, I don't know how Gabe managed to bring it here in one piece.'

'Well, I can't tell you how pleased I am, let alone how pleased the good doctor must be for you being here.'

Marie blushes again. 'Many people have admired my work, but I can't tell you how much this means to me.'

'Well, it means a lot to me too, Marie. I hope you brought your paintbrushes because we can make a lot of money together.'

'Of course I brought them... they're back at the hospital.'

Marie's smile fades. As Paul imagines a future of putting on an exhibition just for Marie, she remembers her predicament.

She shakes her head. She feels her temper rise. 'Paul, please. Don't get excited. I'm afraid that won't happen.'

Paul's smile fades, and he puts the glass down beside him. 'Oh. May I ask why?'

'I'm just not going to be here for much longer.'

He slowly stands. 'Ah, I see. How unfortunate.' He went to offer up some words to persuade her but could see that her mind was entirely made up. 'Just wait here, and I'll get you what is owed.'

Marie sits with her head in her hands until she hears his footsteps approach. She looks up and smiles.

'I've waived my fee,' he says.

'Oh please, you don't have to.'

'No. This is your first professional sale?'

Marie nods.

'Then, if you decide to paint again, please remember you have a friend here. If this is your only one sale, then it makes this sale even more special.' He hands an envelope of cash over to her.

She hugs him and whispers her thanks to him. They kiss each other on the cheek, and he sighs as she leaves.

Marie goes through the archway and onto the street. She looks down at the envelope of cash in her hand. She closes her eyes and sighs. She bites her lip. She'd always thought this moment would be significant, but she thought selling her work would've bought a different kind of freedom. Not her actual freedom. She sees the detonator as she stuffs the money into the bottom of her bag. She'd come close to building a new life for herself, but now it was too late to finish the American's mission. She would have to give herself a new name. She could never be the artist, Marie Cadieux.

As Marie walks through the streets headed towards the docks, she comes across a boutique with a rose marble and mahogany front. She looks in the large windows at the fine dresses on display. She goes in, and once the owner gets over what she is currently wearing, she buys and changes into a corset and a mauve silk dress. It feels tight and restricting after the clothes she has gotten used to over the last few weeks. The shop women braid their hair up as best as possible, which is good. Then she looks in the mirror at herself. She looks good, though she doesn't feel like it is herself looking back.

A man and his wife enter the shop, and his eyes linger on Marie as his wife inspects the dresses.

Carrying a gun on her hip was blunt compared to the power she now wields. A power much more subtle, much more persuasive, she believes. She pays, heads outside, gets a caleche, and is driven to the ticket hall at the docks.

She finds a shipping operator that runs routes to California and waits in the queue. She looks up at the board that charts the various prices of passage and the leaving times to multiple destinations such as San Diego, San Francisco, Lima and Buenos Aires. She has enough money to travel in first class to each destination, but she has to remember that she won't have much left for lodgings when she gets to wherever she decides to go. When she is called forwards to buy a ticket, she hesitates. The people behind her encourage her to move. The man at the booth waves her towards him. She walks forwards.

'Where to Mademoiselle?'

Marie swallows. She looks up at the board. 'Buenos—, no San Francisco,' she says.

The man raises an eyebrow at her, and when she doesn't change her mind again, he begins filling out the documents. 'What is your name?' he asks.

Marie stares through him as she pictures Charlie lying on the bed, dying.

'Excuse me, Mademoiselle, your name please?'

'Marie.'

He writes down her name. 'Marie...Your second name, please?'

She imagines Gabriel being arrested by Inspector Legrand and him being dragged back across the ocean to France and put on trial in Paris. She imagines him decapitated in a public execution by guillotine in Place de l'Hôtel de Ville.

The man at the ticket booth touches her hand.

'Mademoiselle, are you alright?'

Feeling his touch breaks her trance. Marie pulls her hand away. She nods. 'Yes,' she says. 'I am fine.'

'I need your full name for your ticket to San Francisco.'

Marie shakes her head. 'I don't feel guilty for what brought me here. But if I leave now, I will. I'll never be free of the guilt.'

The man frowns. He puts his pen down, leans on the counter and places his hands together.

'Many people pass through here, eager to escape, running from the past. I've never seen anyone with the courage to turn around and face the demons they're running from.'

Marie nods. 'Well, I guess there's a first time for everything then.'

'I take it you don't want this?' he asks, holding the ticket.

'No,' she says, and he rips it up.

Marie walks with her head held high past everyone in the queue who looks on at her. When she leaves the ticket hall, she shields her eyes from the harsh sunlight and waves over a caleche. She asks the driver to take her to the hospital, then she fling her bag inside the carriage and climbs in.

CHAPTER 39

Marie arrives late in the afternoon and is afraid the immunologist, Albert Calmette, may have left for the day. A man directs her to some laboratories. Marie paces in the waiting room as the receptionist goes to see if he is still at work. She goes over to the window to try and escape the bitter smell of chemicals that linger in the air from the labs. A tall man wearing a white lab coat, a beard and thin wire-framed glasses walks out from the lab.

'Yes, you wish to see me?'

Marie goes over to Albert and clasps his hand between hers. 'Yes, monsieur,' she says. 'I believe you can help a friend of mine that is gravely ill.'

Seeing her distress, Albert leads her to a chair, and they sit beside each other. Marie keeps hold of his hands. 'You met a young doctor a week ago who was greatly interested in your work. A man named Gabriel Bertrand.'

Albert looks to the floor as he thinks. 'Blonde, floppy hair?'

'Yes, that's him,' she says, squeezing Albert's hand. She looks down at what she's doing and realises touching somebody doesn't bring back memories of Victor. She shakes the thought from her mind. 'He sent me in haste to seek you out. A good friend of ours was bitten by a snake while in the jungle.'

'Oh,' Albert says.

'Gabe told me that you were our only hope, that you were looking for subjects to test your miracle upon.'

'Anti-venom, I'm guessing the doctor means. It's not a miracle. Just research.'

'But you are looking for subjects to have it tested upon, are you not?'

'Indeed, but as I explained to your doctor friend, any test would be perilous. The grim reaper himself would need to be reaching your friend to balance the risk.'

'That is the case, I'm afraid.'

'How unfortunate.'

Marie can sense Albert opening up to the chance of testing his anti-venom.

'Alas,' he says. 'If I don't know the type of snake that bit him, I will not know which of the antivenins to dispense.'

'My friend said it was a something viper—'

'Pit viper?'

'Yes, a pit viper. I remember it clearly. The snake struck, and I smashed a drilling rod upon its head.'

Albert looks at her as if she is a snake. 'You were there, in the jungle, when this happened?'

'Yes, we were trekking through because the train line was closed because of the landslide.'

'Go on,' he says as he rubs his chin. 'What did it look like?'

'It had a yellowish underside. On top, it was brown with darker triangles running the length of its body.'

'A fer-de-lance,' he says. 'Very toxic. Very dangerous. When was he bitten?'

'Yesterday morning.'

'Really, and he's still alive?'

Marie nods.

'Then the snake must've fed not long before, already administered its fuller dose.'

'That's what Gabe said. Albert, do you have some venom for this snake?' she asks, deliberately getting the name wrong.

248

'Anti-venom, you mean. Yes, I do. Wait right here, I'll get some.'

Albert goes back through the doors into the lab. Marie stands and goes over to the window. She looks over her shoulder when she feels the receptionist watching her back. The young woman looks down at her paperwork and begins typing. Marie leans against the sill and looks out of the small window. She can see a pile of iron bed frames stacked up on each other behind a building.

Albert returns. He holds two vials aloft. 'I wish I could come along and administer these and monitor the patient, but I have an important presentation in the morning to the hospital board. Will you make sure Doctor Bertrand records the patient's hourly progress?'

'Of course,' Marie says.

He hands the vials to Marie. 'Good. One vial of anti-venom should be enough. I explained the process to the doctor. He will know what to do.'

'Thank you, monsieur. I should make haste.'

'Good luck.'

As Marie leaves the waiting room, she hears the receptionist clacking away at the typewriter.

Marie gets a caleche outside the hospital gates that takes her back to the train station. During the journey, her mind wanders. She grows nervous when she imagines her trial. She knows the public will hate her for being adulterous, which will be enough to convict her despite the type of man Victor was. For some reason, Marie pictures Madame Durand watching on from the public gallery, shaking her head that Marie hadn't run when she had the chance.

She pauses in the booking hall when she gets to the station and finds her return ticket in her bag before walking out onto the platform.

'Madame Blanchet.' It is a man's voice. She pretends not to hear it and keeps walking. She gets to the carriage door when she the voice again, closer. 'Madame Blanchet. The time for running is over.'

CHAPTER 40

Marie turns the handle and opens the train carriage door. A hand reaches over her shoulder and shuts it. She turns, expecting to see Inspector Legrand, but it isn't him. The man slides into the gap between her and the train carriage. He is a short man. A smug-looking man. A man with a broken aquiline nose.

'Sorry, I don't know who you are,' she says.

'But I know you.'

'And who precisely am I meant to be?'

He grins. 'You are Marie Blanchet, wife of the late Victor Blanchet.'

She feels a knot in her stomach, but she is sure her face conveys confusion rather than shock. 'Well, I'm afraid you're mistaken. My name is Evelyn Lauren. Do you mind?'

He doesn't move.

'Is this man bothering you, Madame?' the passing train guard asks Marie.

'Yes, he's—'

'No, I'm not. I am Inspector Jean Bonnevay. She's my prisoner. She's under arrest for murdering her husband.'

The train guard nods and begins to walk off down the station. Marie looks on aghast.

'You see, nobody cares, and that's how it will be for you from now on.'

Marie doesn't know what to say. She stands there with her mouth open.

'It's funny watching how people react to being caught,' he says. 'Some try and run. Some stand there like you as it sinks

251

in, not knowing what to do, coming to the realisation that it's all over.'

'You talk too much.'

Bonnevay looks at her sternly. Then he smiles and wags his finger at her. 'You're not the first person to say that.' Then he slaps her across the cheek. It was not hard or soft; the act was enough to shock her. 'But I won't have some criminal, especially a woman telling me that.'

She rubs her cheek. 'What are you going to do with me?'

'Put you in a cell. Here maybe. I'm in no rush. We can wait for the train lines to be fixed. I wonder what the prison is like here? They probably don't even separate the men from the women. That would be fun for you, wouldn't it?' His smile fades when she fails to react to his taunts. 'We'll get a boat back. You can go on trial. They'll find you guilty. Then...' He draws his finger across his neck. Again she doesn't react. 'But first, I'm going to send a telegram and tell my boss I have you.'

Bonnevay leads Marie over to the telegram office in the station. He takes a slip from the tray, and as he starts writing the words, he reads them out for Marie's benefit. 'Blanchet fugitive caught. Pan. City. Call off Legrand from running around France.' He looks up at Marie. 'That last bit will cost more, but what the hell. If only I could see his face when he hears I caught you.'

'Whose face?'

'My rival, the great Mathis Legrand. Pah, I say rival, yet here we are.'

'Legrand's here.'

Bonnevay is surprised as he looks up at her. 'What did you say?'

'Your great rival isn't searching France for me. He's here,

252

in Panama.'

Bonnevay grabs her arm. 'Where?'

'Why? Are you afraid of him?'

Bonnevay grins. 'No. Not at all. I want to see his face when he sees I've got you.'

Marie says nothing. She flexes her jaw and remains silent.

'You can tell me, or I can beat it out of you like any other prisoner I've dealt with.'

Marie looks at the floor. 'Paraiso. He's in Paraiso. The next town down the line.'

Bonnevay claps his hands together. Marie looks up and he's grinning. He scrunches up the telegram note into a ball and throws it at a waste paper bin behind the telegram operator's desk. It bounces off the rim and falls onto the floor. Marie stifles her smile. There is hope, she thinks.

'Come on,' he grabs the crook of her arm and pulls her towards the door.

'Where are we going now?' she asks.

'Paraiso,' he says.

They get onto the train headed east, and Bonnevay sits them in first class. When the train starts, he takes her bag and rifles through it. He puts the clothes onto the table and then her gun belt and revolver. 'Well, well. What would an innocent woman need with a weapon like this?'

Marie says nothing and looks out of the window.

He finds the envelope of cash and one vial of anti-venom. 'What's this?'

She stares at him. She reveals a hint of a smile to unnerve him in any way she can. He just grins back at her.

It is only when he pulls the detonator out that he frowns. 'What the hell have you been doing?'

253

'I'm an eclectic kind of woman.'

He narrows his eyes at her.

'You're a dead woman.'

'Then I've got no reason to tell you anything, have I?' She looks out of the window again and remains silent. Instead, she tries to figure out how to get out of this. So far, she'd had no ideas, and she just hopes to keep stalling Bonnevay until an opportunity presents itself. She hopes there is something more in this rivalry between the two detectives than just bragging rights. Legrand, she'd learnt, was relentless. He'd gone to great lengths to track her down. Maybe an opportunity can present itself, she thinks, that might allow her to escape while the two men are distracted by each other. Whatever happens, I need to get back to Paraiso. I need to get the anti-venom to Charlie, she thinks. She stifles her sigh. Charlie. She wishes he was well. He's the only one that can get me out of this predicament. She isn't sure Gabriel could be of any use.

The train arrives in Paraiso at dusk. They get off and walk past the station hut. 'Alright, where is he?'

'You're very trusting of a criminal. What if I was lying to you?'

'You'd better not be.'

'Else you'll do what? Kill me?'

'Just you keep persisting with that line…'

'Better now than waiting for the inevitable.'

'I'm not going to kill you now. You can wait till we're back in Paris. It just depends on how comfortable you want this period to be.' He stands close to her so that their bodies touch. He holds her chin. 'Because I can make what you have left of your life extremely uncomfortable.'

Marie pulls her chin from his grip but doesn't retreat from him. 'I could persuade you that I'm better alive.'

His serious expression fades into a smile. 'It's a long way home. But my mood depends on finding Legrand. Where is he?'

'He's at the hospital.'

'Really. Why?'

'Looking for me.'

'Lead the way,' he says, stepping aside.

Marie begins walking down the main street, and he walks alongside her.

'What's the deal with you two?' she asks. 'You must really hate him to want to rub his nose in it like this.'

'Shut up and keep walking.'

They get to the hospital and pass through the gates. There is light coming from both the ward and Gabriel's bóhio. Marie's hand is shaking. She rubs the sweat from the back of her neck. Then, as she rubs down from the front of her neck to her chest, she reaches beneath the dress's neckline and takes the second vial of anti-venom out that she's hidden. She glances at Bonnevay as she clutches hold of it. He hasn't seen it. He is looking at the hospital's buildings.

'Which one is he in?'

'Presuming he's still here.'

'He'd better be.'

'It was earlier today that I saw him. He might be anywhere by now. He might've gone looking for me in Panama City.'

Bonnevay glares at her.

'Let's try the ward,' she says, heading towards it. She pushes the door open. Sister Audrey, the older of the two nuns, sees her and strides down the central aisle towards her. Marie goes straight for her and grabs the old woman's soft, wrinkly hands, pushing the vial into her grasp.

As the old woman looks down at what she has been given, Marie looks around the nun's winged cornette towards Charlie's bed. He's gone.

CHAPTER 41

'Where is he? Where's Charlie?' Marie asks.

The nun looks up. Her lined face is grave. 'The patient you brought in passed away this aft—'

'What?' Marie drops to her knees.

'What's going on here?' Bonnevay asks. 'Where's Legrand?'

The nun looks at him. She doesn't answer. She looks down at Marie and puts her hand out to comfort her, but ultimately she can't bring herself to do so. 'You should go and see the doctor. He's in his bohío.'

Bonnevay grabs Marie's arm, hauls her up and drags her out of the ward. He takes her across the courtyard, past the water pump and over to the small wooden bohío and shouts: 'Mathis Legrand. Are you in there? Come on out.'

There is movement inside the bóhio. The door opens. Out walks Legrand. Gabriel follows. Legrand leans against one of the wooden posts holding up the porch. The storm lantern hanging up casts light across one side of his face. The tip of his cigarette glows as he inhales the smoke.

'It's over, Legrand. You see? I have her. I won. I'm going to take her back to Paris. DuVille is going to give me the promotion, and you, you... Well, you might as well stay here.'

Legrand pulls a gun out. He lifts its aim at Bonnevay. Gabriel lurches into Legrand's arm. The gun goes off, and the bullet whizzes into the nearby jungle. The gun flies out of Legrand's hand. As he pushes Gabriel off and reaches down to retrieve it, something hits Legrand in the chest. There is pain. Legrand looks down and sees the wooden handle. The blade is deep into his chest. He coughs. Blood shoots from his mouth. His legs can't hold him, and he falls down the porch steps. The knife pushes deeper into him as he hits the dirt.

Gabriel rushes over to help him.

'Don't!' Bonnevay shouts.

Gabriel ignores the order and kneels beside Legrand. The inspector's eyes are wide, lifeless. 'He's dead. You killed him,' Gabriel says.

'Turn him over,' Bonnevay says.

Gabriel rolls Legrand's dead body onto his back.

The knife handle sticks out. 'Take it out.'

Gabriel looks up at Bonnevay.

'You heard me, do it.'

Gabriel rocks the knife back and forth as he eases it out of Legrand's chest. He holds it up to Bonnevay.

'Wipe it clean,' Bonnevay tells him.

As he wipes the blood off the blade against Legrand's trousers, Gabriel stares at Marie. There is nothing but contempt in his eyes for her. She knows Legrand had told him what she did to her husband, Victor.

'Is it true about Charlie?'

Gabriel nods.

'That's enough talking,' Bonnevay says as he picks up the gun off the floor. 'Go and wash it.'

'No. You should wash the blood off yourself. You're the one who just killed a man,' Gabriel tosses the knife over to Bonnevay's feet.

Bonnevay looks at the knife and then at Gabriel. 'I told you to wash it.'

'Go to hell.'

'Gabriel, do as he says.'

'No.'

Bonnevay aims the gun at Marie. 'Do it,' he says.

Gabriel crosses his arms. 'You're both murderers. Why don't you just go? This is a place for saving lives.'

Bonnevay aims the gun at Gabriel. Gabriel steps back. Bonnevay pulls back the hammer. Gabriel loses his nerve. He walks over, picks up the knife, takes it to the water pump, and cleans it.

'Get on your feet,' Bonnevay says.

Marie is too tired to argue. She is too tired to plot and scheme. Now she will just exist. Gabriel brings the knife back over and hands it to Bonnevay. He smiles as he takes it and slides it into the case on his belt. 'There, that wasn't hard at all, was it?'

'You got what you came for. Why did you need to come here?' Gabriel asks.

Marie stares at the floor. 'You didn't tell me about Legrand,' she says.

'He only arrived today. You should go. I don't want murderers in my hospital.'

'No,' Bonnevay says. 'We're staying here tonight.'

Gabriel looks to the sky. The purple sunset is fading into night.

'Go and fetch me a sedative, and don't even think about saying no.'

Gabriel looks from Bonnevay to Marie and shakes his head. 'Do you see what you've brought to us?' he says, walking past them.

'I'm sorry,' she says, but he doesn't look back.

Bonnevay grabs her arm. He leads her up the steps onto the porch and into the bóhio. He pushes her down into the armchair.

'We should leave,' Marie says. 'I won't give you any trouble, I promise. The saloon will have rooms.'

'I don't trust criminals.'

'I didn't lie to you about him being here, did I?'

Bonnevay finds a bottle of liquor. He uncorks it, sniffs it and then downs several gulps. He winces.

'Why did you kill him?' Marie asks.

He points at her. 'I bet you wanted him to shoot me.'

'Would it have mattered who brought me in.'

'It matters to me.' Bonnevay throws the bottle, and it hits her leg and spins off across the floor, spewing liquid.

She grits her teeth and rubs where it hurts. Bonnevay sits on the end of the bed and waits.

Gabriel returns with some small bottles and a hypodermic needle on a tray.

'Make sure she's out of it till the morning,' Bonnevay says.

Gabriel says nothing. He goes over to Marie and kneels. He draws the contents from a bottle into the needle and turns over her arm. She touches his hand, but he pulls away from her touch.

'Keep still, damn it.'

She doesn't argue. She offers her vein.

'You killed him,' he says as he pierces her skin with the needle.

'Yes,' she says. 'I murdered my husband.'

CHAPTER 42

Marie stands in the dock. She doesn't look up at all of the eyes flicking between her and the judge as he begins summing up. She hears his voice but doesn't take in anything of what he says. The only word she hears is guilty.

They lead her down the corridor in silence. The square is full of people. She is placed in the guillotine. The sun warms her face, and she smiles because it reminds her of Panama and riding the horse with Charlie. Then the blade drops.

Early morning sunlight fills the room and urges Marie to wake. Her throat is sore. Her eyes flutter open. She goes to turn, but her arms are tied to a chair. Gabriel, slumped over his desk, snores. Bonnevay sleeps on the bed. She tries to pull her arm free of the rope binding her to the arm of the chair. Bonnevay sits up on his elbows and looks at her. He swings his legs off the bed and stretches his arms above his head.

'I'm surprised you're up so early. It seems the good doctor's medicine worked better on him.'

'What happened to Legrand?'

'Buried him.'

'Hid the evidence then?'

'I have nothing to hide. It was self-defence.'

'No different to what happened to me. Yet I'm here, tied up.'

'I'm just doing my job,' he grins at her. He walks over to Gabriel, who doesn't even stir. He lights a cigarette. 'Time to go.'

'Where?'

'Back to Paris.'

'Well, I'm guessing you haven't heard. There was a landslide. The train line's out. You can't get across to Colón.'

'And the canal's not finished either, so we're going through the jungle.'

'Don't be ridiculous. We'd never find our way through.'

'Really?'

'The doctor told me you'd come with that man who'd died,' Bonnevay says as he picks up Marie's bag. He pulls out the maps she and Charlie had used and drops them into her lap. 'It looks like you managed to get here through the jungle. You can lead us back through and tell me all about this dam you were going to blow.'

Bonnevay unties Marie and makes her pack what they'd both need for the trip. She takes off the mauve, silk dress she'd bought in Panama City and changes back into the long skirt, her boots and the shirt she'd worn while trekking through the jungle. She isn't allowed to put her gun belt on, and it feels strange to put her hand on her hip and not feel it. Lastly, she puts Charlie's hat on and adjusts it in the mirror. In the reflection, she sees Gabriel shaking his head at her.

'I don't recognise you at all, Marie.'

'Then I guess you never really knew me, Gabe.'

When it becomes time for them to leave, Gabriel walks with them across the courtyard. Bonnevay goes to the stables and takes Legrand's horse from Sister Aceline, who'd saddled it. 'After all we've been through, you have nothing to say to me, Gabe?'

Gabriel sighs. 'I'm sorry it came to this.'

'Not as much as I am.'

'Why didn't you tell me?'

'I don't know.'

He shakes his head. 'It doesn't matter now.'

Bonnevay leads the horse through the gate and then climbs on top of it. Marie and Gabriel follow, and he stops on the threshold and folds his arms. Marie looks back at him. 'Goodbye, Gabe.'

He turns his back on her and goes back into the hospital.

Marie doesn't look back at Paraiso as she leads Inspector Bonnevay into the jungle. He sits on the horse above her, and she walks in their shade. After a couple of hours along that straight dirt road through the jungle that she'd spent most of a day dragging Charlie along, they get to the rope bridge.

Bonnevay is getting burnt by the sun. His forehead is red. He finishes his canteen of water and looks down into the canyon of raging water. Marie sips from hers.

'Give me that,' he says. She holds her canteen up, and he grabs it from her. He can feel by the weight that there is still a lot of water inside it. 'Why have you hardly drunk anything?'

Marie shrugs her shoulders. Then she walks out onto the bridge.

'Where are you going?' he asks.

'It's this way.'

'Wait.'

'You're not scared of heights, are you?' she asks.

'No.'

'Well, come on.'

He climbs down from the horse and stands at the foot of the bridge.

'I could just run away,' she says.

He begins leading the horse onto the wooden slats. She goes on out into the middle, making sure to hold onto the rope. The water crashes around the rocks below.

'Stop,' he says. 'The horse will never make it across.'

She faces him and sighs for his benefit. 'If we don't hurry, we won't make it to the camp for nightfall.'

The horse resists being pulled further, and it edges backwards. 'Enough. Wait there,' he says. 'We'll have to go the rest of the way on foot.'

'It makes no difference to me,' Marie says, then she curses under her breath. Bonnevay leaves the horse and comes out towards her as she contemplates swaying the bridge. It would be no use. It wouldn't be a surprise, and she doesn't have the weight to make it rock like the horse had.

After crossing the bridge, they continue along the cliff's edge, where she'd encountered the snake. Bonnevay follows her, so there is no opportunity to push him off. When they reach the point where Marie had broken free of the jungle, she points into the thicket. 'Through there,' she says.

Bonnevay looks into the jungle, and his brow creases.

'We'll have to cut through,' she says. 'You'll have to trust me with a machete.'

Bonnevay smirks and shakes his head. 'You must think me mad. Besides, I don't think a woman could cut through that. Just you navigate us, I'll cut.'

CHAPTER 43

After a couple hours of hacking through the vines and branches, Bonnevay is exhausted. Marie is surprised she has managed to navigate them back to the cave where Charlie had been bitten by the snake, but she is also nervous. 'We stored the dynamite in that cave so it wouldn't get wet.'

Bonnevay narrows his eyes at her.

'Lead the way,' he says.

Marie takes a deep breath and leads him into the cave. She points to the group of rocks where Charlie placed the dynamite box. She folds her arms. 'It's there. Behind that rock.'

Bonnevay sees the box covered by the sack. 'Why have a dog and bark yourself. Go and get it.'

Marie's eyes grow wide. 'I couldn't,' she stammers.

'Why on earth not?'

She edges back towards the cave's entrance. 'It's too heavy. I couldn't lift it before.'

'I don't care, do it.'

'If I drop it, the dynamite is liable to blow.'

'At this point, I don't care.'

Marie swallows. She takes a deep breath. She walks over to the rocks and hesitates.

'Pick it up,' he says.

She shushes him and listens for any sound of a potential snake. She reaches down. She stops. 'I need some light. I can't see.'

'Sure, I'll just hold a flame over the dynamite, shall I? Pick it up.'

Marie curses him. She steps closer with her arm outstretched. She doesn't know whether to move slowly or fast. She reaches down, takes hold of the sack, and slowly lifts it. As soon as it is clear of the rocks, she staggers backwards, keeping it at arm's length and her head angled away from it. When she gets to a part of the cave that is clear of large rocks and hiding places for anything that slithers or crawls, she all but drops the sack containing the box of dynamite onto the floor.

'Are you trying to blow us to kingdom come?' he says. 'Open it up.'

Marie looks to the heavens. 'Well, you won't be able to see from over there, will you?'

He crouches opposite her beside the sack. Keeping her distance, she reaches out and pulls the folds around the box. There isn't a snake inside. She sits down and stops holding her breath.

Bonnevay shakes his head at her. He reaches out to the box, opens the lid and looks inside. 'Well, I'll be damned.' He picks up a stick of dynamite. 'There's a lot here. Are you going to tell me what you aimed to do with it? Though I'm already piecing the clues together.'

'What's there to say. Charlie is, was a spy. A saboteur. He was going to blow up the dam—'

'Where do you come into this?'

'I stopped him. I sabotaged his sabotage.'

'Why were you with him in the first place?'

'I hired him to guide me.'

'So you're a killer and a hero?' He grins. 'It's still not going to save your neck. Take me to the dam.'

CHAPTER 44

Marie leads Bonnevay down the river. He doesn't know the direction she's taken leads them away from the dam. She further distracts him by talking to him, and the humidity and the jungle aid her.

'What made you believe I was in Panama?' she asks.

He smiles as he looks over his shoulder. 'A reliable source.'

'Who?'

'She was an acquaintance of yours, apparently.'

'Don't tell me then.'

'The wife of some diplomat.'

Marie sighs. 'Madame Gage?'

'Yes, that's her. She saw you on a train headed to Le Havre with your lover. She was in London when she heard of your husband's death and thought we should know she'd seen you.'

'I bet she did, the bitch.'

Bonnevay is laughing when he trips over a root. He pushes himself up and strikes at the root with his machete. It barely makes a dent. He hits it repeatedly but doesn't even cut through. Such is his fatigue. He gasps for breath. Then he stands. 'Why isn't the jungle affecting you?'

'It is. I feel quite faint,' she lies.

He narrows his eyes and studies her.

Marie shifts her weight onto her other foot. She wipes away the sweat from the back of her neck. 'We should keep going. It saps you just standing still as much as it does moving.'

He keeps watching her, his lip twisting in disgust.

'I'll hack for a bit if you wish,' she says, offering her hand.

'I'm not giving you a machete. Which way?'

'This way.'

'Are you sure?'

'I don't want to be here any more than you.'

'If I was in your position, I wouldn't be in any hurry to return to France.'

Marie doesn't reply. She keeps walking, pushing branches out of the way.

Bonnevay looks at the river. He frowns. The water flows in the same direction they are headed. He looks back. They are walking downhill. It isn't a steep decline, but they are definitely descending. 'Why are we heading downstream? Shouldn't the dam be upstream?'

'I'm an artist and a woman. What would I know?'

'That's what I'm afraid of.'

They keep walking, following the river.

After a few minutes, he says, 'If we're heading towards a dam, shouldn't all this be underwater?'

'Do I look like an engineer? Listen. The dam is only partially constructed. It's being built around the river. I guess that's why.'

'Don't test me,' he says, holding the tip of the machete to her chin.

'Well, let's go back that way. But at what point do you believe me and we arrive back here. Hours later? Days later?'

He keeps the blade to her chin as he regards her with suspicion. 'There's one thing you haven't asked me,' he says.

'No need to ask when you're going to tell me.'

'Ask me.'

'What am I asking for?'

He pushes her chin up with the machete, and the tip digs into her skin. 'Ask me,' he says.

'What? What is it that I haven't asked you?'

'Do you think I came all the way to Panama and didn't think to seek out where Gabriel had been stationed?'

She swallows. 'Tell me,' she says.

'I did think to seek him out. Oh, I met Gabriel. It must've been a week before you arrived. He'd just started in Paraiso. I could see from how he reacted that he had no knowledge of you having killed Victor. Oh, his surprise made way for disgust so quickly. We didn't think you'd show. I thought I'd lost the race with Legrand, and I got suitably drunk in Panama City. Lo and behold, the good doctor was true to his word. He said that if by some miracle you were to show up, he'd let me know. And he did.' Bonnevay lowers the machete to his side. His words cut her deeper than the dull blade of the machete. 'He sent me a telegram. I got it late and thought I'd missed you when I arrived at the hospital, only to find you'd been and gone. Then luckily, I found you at the station.'

Marie remains expressionless. 'Are you done?'

'Have you nothing to say?'

'The dam is this way,' she replies and begins walking. 'It's not far.'

'You're one cold, calculating bitch, do you know?'

Marie looks over her shoulder. 'And so you should be scared.' She runs. Bonnevay is caught flat-footed. He begins after her. She is fast. She reads the jungle with supreme accuracy, dodging vines, leaping over rocks and avoiding branches. Bonnevay pulls the revolver from the bag as he runs, which serves only to slow him. With the gap between them growing, he fires a shot at Marie. It misses. The jungle thins. She breaks free onto the riverbank and keeps running. She can see the Emberra tribe's village. She can see them.

Women run away at the sound of the gunshots. The men rush towards the noise of the gunshots with their bows and arrows in hand. Then she trips. The sky and the earth roll around her until she stops in the dirt and dust. She is dazed when she hears the running footsteps approach. The pain in her knees and hands is matched by the pain in her scalp as Bonnevay grabs a fistful of her hair.

'Stay where you are,' he shouts at the five tribesmen coming upon them. She winces and opens her eyes. She recognises Enerdo. He pushes between the men with the bows and raises his own.

Bonnevay fires a shot off into the air, but as he lowers his aim at them, a flurry of arrows whistle through the air and embed into his body.

His grip on her hair loosens. The gun falls to the floor. She edges away from him. He staggers forwards, then he sways and falls onto his back.

Marie leans up on her elbows. Her plan had worked. She looks at Bonnevay as he takes his last bloody cough. She looks at Enerdo. He simply raises his eyebrows at her, then smiles.

EPILOGUE

It is afternoon the next day, and Marie stands knee-deep in the cool, calm river. Enerdo and his daughter intently watch as Marie plunges her arms in elbow-deep and picks up a large stone. She hauls it over to where she's created a small dam in a channel running off the side of the river. She places the rock on top, blocking off the overspill. Behind the rocks, the water pools increasing its surface area.

She goes around this small dam to the fine river sand revealed by the lack of water. She lays out some pieces of wood. She points over at the village, at each house in turn. Then she lays out the pieces of wood to roughly match the village's layout. Enerdo's expression grows serious. She points back at the houses in the village and then back at the pieces of wood. Enerdo nods. Then, Marie pulls out two blades of grass from the riverbank, indicating that one is Enerdo and the other is his daughter. The young girl smiles, but Enerdo frowns. Marie sticks them into the ground next to the largest trickle of water, which she indicates is the river.

When everything is laid out. She points back upstream along the river. Then she points at the dam. She picks up another rock and lifts it above her head before launching it at the pretend dam. As it hits, the dam tumbles apart. The pool of water rushes, and the wave engulfs the model village. The two blades of grass are swept away. Enerdo jumps to his feet. When the water flow has returned to its previous state, the pretend village has been swept away. Marie points to where the dam had been, and she points up the river.

Then she points at the actual village and makes hand ges-

271

tures, indicating that it should be moved back. Enerdo nods. She smiles. He has understood.

That evening just after sunset, Marie sits around a fire with the whole tribe. There are about one hundred people, including the children, a lot more of them than she had initially thought were in the village. She watches as Enerdo tells them what Marie had told him about the dam and how it will flood the village if they do not move. Some of the younger people complain and point fingers at her. The elders of the tribe nod and watch on, deep in thought and concern, as Enerdo speaks.

Marie wonders whether she is doing the right thing in pursuing the plan to blow up the dam. At the forefront of her mind, she knows her motivations are selfish. She knows she can gain the greatest from blowing it up; money and asylum. But then she has seen what the French have done to Panama. How they've destroyed the landscape, reducing lush forests teeming with life to muddy trenches. She's seen how they will flood kilometre upon kilometre of land and jungle. What will be left for people like Enerdo and his tribe? What would be left for people that simply want to live off the land? If she acts, if the frontier could finally be seen as untameable, maybe Panama would be left alone. But she knows the Americans will move in the minute the French leave.

She is pulled from her thoughts when a mosquito lands on her arm. She splats it into mush and then flicks the residue away.

Enerdo's wife, who is sitting beside her, smiles. She touches Marie's arm to get her attention. Then, just like Marie has communicated to Enerdo with a series of hand gestures, the woman tells Marie how the tattoos they wear keep the mosquitoes away from them. Marie can see the design on the woman's arm differs from when she'd last seen her, meaning they mustn't be permanent. Marie nods.

The woman goes away and comes back carrying a cloth which she lays open on the floor. Inside are some green fruit, a knife and a bowl. 'Huito,' the woman says, holding up the fruit, then she turns the piece of fruit into a paste. The woman applies the paste to Marie's exposed skin; her forearms, chest, and neck up to her jawline. By the time she has finished being painted, Enerdo has convinced the tribe that they must move the village.

The following day, the tribe wakes early and pack their possessions. They all gather beside the river where they'd had the fire the night before. Marie embraces Enerdo and his wife. When it comes time to say goodbye to his daughter, she kneels before her, so they are the same height. From behind her back, the girl reveals a turquoise beaded necklace, which she places over Marie's head. Marie lifts it up and admires it. Then she reaches into her bag and withdraws her wedding ring Victor had given her. She holds it between her thumb and forefinger and offers it to the girl, who smiles as she takes it.

Marie and the Embera tribe part ways. She watches as they enter the jungle heading away from the river in the opposite direction. Then she is finally alone. She looks at the deserted village on the banks of the river as she picks up her pack and swings it onto her back, adjusting the weight so that it sits comfortably on her shoulders. Parrots whistle and glide across the dry river from one side of the jungle to the other. Monkeys call to each other in the distance, and uncountable frogs and insects click and clack and croak. A sloth crawls upside down along a nearby branch. She takes a deep breath of clean jungle air. She smiles. Then she sets off along the river, upstream, once more towards the dam.

Marie Cadieux is a free woman, about to let her presence reverberate across the world.

REVIEWS

Thank you for taking the journey with Marie and reaching the end of Marie Cadieux and the Fever Coast. I hope you enjoyed this story.

As an independent author, without the backing of a big publisher, your review would really help me to reach a wider audience. If you have a spare couple of minutes, I would really appreciate it if you could post a review from where you purchased this book.

Each positive review I receive makes a huge difference meaning more people discover my writing.

Not only that, I love hearing how you felt while taking the journey with Marie.

Thank you once more.

David

ACKNOWLEDGEMENTS

There are many people who have given help, advice and support over the course of my writing career to date. Every conversation, interaction and experience a writer has feeds into their work.

With my stories sitting on my laptop, my dad always urged me to get my novel published. Now I can finally say, dad, I did it! So to mum and dad, thanks for all your support on this storytelling journey.

Grateful thanks to all of the writers who have read my work and critiqued it over the years. Jan Cabral-Jackson, Phil Olsen and Paul Thomas your thoughts are invaluable, and sharing our writing is always a pleasure. Lisa Bentley, your eye for detail and story is indispensable. M.J. Hyland, your advice on this story helped shaped the books I love to read to this day, but your belief and guidance also had a profound affect on my writing.

And to my family. To Liz, Lauren and Evie. Thanks for listening to my endless debates on character, plots and storytelling. Your support and belief makes things like this happen. This book is as much yours as it is mine.

ABOUT THE AUTHOR

David Gennard graduated from The University of Manchester with an MA Creative Writing studying under M.J. Hyland, Jeanette Winterson, and Ian McGuire.

When not writing, David can be found on set shooting promotional photographs on films such as The Unlikely Pilgrimage of Harold Fry and TV shows like Billions. He's also often found out in the countryside, on a beach or paddling across a lake. David lives on the Wirral with his partner, two children and his border collie, Buddy.

Find out more about David's writing and sign up for his reading crew at: www.davidgennardauthor.com

COPYRIGHT

www.ingramcontent.com/pod-product-compliance
Lightning Source LLC
Chambersburg PA
CBHW011033190726
48290CB00011B/2831